STANDARD TIME

Standard Time

KEITH RIDGWAY

faber and faber

First published in Great Britain in 2001
by Faber and Faber Limited
3 Queen Square London WC1 3AU

Photoset by Parker Typesetting Service, Leicester
Printed in Italy

© Keith Ridgway, 2001

The right of Keith Ridgway to be identified as author
of this work has been asserted in accordance with Section 77
of the copyright, Designs and Patents Act 1988

'Never Love a Gambler' was first published in *Granta*; 'The Problem with
German' was first printed in *New Writing 6* (ed. A. S. Byatt and Peter Porter)

A CIP record for this book
is available from the Briish Library
ISBN 0–571–20588–7

2 4 6 8 10 9 7 5 3 1

Thanks to

The Arts Council of Ireland
Conor Toomey for 'The Problem with German'
Peter O'Connell & The St Judes for 'Headwound'

Kenneth A. Armstrong for everything

Contents

The First Five Pages

We came in over the sea, we came in the morning, just after the sun, coming low out of the east across the flat sea, on time, the two of us. We watched boats scratch the surface, we put our seatbacks in the upright position, we called for more drinks, but they were having none of it, they were cross with us – they wouldn't let us toast your first sight of Dublin.

We crossed the panel sea, the grey-blue web of waves and routes and trawlers, across the humming radioactive sea, over submarines and the drowned, over the cables and the pipes and the deep connections, and we craned our necks and looked for the city. It came at us as islands, small islands which I could not name, and the two pencil-thin chimneys then, which I had forgotten, and finally the bulk of it, split by the river, a huddle of colours and a shadow in the foothills, a gathering of times, a city on the edge of Europe, on the edge of the world, a city from the back of our minds, shot suddenly forward, in front of us, offered in the early sunshine, the clouds rolled back for us, the whole place gazing upwards for us, waiting.

I told you that I wanted to set my watch, and you misunderstood, thinking that I was confused about time zones and had over-estimated the distance we had travelled. But that is not what I meant. I wanted to set my watch. I was coming home to see how I had changed, to see what you really looked like, sounded like, to find out how wrong I'd been. But I couldn't tell you this.

We descended over housing estates and motorways that I had never seen before. We skimmed the tops of call centres and warehouses, distribution networks and technology parks, software development clusters and the green belts tightened by a future that I had missed.

The plane hit the ground.

'Welcome home,' you said, your hand on mine, your accent sounding suddenly wrong, sounding wrong for the first time in five years. As they made announcements and we tried to remember the last time we had seen a living farm animal, I thought that at last we were on my territory, that at last I knew more than you did, that at last I could place you. Which sounds cruel, and it was cruel, and it was cruel enough for me to wonder whether I could get away with actually leaving you at the airport, abandoning you there to fend for yourself, with your half English and your appalling sense of direction. I was amused at the thought of it, but decided that it would be better to get you nearly settled first, almost confident, with the first tender hint of security. And do it then.

In the baggage hall though, I had to stop myself, as you perched on the edge of the carousel, your arm dangling, as if you were sitting on the edge of a lake, testing the water. I could so easily have headed for the bathroom and turned instead for the green channel, for the arrivals hall and the waiting faces, and gone out into the sun and found a taxi, and just left you there, with your plastic bag and both our suitcases, frantically looking for the section in your phrase book which covered the reporting of missing persons.

So I found a trolley instead, and told you to watch that you didn't get dragged into the machine, that you didn't lose an arm to the revolution, at which point you sneered at me, and told me that I was not to boss you now, now that we were in my place instead of yours. Which made me think. About how much you knew.

No one waited for us. No one knew we were coming. Which is what I wanted. I wanted to get my bearings and lose my boyfriend before going for a pint with the locals. Not that you understood this. You complained about the expense of the hotel I had booked, which was a laugh. We had flown to Dublin via Bonn, of all places, and London, so that you could take care of some unspecified business and leave me to wander and plot. You owe me more money than it is possible to count. And that is only money.

Our taxi took us on roads which I didn't recognise, past homes and businesses which I didn't fully see, so perplexed was I by the traffic and the look of the people and the voices on the radio, all familiar, somehow, but altered as if by special effect, which is I suppose, what time may be. My confidence that I had the measure of you here was a little dented, until we reached the city centre and I saw that, fundamentally, although the streets were crowded and the sun was out, and the faces were healthy and varied and the money was obvious, fundamentally I knew where I was.

At the hotel I made a point of talking quickly at the reception desk, and of using words which I had not used in many years, wondering not, for example, if there was a shop nearby, but whether there was a newsagents in the vicinity. I asked about the times for everything, knowing that you were not good at time, and about the hotel itself, whether it was busy, how new, etc, and whether, flirting a little now, it was a good place to work, all the time aiming for a vocabulary which you did not possess. It made the receptionist and I best of friends, and left you silent and a little wide-eyed. Which was lovely.

Our room was from the book of rooms, taken straight from a Habitat catalogue and placed three floors above a clogged street, with a glimpse of a cathedral and a three-inch ration of river. You liked it. Immediately you turned on the television and concentrated on the meaning of things here, while I showered and wondered exactly how to proceed. I thought it would be polite to pay the hotel bill for a few days in advance. Or rather, I thought that kind of politeness would be a nice touch, a tiny little twist which you might not notice but which would give me a minor, private glow. Standing naked under the water I plotted your abandonment. I weighed my options, I caught the water in cupped hands pressed to my chest, I held it briefly and I let it go and I did it several times, and thought of whether or not a note would be good. What would it say? What language would it use? Mine, I decided. My language. I was reminded, showers being what they are, of other times, and I allowed myself, in my six square feet of rain, to go over tiny patches of the past, as if to steel myself, or to reassure myself, or to overcome the noise of you from the other room, flicking through the channels, repeating phrases in English that you would never use, like 'an area of low pressure' and 'separated egg whites'.

We met in the cranked up part of ourselves, on a beach I think, or a road near the sea – outside certainly, and away from the city, close to the edge of something, in ourselves I mean – water in the air, salted skins, passing through and halting. I think it was France. I know it was France actually, but pinning these things down is so difficult; not difficult in the way of putting my hand to the facts, but difficult in picking them up, holding them, setting them out in a row. Everything seems so meagre.

I liked your body. You liked my manner. I bought you food and drink. You made me laugh. A series of small exchanges like that, and both of us were so placed, so poised, that such deals, such trade-offs, were enough to mesh us. Interlace us. I thought again, with the water hitting my shoulders and my back, with the water running off me, about how that might have happened, how I had been so easily filled by you. What was it about that place? What corner of me had that fled to?

I followed you home. I trailed after you across half the continent, splitting something in two, mostly me I think now, giving you money, learning your language, making myself small enough to fit in your pocket. Where I was warm and eyeless and content. Until I somehow noticed the time. Without really having thought about it before. I realised that we were five years into it. Five years. Into it. Which is too long for a seaside romance with a man you hardly understand. And I entered the counting room – located somewhere between the heart and the stomach – that dour, fearful little place where the books are kept, where the tallies are made and the sums done and the imbalances are justified, and where the present is divided by the past to give the future. And other formulae follow. And there I tried to make sense of you and couldn't. I pored over the ledgers and the receipts and I tried to make us solvent. And all I found was an accumulation of debts and promises and failures and dodgy practices, and I came to the conclusion that we had been simply an accounting sleight of hand, a convenient, unexplained statistic, a false item, a fraud. That we were not a couple at all – we were a category, a sub-category, a ghost heading, a non-existent overhead, created to cover the siphoning off of five years of my life into the slush fund of your own. Thus was the finding of my audit.

You came into the bathroom wondering what 'compliments' there might be, and I chose not to understand your English and let you lapse back into your own watery native tongue. Complementary toothbrushes, soaps, shower caps – that was what you were after. You paid no attention to my naked body dripping on the fretted mat, and rummaged in the presses instead, testing the softness of towels and the scent of shampoo sachets and the size of the soap. You asked me what the water pressure was like in the shower, and wondered then whether you mightn't take a bath instead, looking at yourself in the mirror, yawning, asking where I planned to take you that night, what part of my home did I think would impress you? I told you to take a bath, and as I left the bathroom you kissed my cheek, and I ran my hand along your shoulders, and it meant nothing to either of us, having as much value as words of parting or greeting, habitual, ancient, semaphore, an old dead language, entirely ceremonial. And I would not have thought of it if I was not busy recording it, jotting it down, tucking it away. Before I closed the door I had a sight of you undressing, unbuttoning your shirt in front of the mirror, your eyes on yourself. If there was any doubt in my mind I do not remember it. But there was regret, I'm sure, and sentimentality, and five years of clutter. You caught my eye, and said in my language 'What?' and I said in yours, 'Nothing,' and I closed the door on you and looked for something to write on.

My idea was a stupid one. The idea that I could take you to a place that you did not understand, and leave you there, and that the leaving would fix me. It was badly conceived and badly executed, and it lacked grace and it lacked style and it lacked substance. It was like the start of a joke which has no punch line. The structure was all wrong.

I wrote a sort of letter to you, scrawled in simple English on hotel notepaper, with occasional, minor clarifications in your own tongue in case you misunderstood, in case you thought I had gone to the newsagents or to take some air, in case you thought I had not left you. I did not attempt to explain, but I made some mention of the time span, and I believe I wrote cruel things, and I believe that it was a hateful, stuttering, spittle-flecked rant, and I believe that I slammed the door. There, I thought. There. See how you like it.

And of course therein lies the flaw. Because I could not see how you liked it. I could not watch you read, reaching perhaps for your dictionary, scratching your head, wrapped in a towel, perched on the edge of what would not now be our bed. I missed out on the upshot of my little scheme, and I began to realise it as soon as I was out on the street.

What do you do once you've written yourself out of your own story? You start a new one, or you try to write yourself back in.

Why did you want to travel via Bonn? What business had you there? I could ask you a million such questions. You disappeared for the best part of a day, and I wandered and sulked and plotted, and ended up in a bar which looked like a railway carriage, where a boy approached me and said something which I of course did not understand. I muttered or stumbled sufficiently for him to break into clear English, clipped and precise, and almost entirely without accent. We got chatting, and talked, as people tend to, of our homes. He was from Bonn, and wanted to know how I liked it. I had seen little enough – I mentioned the wedding cake building, at which he frowned, and the Rhine, along which I had walked without you and which had appeared to me to be monstrously wide and fast. The boy agreed, seemed particularly proud of the river, as if it was an achievement. He told me that when it had last broke its banks it had risen so high that the river rats had found refuge in the trees which lined its sides, and that some of them lived there still. This also was related with a solemn nodding, as if it too was an achievement.

Rats in trees.

When you reappeared, shrugging, not knowing what you had done to provoke me, we walked a concrete stretch of the Rhine and fought loudly. I kept a careful eye above us, and although I cannot say for certain that I ever saw anything, I'm sure that up ahead, in a place we had not yet reached, the smallest of moving shapes could be seen, blurred on the branches, birds or squirrels or rats. And I was only half fighting with you, softened as I was slightly by the beer, and the conversation with the boy, and by the predictability of what each of us was saying, and the breadth of what we were *not* saying. I was following the plot, but my mind raced ahead, and I saw what I saw, and I listened to you as you moved as ever, skilfully, beautifully, brilliantly, from secretive to insulted to conciliatory to apologetic, without conceding anything, without revealing anything, without once saying anything to make me change my mind. I gave you till Dublin. I decided that, as you might look out the window of a bar and decide that you will go home when the street light on the corner comes on, or as you might leave for work at the end of the second next song on the radio. I picked my place, or more correctly my time, and I relaxed a little and let you get away with it.

And now that it's done, now that I have put you from me, I am left with the debris, the rats in the trees, the clicking of the minutes from zero upwards, the new calendar, the rats in the trees. I do not know what you did. I don't know if you stayed or you left, whether you simply took a taxi to the airport and flew home, or whether you looked for me first. I do not know what you thought, I don't know what it meant to you, and I have lost the clues, I have lost even the signals, tired and all as they were, which might have suggested whether you were as little as you seemed or whether there was more.

Months later I called your city. I called your apartment and you were not there, someone else was there. You had moved out. And later still I called some friends of yours, and they would not talk to me other than to say that you were gone and they did not know where and that it was all my fault. I am puzzled by the sense of having put something in train which I have now lost track of, which has escaped me, which is loose and ongoing, while I am here, still eyeless, but cold, and ill at ease.

Where the hell are you? Where?

I have come to look for you. I have deserted Dublin. Dublin has failed me. It has failed to act, failed to facilitate me. It has simply carried on, as if I had never been away, as if I had never come back, not seeming to realise that it was the major player in my plot. It has been such a disappointment. So I have returned to your city to find you and to make you forgive me, or to end it. But you are hard to find. I live in an apartment within walking distance of the one we once shared. I look for you and I come back. I go out and look for you and I come back, and I find only that I am self-contained. That with a packet of cigarettes, with the television, all of the wide world can be held inside the lace curtains and the grubby glass. And I can sit here and wonder why the time is such as it is, this late already, and nothing done, nothing done at all, as if there has been a gap bridged between where I was and where I am now and that nothing in the interim has kept me alive or awake or meant or uttered a thing.

Except of course that there are scars and watermarks, and tidal debris, and the stains on my fingers and my teeth, and my skin newly fleshed out, enhanced, made large in the small stricture of what I say to myself and the little that others expect of me. Here I am now, fattened on the blink of an eye, made old in an instant, failing and fading and faltering fast, my blind piggy eyes stuck on the rump of a day retreating before me, my days retreating before me, and I in pursuit, in my hairshirt pursuit, catching nothing but the trailing gasses of the future, come back on us with poison, stories of flood, and of what crawls from the flood and where it clings and what it clings to.

Put one story behind you and start another. That is the theory. But I find that what should be new is polluted by what should be old. That there are no endings, that all stories overlap, and that all you can do is decide where to begin. When to begin.

I don't know where you are. And that is the start of it.

Never Love A Gambler

There was the roar of a bus, a shuddering agitation in the warm air, and then a rotten smell that came wafting in the open door from the street, and then a second later a dog, an awful nightmare of a dog, a cur, who strolled by with something dead in the clamp of his jaw.

'Ah Jaysus,' moaned Dodo, hiding her eyes. 'What's he got? What's he got?'

The dog went on, dripping, and there was a trail left after him, of something dark and thick that was not blood.

'A rat I think,' said Jimmy, squinting.

'Or a cat. A little kitten.'

Another bus roared away from the lights and Dodo picked up her half of stout and put it down again. Jaysus. The smell lingered. It hung and she could see it, a red-black colour like a winter nosebleed. In her leg the pain began. She glanced at her son and burst into tears.

'Ah Mam, don't cry for Christ's sake. What's wrong with you?'

She put down the glass and pulled a sky-blue handkerchief from her pocket and blew her nose and dabbed at her eyes and picked up the glass again and drank. A skinny drunk woman looked down at her sideways from the counter of the bar.

'Nothing,' she said.

'Is it Da?'

His father, his father. Her son and his father and the pain in her leg.

'No.'

'What then?'

'My leg hurts.'

'Is that it?'

'Feels like there's something living in me knee. It's killin' me Jimmy. Turns and twists and turns like it can't get asleep.'

'We'll go to the doctor tomorrow.'

'What do you want to go for?'

'You go on your own so.'

'He's useless.'

'He's all right.'

'He looks down at me, turns up his nose.'

She drank, and watched him out of the corner of her eye as he stuck a finger in his whiskey and sucked it. Her knee twisted itself again and she scrunched up her face and stuck out her tongue and let a moan out of her till it passed.

'All right Dodo?' the barman called.

'Oh yes. It's me knee. Awful in the heat.'

'Awful in the cold. Awful in the in-between,' said Jimmy huffily, his eyes front ahead, his mess of hair in a greasy tumble over the bad skin of his forehead. Forehead from his father. Great domes the two of them – made you think of clever, complicated men. They weren't that.

'I'd have thought it'd be better when it's dry,' said the barman. 'Dry and hot like it is. I thought the damp'd be worse.'

'No,' said Dodo, conscious of Jimmy smiling and shaking his head.

The barman lit a cigarette and flicked the flame from his match and tossed it smoking towards the door, but it fell short, landing on the colourless mat.

'Joints are awful things,' he said. 'Never trust them.'

Dodo nodded and stared into her stout. Jimmy watched the barman for a while and then lit a cigarette of his own, drawing in a great big lungful of smoke and pausing for a long moment and hurling it out of him then in a great big rush towards the bright street.

'I wonder is it cigarettes?' said Dodo.

'You've been off them for years.'

'Not as long as I was on them. Rose Kelly's sister-in-law

11

had a leg amputated and she was on forty a day and I was on forty a day too.'

Jimmy said nothing, only shook his head and drew again the soft grey smoke into himself and held it, as if it were necessary to test something, in his insides.

'There's that dog,' said Dodo, and Jimmy breathed out.

'He's eaten it.'

'Ah don't say that.'

'Swallowed it whole.'

'It's a fierce smell off him.'

The dog paused in the doorway and looked in, one eye gooey and the other colourless and blind. His coat was dirty with dust and filth and he was of no particular breed. A scar ran down one side, and he dragged that hind leg, and he smelled hugely.

'Poor fella,' said Dodo. 'Bad leg too.'

'Forty a day man.'

Dodo smiled.

At the other end a door opened and in stepped Mossie Russell, and all the bar glanced up at him and away again, and there was a slight hush, all eyes. The skinny woman got up and left, going out the side door, stepping, almost falling, over the old dog who now lay panting on the pavement staring at Dodo.

'Shite,' muttered Jimmy, cleared his throat, shifted in his seat.

Mossie Russell walked smiling across the room, for all the world like he had stepped out of a game show, as if there was applause going on, as if he was delighted, delighted, to be here, my word, with all these lovely, lovely people. He nodded hugely at the barman and made a gun with his finger and fired it, clicking in his mouth, just a couple of times too often, so that it was funny, or past funny, a parody of that type of man, so that he showed that he had the measure of himself, contained himself, stood beside himself, watched you watching, letting you know he was cleverer than he

12

seemed, but keeping a secret still just how much cleverer, as if the parody might itself be a joke, a double cross, a parody of your smug amusement, a way of getting at you no matter who you were or what you thought. Here was Mossie Russell. And without once glancing at them as far as Dodo could see, he strode the length of the place in his swagger and came straight to her and Jimmy. He clapped his hands and rubbed them.

'Mrs Fitzgerald,' he said. 'Jimmy,' he said. He smiled at them and held his arms out wide and stood like that for a moment, a beaming cruciform shape, an exaggeration of himself, tempting comment. Jacket a kind of yellow. Go on. Say a word.

He sat at their table on a low stool with his back to the door and the dog. 'Mind if I join yous?' This after he was seated.

'We do yes,' said Jimmy.

'Ah shut up Jimmy,' said Mossie, delighted. 'What are yous havin?'

'I'm fine thanks,' said Dodo, chewing, which was what she did.

'Jimmy?'

'What?'

'What can I get you?'

'Large Black Bush.'

Mossie laughed and nodded at the barman. He reached into the pocket of his jacket then and pulled out a box of Extra Mild Silk Cut and a gold lighter and offered cigarettes to Dodo, who shook her head, and to Jimmy, even though he had one lit. Jimmy took one and dropped it into his shirt pocket. Mossie laughed again.

'You're great fuckin' fun Jimmy do you know that? What's that fuckin' smell?'

'It's the dog,' said Dodo quickly, and nodded her head towards the open door. Mossie turned and looked and stood up then and went over to the dog and aimed a kick. But the dog had seen him coming and got out of the way with a speed that was shocking for a dog in his state. Gone he was.

Mossie came back to the table shrugging his jacket and nodding, as if acclaimed. Squinting eyes brought on by smiling. Smiling brought on by squinty eyes. The barman put down a pint and a large whiskey and went off again without asking for money.

'Grand,' said Mossie, sitting on the stool. 'Are you sure Mrs Fitzgerald that you won't have another?'

'No thanks Mossie. I'm fine now.'

'Right.'

He fell silent and stared at the table, and Dodo looked at the horseshoe of hair that sat on the top of his head, and at the taut honey-coloured scalp that he scratched now, as if her gaze was an irritation. He looked up at the ceiling and rubbed his chin and his throat, and Dodo looked at the two rings that he wore on his left hand and then glanced at his right hand that rested on the table top and saw the three rings there, and looked at his neck, expecting to see a chain, but seeing no such, just a tuft of dark hair poking out from under his black denim shirt. He wore a yellow, well, sandy, mustard, she wasn't sure, sports jacket, and black jeans and a big buckled belt and soft brown shoes. There was a scent from him that was fresh and clean, and he held his cigarette between his pale fingers as if it was a permanent fixture, forgotten. But then, her irritant eyes again, he took a drag and blew the smoke upwards, away from her.

'Isn't this the weather?' he asked.

Dodo nodded. Jimmy scowled.

'It's global warming,' said Mossie. 'Global warming. The sun goes lethal and we get more of it. Get worse before it gets better. And of course some fools lap it up. Always have. Billy Lawlor from Phibsboro out on the grass in his knickers the first sign of it. That's some sight. Every time Mrs Sullivan looks out her window there he is spread-eagled like he's fallen off the roof, his shite brown legs and his scrawny body.

She complains about it but you know I think it's the only reason she listens to the weather forecast. Makes sandwiches the
night before if it's going to be hot. Sits there all day long
drinking diet coke and munching her sambos, her eyes crawling all over Billy Lawlor's sorry corpse.'

He gave a great laugh, winked at Dodo, sipped his golden
drink.

'Then Mrs Grealy calls by and wants to see the new wallpaper in the upstairs bedroom, new since 1979, and they sit
there the two of them making Billy Lawlor wonder why he's
so bleedin itchy. I'm a winter man. Warm coats and coal fires
and hot drinks. But some people. Lie in the fuckin' sun from
dawn to dusk and not move a muscle. I never understood it.
Jetting off to Spain and fuckin' Florida. When I go away I go
to cities. I go for the culture.'

He gave a wide smile and nodded. Roar of the fuckin'
crowd.

'Paris. Venice. Rome. Travelling to the sun is a fuckin' joke.
If you're looking for a holiday Jimmy take your mother to
Paris. Take Mrs Fitzgerald to the Louvre.'

He took a drag of the cigarette and stared at Jimmy.

'It's an art museum. Mona Lisa.'

'I know.'

'Mona Lisa, Mrs Fitz. About the size of a postcard. Big
throng of nips around her yapping away. Mona Lisa and the
way she might look at you. There's better pictures there. Better stuff than that.'

He sighed as if it was a great shame. He looked at his
watch.

'Can't find Frank,' he said.

Dodo's knee twitched and she gasped and closed her eyes.

'What is it Mrs Fitz?' asked Mossie.

'My leg. My knee.'

'Hurts does it?'

She looked at him. His face that he lived in. His face that he
pulled around and pushed at, him behind it somewhere, a

skeleton with a smell, an earthy breath of bad thoughts. He could stay looking at you with the same expression for a long time, unflinching. While inside he ran around the angles. And even when he had not asked a question, he always looked as if he had.

'Yes,' she said.

He nodded.

'Where's your husband missus?'

Dodo sighed and sipped from her stout, the thin head gone warm in the heat.

'Why do you want to know?' asked Jimmy, making his voice hard and slow.

'I have business with him.'

'What kind of business?'

'He's in the flat,' said Dodo.

'What kind of business?'

'I was at the flat. There's no one there.'

Dodo shrugged.

'I asked you a question,' Jimmy said.

'I'm sorry Jimmy, I missed it. What did you say?'

'What kind of business do you have with my father?'

Mossie looked at the table top and ran his fingers along the edge of it, his cigarette burning low, his rings bright.

'None of your business business.' He laughed and looked up. 'You know the kind of thing.'

He stared at Jimmy, still smiling, and did not blink. Jimmy nodded and looked away. Mossie turned to Dodo.

'I was at the flat. There's no one there.'

'Maybe he has the telly on,' said Dodo. 'Can't hear you. Maybe he's fallen asleep.'

Mossie took a last sharp drag from his cigarette and stubbed it out in the ashtray, it hissing in the water and smoking and dying. Mossie drank and put his glass down and folded his arms.

'I thought that,' he said. 'I thought that might be it. But no. There's no one in the flat at all, asleep or awake.'

16

His smile was gone and Dodo could not look at him.

'What do you mean?' asked Jimmy.

Mossie said nothing.

'Did you break in to our fuckin' flat?'

'Didn't know you still lived with your Mam, Jimmy.'

Jimmy made a small hissing noise and Dodo glanced at the ashtray.

'Now Jimmy,' said Mossie. 'There's no call for that at all. Your Da invited me by not turning up. Me sittin' like a fool on the steps outside the gallery, that's an invitation. Half hour I was there. That's an invitation Jimmy. Given the circumstances.'

Jimmy did not say anything. He lifted his whiskey, the one he had bought for himself, and drank it all. The double Black Bush stayed where it was. Mossie watched him and turned again to Dodo.

'Lovely place you have missus. Nice view too, of the world. And you have all the gear. The telly and the video and all that. Deep fat fryer. Microwave.'

'We don't have a deep fat fryer,' said Dodo.

'Lovely view though. That height.'

'I don't know where he is,' said Dodo, and she sipped her stout.

Mossie nodded. He traced his fingers on the table top and cleared his throat.

'I've left a fella by the flat in case he comes home. You don't mind him. He's outside the door and he's a nice fella and you won't know he's there. In the meantime if you know where Frank might be, if it occurs to you suddenly like, then I'll be at my place and I'd love to hear from you. Right?'

Dodo nodded.

'Fuck off,' said Jimmy.

Mossie stood quickly and his stool fell over behind him and Dodo crouched back out of the way as he leaned across the table and grabbed Jimmy by the shoulder of his shirt and lifted him to his feet, the shirt ripping a little and a button popping out into the air, Dodo watching it, up and across and down like it was taking forever, through the air with her eyes on it all the way, and down then, plop, the sound maybe only in her head, who knows, into the Black Bush like a body in the canal in the sunset. Dodo was stuck on that for a moment. By the time she was back, tugged round by a shaking in the surface like a nice evening breeze, Mossie had pulled Jimmy towards him and the table was pinched by their thighs.

'Now Jimmy. Stop being a thick little shite and keep your fuckin' mouth shut or we'll have to see how well you dangle. Do you hear me Jimmy?'

His face was so close to Jimmy's, and his voice so loud, as if Jimmy was in another room, that he spat on Jimmy with all the openings and closings of his mouth. Then he was still for a minute, glaring, with not a sound in the place, not even in the street or the whole of the city, so it seemed to Dodo, then he sniffed and let go, and Jimmy dropped to the seat wiping at his mouth.

'Fuck's sake,' he muttered.

'I'll be off,' said Mossie. He nodded at Dodo and his smile was back. He ran his hand over his head. 'I'll see you around Mrs Fitzgerald. See you soon.'

He nodded at the barman and walked back through the bar, stopping to talk to a couple at a table by the door, shaking hands with an old fella who stood up for it. He did not look back. Then he was gone, and the barman looked towards Dodo and Jimmy and shook his head slowly.

'Jesus Christ,' said Jimmy. 'He's a fucking bollox.'

'What does that mean?' Dodo asked.

'What?'

'We'll see how well you dangle. What does that mean?'

'They hung a fella off the top of the flats last week. Tied a rope around his ankle and the other end around a chimney stack or something and pushed him off. Fucking left him there. The fire brigade had to come. It's his new thing. Bungee jumping. The fella's leg was nearly ripped out of him.'

18

Dodo drank what was left of her stout. She reached for her stick.

'Come on,' she said.

'Where?'

'To find your father.'

Jimmy sighed and shook his head, but he did not argue. He fiddled with his shirt, looked for his button, felt the cheap material, patting himself, as if it might have slipped inside and be against his skin. Dodo watched him. As if something would be against his skin. She closed her eyes and told herself that that was a wrong thought. You love your son. Your children. Love.

She was about to tell him where it was, but that would give her away. Let him know that at his moment of danger, his pale body threatened, she, his very mother, had chosen to watch the gentle arc of a plastic button through slow motion air into whiskey. Which was, she thought, shocking. They moved away, her son helping her, a sash of his white stomach visible, the Black Bush staying where it was. She thought of some poor man coming across it and delighting in his good fortune and knocking it back and choking to death on the button of her son's shirt. The barman called 'good luck' and Dodo groaned with the pain in her leg and told her son that it would be fine after a minute. Once they got going, she said. Once they got going the pain would fall away.

Outside the evening was still as hot as the day had been and traffic waited at the lights and two children played on the steps of the wax museum. The dog was there, dozing by the wall in a shaft of sunlight. He looked up at them and got to his feet.

'Are you all right Mam?'

'I'm feckin crippled. I'm like that fella.'

She stopped and looked at the dog who took a step towards her and wagged its tail.

'We're for the vet's,' she said to him. 'You and me son. They'll be putting us to sleep soon the two of us.'

The dog nodded and turned in a circle and wagged its tail and seemed happy at last. Happy at last. The end of the day and happy at last.

'Where'll we look?' asked Jimmy.

Dodo leaned on her stick and patted the handbag that was slung around her shoulders and pulled her handkerchief from the pocket of her cardigan and dabbed her mouth and her nose.

'I don't know love. We'll go around by the gallery I suppose. By the Garden. Maybe he's over in Barry's.'

She set off slowly, taking small steps. The dog watched her, Jimmy held her elbow. She remembered being other than this. Always that memory at the start. Fell away when she got going. Everything falls away when you get going.

After a few yards they moved a little faster. The pain in her leg made itself smaller. The dog followed. At the pedestrian crossing past The Granby, at the corner of the square, the lights were against them. If she stopped she'd have to start again. There was a bus approaching. Always a bus. She shook Jimmy loose and strode across the road against the red man.

'Jaysus mam. Will ye fuckin' wait.'

The bus blew a loud horn and Dodo hurried. The dog ran ahead of her, telescoping its arse up to its ears. Dodo tried something similar, regretted it, something in her hips clicking.

'If I stop it'll hurt,' she said.

'If you don't stop it'll fuckin' kill you.'

The bus had slowed and moved around them. The driver leaned out of his window and shouted.

'Yeah yeah' said Jimmy. 'Yeah yeah.'

They walked with the dog in tow and the leg pain diminishing, like a toddler rocked silent by travel, leaving off its scratching and its squeaking and fading into sleep. Dodo thought herself a ship with a child aboard, as she had in pregnancy, sailing through all those days of her life like a liner, and the thought made her thirsty again. They went on. Past the school and the parking meters and the cars parked head on, and into the clear space in front of the Hugh Lane Gallery Of Modern Art. She squinted at the steps and slowed. Jimmy regarded her with suspicion as she tugged at him and dwindled and came to a stop. They looked at the closed doors.

'He's not here all right,' said Jimmy.

'Why meet here?'

She felt her son shrug and mutter something about Mossie and culture. She had met Mossie's mother once, a delicate woman, thin and smoky, a tireless talker, long hands that tapped ash and fear, fear and ash. Dodo stared upwards at the gallery, at first floor windows and then at second floor windows. A face looked down at her. A pale circle in the dusty air. Straight into her eyes. She gripped Jimmy's arm tightly and gasped, and he must have thought that it was her leg at her again because instead of looking up he looked down, at her knee, crouched and stared at it, as if he might catch a spasm, a ripple in the skin, a flutter of the kneecap. Dodo tugged at him, her eyes impatiently wandering for the slightest of seconds, but enough. Enough to lose it. Jimmy straightened and looked where she looked and saw nothing for there was nothing there.

'Oh,' said Dodo.

'What is it?'

'Nothing.' The dog wet a parking meter and nodded at her. It was his bad leg he lifted. 'Let's go on.'

They walked, the leg pain oddly quiet. Dodo could not glance back without stopping and they did not stop. The face had been a man's, and Dodo had been sure that he had looked directly at her, and that he was pale and saddened, and that he was dead and a ghost, or a spirit, or a memory in her own mind of a previous life, shone up on the glass of the window like a cinema or an old party trick from her days as a girl. Or perhaps God, or the devil, or a murdered soul, trapped, or an angel. One of those many things.

'What was that house?'

'What house?'

'The gallery. Who lived there before it was a gallery?'

'I don't know Mam. Some old English Lord or something. Maybe. I don't know.'

Dodo shuffled, her sore feet scuffing the ground.

'There'd be a lot of history there then.'

'Yes.'

'All old stories of murders and sad ladies and candles.'

Jimmy sighed. He was looking over towards the Garden Of Remembrance.

'There'd be ghosts there too,' said Dodo. 'Or the hope of ghosts.'

She thought of the dead. They would be flighty. They would be cautious like children, like parents, conscious of the difference. They'd know the trouble of living and have soft sighing pity on her. On her and her husband and her sons and her daughters and their children who ran in small circles around her and dizzied her with giggling. They'd watch, the dead. She raised her eyes and sniffed the air. Over by the cross pool and the children of Lir. Ghosts. The uncertainty of them. Marks on the ground for them. Signs they might know. Calling out to them. Come here and hover. We shaped you a pool.

'Barry's Ma?'

'We might as well have a look.'

They passed the tall mast of Findlater's church and waited at the lights this time, her leg very calm. Jimmy monitored her. The dog sat politely, its raggy coat splayed on the ground, some connection made in its simple brain between Dodo and the scent of its dreams. They crossed and she thought of sending Jimmy into the shop for a can of something, but said nothing and they went on into Gardiner Row and the high lights. It was gloomy now, the sun sickening behind them. They walked to the crack in the pavement that marked the end of Gardiner Row and the start of Great Denmark Street.

She waited on the footpath with the dog, a hand on the black railings, while Jimmy ran into Barry's. She watched a grey-dressed schoolboy slowly idle by her, his big eyes on the ground. They were back then. Poor things.

'Back already?' she said.

He heard her. She knew he'd heard her. It was in those big eyes, and in the tiny stiffness of his little head. But he didn't look up. He set his small mouth shut and went by, his hands in his pockets, his schoolbag shrugged up on his narrow back. He was a low thing, not up to her elbow. About eight maybe. First class. New to the middle of the city. Don't talk to strangers.

Dodo let go of the railing and glanced at her palm. Black paint flecked. She gripped things tightly now.

'Were you not collected?' she called to him.

He sort of paused, then continued, as if he'd stepped over a little bump in the ground.

'Belvo is it?'

He glanced back. Whatever she was to look at she was not a worry. She didn't look like a stranger. He stopped and nodded.

'Not collected? Did your Mam not come?'

'My father,' he said. He stayed where he was. He looked up the street and squinted. As if it was an inconvenience. Can't get good parents these days. But Dodo could see glinting trails on his baby cheeks.

'How late is he?'

'He was supposed to be here at five o'clock because I had to go to swimming at half three. But he usually comes at half three because that's the time that I usually finish so maybe he did and couldn't find me.'

He gave an awful moan out of him and a stuttering sob and his hands came out of his pockets and went to his eyes and he crouched over and before Dodo could think she was at his side with her arm around him telling him hush and not to worry and such things that she had not had to say in a long time and which filled her with memories of her own so that it was nearly the two of them in floods. And the dog dancing in a circle, wagging a terrible tale.

'Can you not ring him?'

His face jerked and his nose was a mess and Dodo gave him her handkerchief.

'I have no money.'

'Did the priests not help you?'

'It's too late. They're all locked up.'

She could give him the money. They'd take him to a phone box and he'd call home.

'What's your name?'

'Kilian.'

The poor child.

'Mine is Dodo.'

He looked at her.

'No it's not.'

'It is.'

'Dodo?'

'Yes. It's short for something.'

'What?'

She laughed and reddened and pretended that she was a little embarrassed and didn't want to say, which seemed to cheer him up a touch. But the truth was that she couldn't remember what it was short for. Something regal she thought. Something posh. But couldn't bring it to mind. Doreen. Dolores. Deirdre.

'Will we ring your parents?'

'I only have a father. I know the number though.'

'Will he not be worried?'

The child shrugged and hurt his shoulders with the weight of the bag. She helped him off with it and told him that they'd just wait for Jimmy and then go and find a phone box. He squinted up at her and wiped his face and offered up the sodden handkerchief. She took it.

'Jimmy is my son. Used to be your age, but is no longer.

He's inside looking for my husband Frank who owes money. We're wandering around looking for him and finding ghosts and small boys instead.'

'Ghosts?'

She didn't answer. The dog sniffed the boy's shoes and fixed his rotting eyes on the schoolbag. It was a great mystery.

'What's your dog called?'

Dodo patted her cheek.

'Let's see now. Mossie. Little Mossie with the yellow tongue. We've been places me and him. Her. Him.'

'It's a boy dog,' said the boy. 'He's very smelly.'

Jimmy bounded down the steps shaking his head, the gap in his shirt shifted now to reveal his dirty navel, a black eye in the dusk of a September evening. Dodo would have said something, but he saw the child.

'Billy's there hasn't seen him since Thursday. Who's this?'

'This is Killin.'

'Kilian.'

'His father was meant to collect him and didn't so we're going to help him phone. Isn't that right love?'

'Jaysus. Are you from the posh school?'

He nodded, ashamed.

'Jaysus. Do you not have a mobile or a car of your own or something? A credit card? Take a taxi for God's sake.'

Dodo sighed, ashamed. There was a pause and the sun was gone. They stood in a second of quiet, broken by the click of the bulb at the top of the curled silver wand that stood high beside them. The boy craned and saw it. Jimmy grinned. Dodo wondered whether Mr Kilian might not have had an accident. She wondered what had happened to the mother. Could she ask? Could she ask that question in the rattle of traffic and Jimmy's thin leer?

'You said ghosts.'

'I'll tell you later. Jimmy, where's there a phone?'

'Inside.'

'Oh. Right. Inside then.'

It was the steps. Only four of them but steep and tiled and the colour of sand. Mossie's jacket colour. Shifting in the dim light. The boy before she knew it was watching her approach, standing in the doorway of the hotel with his hands back in his pockets, sniffing. Jimmy held her. Helped her. She put her head down and stared at her awful feet. Then the boy before she knew it was moved again, this time to her side, his little hands on her swollen arm, his baby head whispering encouragement to her breast. The wholesomeness of it nearly sent her flying. And her knee. Waking up.

'Oh.'

'All right Ma. Last one.'

The whispering boy. What was he saying? Was his mother dead in a car crash? Crushed? Had it happened again? Hmmm? Could that happen? Would they let her adopt at her age? Not at her age surely. With Frank dangling from the chimney and her unwashed son always smoking in the kitchen? Hmmm?

'Here we are. Top of the hill. Thank you boys. You're a good strong fella Killin.'

'Kilian.'

'Very strong love.'

He bent his body and picked up his bag and straightened again and was up the door step and down again, three steps ahead, turned, back again, a little jump, reaching his hands up on the wall to feel the wallpaper. Dodo was dizzy. Her knee was building up to a rage. A pure rage.

Behind her there was a little whimper, barely heard. She turned and waved.

'You stay there boy. We'll be back in a minute.' Mossie the dog nodded and flopped on the footpath, his chin at rest on two soft paws. Dodo envied that. Wished she could settle down for a snooze.

'There's the phone Ma.'

She stuck out her hand and Jimmy rummaged in his pocket and blew out a breath and Dodo didn't breathe in while it

26

flowed by her. The boy was looking happier now. He swayed on his little legs. A couple came by them, arm in arm, going in. A barman swung a bunch of keys and nodded at Jimmy and glanced at the boy and went through glass doors whistling.

'What's the number love?'

He told her, one number at a time, as she pressed the buttons and heard the tones in her ear. It rang. And rang. No one exactly sitting by the phone. Then it opened onto air, a hiss, a space. A sleepy man's voice said, 'Hello there.' Her knee was on the verge of bursting.

'Hello. Mr . . .' She held her hand over the mouthpiece. 'What's your surname love?'

'Hickey.'

'Mr Hickey. My name is Dodo Fitzgerald . . .'

'Who?'

'Dodo Fitzgerald. I'm here with . . .'

'Dodo?'

'Yes. I'm here with your son. With Killin. Oh sweet Jesus Christ.'

It was her knee. It buckled and flexed like a fish. Something electric shot up her thigh and spewed a thick syrupy pain through her bowels and her pelvis and her shivering flesh. She vomited pain sounds.

'Hello?'

'Mam? Leg? Here.'

Jimmy took the phone while Dodo grabbed her knee and pressed, and backed her backside into the wall. She stood one foot on the other in an effort to confuse her senses. She thought she might faint. Through a dripping mist she saw the boy stare at her with an open mouth, fascinated. Wondering if she'd die maybe. Perhaps thinking of his mother. Dodo bit her cheek. Cried.

'We have your son Mr Hickey. What? No he's not, don't be stupid. You never collected him.'

It found a way across her hips, turning them to dust, and

shot down the other leg. To the other knee. She was now dying in stereo. Being shot would not be as bad.

'Well whatever. We're at Barry's Hotel on Denmark Street and if you're not here in fifteen minutes we pull the trigger.'

And Jimmy hung up. The boy looked at him and Jimmy grinned.

'All right Ma?'

'Don't mind him love he was only joking with your father. Good lord.' It echoed through her like a bomb. Everything shook. Her body was a trembling bag of soft fraying strings and bubbles that burst.

'Are you all right?'

'I have a bad knee. It hurts sometimes very badly.'

She thought from his half open mouth and his big eyes, blue as it happens, that he was about to say something, perhaps that his mother had had the same complaint and he hoped that Dodo would not die too, and she thought as well that maybe she had the same name as his mother, which was, which was . . .

'Is my father coming?'

'He is,' said Jimmy, looking out the door, lighting a cigarette. 'He's coming to get you. Be here soon. Thought someone else was doing it. Fuckin' mortified.'

Jimmy showing off in front of a child, swaggering, being like a film star with his cigarette, spitting towards the dog. Dodo leaned on the wallpaper, swung her leg from the knee, eased it like turning on a cold tap. She limped to the door and across to the steps, past Jimmy and his smells. The boy followed, scurried to the footpath like a dancer, offered her a white hand. Gentleman.

'Good fella. Thank you love. I need to pace. It calms the soreness.'

'Did you fall?'

The dog was on its feet, watching her carefully. Ready to catch her. It was easier going down. No sign of Jimmy. She put her weight on the little man. He took it.

'No. Thank you love. That's it. There we are. It grew on me. Crept up.'

'Like a ghost.'

'Exactly like that.'

'Where did you see a ghost?'

'I'm not sure love. In an old house maybe. It was probably just a cleaner. A man looking out the window. It was probably just that.'

He nodded. She thought that he would have pondered death. That ghosts would have a hold on him in more than just the scary way. That he might have seen his mother in the dark of his bedroom just before the dawn.

'Have you ever seen a ghost?'

'No.'

He had forgotten crying. He lugged his bag and paced with her, turning at the end of the railings and coming back, turning again opposite Jimmy, the dog keeping up for a while then sitting at the kerb, puzzled at this nonsense.

They talked. He held back a bit when it came to his new school. He seemed undecided. He seemed to think it very old, odd, as if he had stepped into the past. 'The classes have funny names. Some of the teachers wear gowns.' She nodded, uncertain. Had no advice for that kind of thing. She told him about her children and their schools. Smoking rooms and clatter palaces. Stained, drizzling places to which she was occasionally summoned to be sneered at in words only understood later. 'Your daughter's behaviour is inappropriate Mrs Fitzgerald.' Much later. Told him Jimmy had cried his eyes out for days when he first went to school, which was not quite true, though nearly, there having been at that time in her family's life a general wailing, unconnected to circumstances, as far as she could remember, beyond the front door. The child chewed on the news, glanced back at Jimmy with a little admiration and a little understanding. He told her that he had two sisters and a brother who was nearly a doctor. That was nice. Told her that they lived in Clontarf, and he could see the sea from his room. She sighed at that, thought it lovely. Told her that he was a good swimmer, probably the best in all of Elements. And probably better than anyone in Rudiments as well. As good as that? Yes. Told her that his father was a businessman. And that he was left-handed, (this information was half whispered), and that he took the boy and his two sisters to the cinema practically every week. Popcorn sickness was a family ailment. Told her that his friend in Clontarf, Paul, had fallen off a wall and broken a cheekbone. He had touched it and felt a soft mushy give, and he shuddered slightly as he recalled it. Said Paul had screamed his head off.

About his mother, nothing.

'My mother,' said Dodo, trying to remember, 'was a singer.'

Silence. The dog was yawning.

'She sang old songs that you wouldn't know. Was an angel at a party or a wedding or a funeral or any class of gathering at all. She met my father in a chorus line. He was a chorus boy. She was a chorus girl. They fell in love and lived in Primrose Street. Music always. I had four brothers and two sisters. We were always fed and clothed and cared for. She lived to nearly ninety. She did. My mother.'

Nothing. Then he sighed. Rubbed at his nose.

'My mother left us.'

'She what?' It was a way of saying it surely?

'She left. She had this problem and she had to go away for it. Not to jail or anything, but she couldn't stay because it wasn't good for her to stay. Or for us. Or something.'

Well. She stood still for a moment, paused. Felt a tension start in her knee, a turning of a clammy screw. Looked at the light on the head of the boy. Moved off again.

'That's very sad.'

He gave his sigh.

'She writes.'

What did she write?

'Liked a drink did she?'

'No, not really.'

Well. Dodo frowned and tried to work it out. A lover. But her children? Was the woman maybe dead and the left-handed father and the doctor son telling lies and forging letters? Maybe she really was in jail. Though probably a lover. So easily found these days. So easily taken. A lover. A bright flame in a far town. Perhaps there was, oh, she knew, a break-down. A mental collapse. An asylum.

'How long ago did she leave?'

'I don't know. A few years.'

Could a mad woman write letters?

They turned and came towards Jimmy again. Mulling things over. The boy seemed to whisper, or hum. Dodo tried to hear, but it was hard, above the traffic from the square, and the odd car that passed them, and the one or two people, and the planes in the sky. Jimmy cursed. Dodo looked at him frowning, fed up with his bare belly and his nicotine and his sharp skull. But he was staring off down the street nervously. Dodo looked. The night almost down. Figures in the gloom, moving into the light's glow, one of them briefly open-armed, as if advancing on an embrace. Not a specific embrace. A gen-eral embrace. The glad arms of many. Mossie Russell.

He sauntered. Up the street from Findlater's church as if the path disappeared behind him, a cigarette in his hand, a big thug at each shoulder, two thieves. Brutish shadows and Mossie bringing light. In the sky there was a red line like a cut on a black man. The evening smell. The chill air. Mossie dropped his arms and changed his tune. Slightly hunched now, not a television colour any longer but a late night black and white gangster, bright grey but for the red gash in the skin of the sky.

'You wait here love,' Dodo told the child, pressing him back a little so that he leaned against the railings. She moved away. Moved forward. Halted. Mossie in the open air at night time was not a thing she'd choose. Jimmy was small in the door, not crouching, but small. Mossie Russell said something to his entourage. There was a nod.

'Mrs Fitz.' He stopped and beamed at her.

'No luck then?' Dodo asked in a shakeless voice.

'No.' He seemed delighted. 'Nor you?'

'No.'

'Isn't that an awful shame?'

He was beside her, laid an arm across her shoulders, turned her gently to face the road, her back to her son. His party was lost to her, just shapes pushing gently at the air on her back.

'Not sight nor sign. Odd how a man like your Frank can be so, so, ubiquitous, that's the word, then gone. Gone! Like a ghost. Flitted away into the cracks in the ground. Like a ghost! Whooooosh! Poor Mrs Fitz.'

Behind them there was the sound of a scuffle, Jimmy cursing, protesting, flapping. Mossie's voice dropped into confidence. Between you and me.

'I'm just taking Jimmy off to the flat Mrs Fitz. You don't come home for a while now all right?'

She nodded God forgive her. Nodded in the smoky light. From the corner of her eye she could see the boy, still as a pillar, small as a bead.

'We'll just see about settling Frank's account via a fair estimation of goods and such like. Nothing excessive I assure you. Sort out the whys and wherefores at a later date. No need to worry yourself. Suffices tonight to reach a round figure in terms of items in lieu. Need Jimmy for, eh, for guidance.'

Jimmy squealed like a pig in a dream and Dodo turned just enough to see his arm twisted up behind his back and his face in a scrunch. The gap in his shirt had grown bigger. It seemed to hold a patch of the ground. He was marched by one of the big men back down towards Parnell Square. His insect shadow attached to a tree.

'Don't do that thing with him,' said Dodo.

'What thing?'

'Dangling or whatever.'

Mossie looked at her. Looked into her eyes. Sucked his cigarette.

'OK.'

She nodded, but it was the way he held her gaze. It was too straight. Too solid. Honest and sincere and his word as a gentleman. Liar.

The dog brushed her leg. The second big man was out of sight. Somewhere back there, hands held loosely at his crotch, chewing probably, looking this way and that. Under control Mr Russell. Again the brush of the dog and a waft of his decay. Mossie made a face. Looked down. Made a blubbery noise, shooed at the creature. The creature persisted.

Dodo glanced. And then, oh then, in the night that had finally fallen, with the cold air lapping her shoulders, Dodo heard, and it stopped all the clocks in her faltering world, the thin lovely voice of the boy.

'Mossie. Mossie. Come here.'

She opened her mouth to gasp or gape, or something. But her mouth caught the city and tasted the slowness of all things, the patience of time.

'Come here Mossie. Come here.'

Mossie the man let her go. Stood and peered into the gloom by the railings. Mossie the dog stayed where he was, looked up at Dodo. Dodo wondered at the sloth of sudden things. How they unravel.

Mossie the man stepped towards the boy, who cowered.

'What?' said Mossie. Astonishment really. The heavy squinting too. The boy shifted slightly. Straightened. Took stock of the state of things, his place in the world, decided now might be a good time to be more than he felt he was.

'I was not talking', said the brave, brave boy, 'to you. I was talking', and here he flung out his small exasperated arm, 'to the dog.'

Dodo saw it all as if she was a ghost, hovering in living space, watching the play of small mistakes, the breath of lives, the teasing out of moments.

'Fuckin' cheek,' said Mossie and grabbed the little stick of flesh and pinned it to the black iron, and raised an arm of his own, and swept his hand down twice, the first time only brushing the boy's hair, the second time harder, the second time coinciding, (and here is where Dodo came into her useless own, seeing all things from all angles without moving an inch), coinciding with the appalling arrival of sharp brakes, the Jimmy squeal of them, the opening of a car door, the flashing run of a strange man, eyes lit in fury, his raised left arm crashing past Dodo towards Mossie the man, just as a shout rings out – 'BOSS!' or something – and Mossie turns and seems to arch in the air and come down somewhere else, his shoulder sinking into the man's ribs, the man faltering, the brute shadow arriving with a downward crash of doubled fists and a quick upwards kick to the man's lowered head, the man collapsing, Mossie cursing, Mossie kicking, the brutal shadow kicking, both of them kicking, the dog a mess of barking, the boy a huddle on the cold ground (Dodo watching, altered into infinity, as if the scene is a show in the heavens, the hells), the wretched flexing of the man on the hard ground, his head cracking, his back strangely shaped, Mossie kicking after his shadow has stopped, the shadow taking Mossie's arm, telling him to leave it, 'LEAVE IT!' Mossie patting down his hair, leaving it, cursing, kicking again one last time, the boy jerking, the father jerking, Mossie and his shadow leaving, leaving, walking off, Mossie spitting, tugging at his sleeves, tugging at his sleeves, a groaning from the body on the ground, the pool, the boy moving closer, his hands unnaturally stiff, pale, his white face holding nothing, and then from somewhere else, a gentle crash, seen without turning, a meshing of metal and a sprinkling of glass as the father's abandoned car rolls, with all the time in the world, as if everything, absolutely everything, is inevitable, written down and predetermined, into a parked white van with a side of gothic black lettering which reads 'Charlemont Catering.

34

Fine Food For Formal And Informal Functions. Business Lunches A Speciality.'

Mossie and his men were gone. The dog ceased barking and sniffed at the beaten man until Dodo chased it away. It. The boy sobbed and held his father's hand. There was a red mark on his shocked alabaster skin, where Mossie's hand had found him. He sat on the ground with his feet before him. A small crowd gathered. Someone called for an ambulance. By the time it had arrived Dodo was on the ground too, her knee a roaring furnace, her eyes scorched, her hand on the poor child's head, her voice ragged in the night, her mind a haul of wrong turns and missed chances and good ideas she had forgotten.

'Blast you Frank Fitzgerald,' she cried. 'I hope he finds you and I hope he hangs you and I hope it snaps, the rope, I hope it does, I pray to God the rope will snap.'

And in the gentle night, the swollen clouds roll across the city. And unlucky dogs bark at empty windows. All falls away when you get going. When you get going it all falls away.

Ross and Kinnder

The house was in darkness but for one sullen candle in an upstairs window that flickered for a moment and died. Nothing then. Just the hum of the night and a distant clatter of hooves, some cart dragging noise through the streets.

I read my hands, turning them over and squinting at the backs of them, unsure of a word here and there but getting the gist. There was light from the moon, bits and pieces of it flowing down the edges of things at the corner of my eye, stopping when I looked, and in the near distance a new house was filled with a glow – a gathering started in the middle evening. I thought I could hear music, but perhaps not. There were coaches parked in the roadway, and a cluster of sedans, and men tended their horses while some heavies smoked at the gates and two old Charleys paced up and down swinging lanterns and coughing.

I counted to forty-eight, on the way to one hundred, and my mind drifted then and I lost where I was and started again and counted to thirty, and waited for a while and checked the street up and down and made my way across it, slipping into the shadows of the house, leaving the gate half closed as it had been, not touching it with any part of me. I counted the plants on the left, having to stoop to see if something was a plant at all or just a tuft of grass or rubble of clay, until I counted to the seventh, a big bushy thing up to my thigh, and I wondered what it was called and why it was called it, with its soft pale flowers and its scent like elsewhere oranges. I wondered because I wondered on top of it whether the name, or the story of the name, might tell me something about his reasons. For counting out shrubbery in the gloom is not an accurate thing, and it might have been managed better with a direction towards the first plant or the last plant, or the highest or the lowest. But he had clearly written the seventh. Which might in itself be the thing. But he is not a numbers man, does not pay any due to that, and I don't either, not that way. I am good at them and like to use them – like to count and measure and tally them up – they are easy company and good for the mind, and while I know they hold qualities and cruelties for some, for me they follow simply one after the other, as do the qualities and cruelties of any life.

At the foot of the seventh plant, half buried in the cold earth, was a small leather purse containing the key of the house before which I stood. It was a small key for such a big house. I climbed the steps, six of them, gently, and found the lock and turned the key. There was nothing else to stop me. I clenched my heart and held my breath and stepped into the hall.

Cold. Dark and cold like a touch in winter and I couldn't understand that. Silent too, quiet as sleep, the hum of the night cut off like putting a lid on a jar. Not a sound. Lifeless. I waited, counting again, backwards, from twenty, slowly, moving my lips.

My eyes became useful, but not very useful. I picked out what I needed though – the stairway, and the door to the downstairs where the two housemaids would be sleeping and the old man would be turning and sighing through his wild dreams of horses. I saw the door to the Scottish woman's quarters, the lodger, solid shut. Timid, he had written, newly arrived and ill at ease. Nothing would bring her out. I put the key back in the purse and slipped it into the long pocket of my waistcoat. I peered at the walls and followed them, making my way to the stairs, sliding my feet onto the floor rather than stepping as such. Quieter. I pinched the cuff of my coat in my hand and touched it to the banister and carefully stepped up, afraid that my bones would crack, but they did not.

Slowly I climbed, concerned with my breathing and the gaps between steps, my head tilted always upwards, picking out the features of the landing. A portrait of her mother, a table with flowers, a waxy candle in a plain china holder, a vase on a three-legged table, doors. I paused near the top and tried in the gloom to read my hands once more, but there was not enough light coming through the battered slats of the stairwell window's splintered shutter. There was little money left here. No light, no money. I peered at the delicate black veins on my hands, at the latticework of what he wanted. I knew exactly what was written there, but I felt the need to see it again. Details compel me.

I slipped my security blade from its place in my sleeve and into my palm, snug. I call it my security blade because it's the one I would not be without, ever, under any circumstances. It's six inches, a snub point broken on bone, gleaming edges that rise and meet in the middle. Inch across, tapered. The handle is old wood, I don't know what kind, and it has my sweat soaked into it now so that it smells slightly. I had my initials on it but I scratched them out a year ago or so. I scratched some numbers then, but stopped.

I reached the landing and stood in the cold and waited and counted to fifty. Not a sound. Nothing from outside even. He said that she was a light sleeper and kept things quiet. Told me that the opening of her door would wake her because there was a creak in it and that there was nothing I could do about it other than hurry.

I reached fifty. Quick as I could I made my way across the landing, short steps. I opened the door with my free hand and did not pause. I glided across the room and reached the bedside as a flame rose in the lamp and the birth of a scream broke dribbling from her mouth and her face stared up at me like the face of a child. I got her hair in my fist and with my security blade I sliced her throat, at the same time trying to turn her away from me so that I wouldn't get the full force of the spray. It shot out all over the bed, hitting the floor beyond, and I could hear it. Her eyes rolled and there was a noise in her throat and she clutched at it but went limp very quickly. I stuck her in the back anyway, let her arch. There was quiet then and I felt her slump and I let her fall back down to form a pool on the bed and I moved away from her and checked myself for spray but apart from my hands and my cuffs, and a little on the corner of my coat, I was fine. I doused the lamp.

I spent a moment there in the room with her.

I used a sheet to clean myself and clean the blade, and I slipped it back into its place and quietly left the room. I counted my way across the landing and down the stairs and out the door. Twenty-three. They would not have heard a thing, the lodger in her fretful sleep, the maids clutched in the short dark, and the old man galloping, down in the basement. He rambles and is too old. But she keeps him on all the same. Or she did. He'll have to fend for himself now.

I drank gin in The Lost Child, enough to get me calmed down, relaxed, and made my way then over the river to The Broken Pony, near the cathedral. There was a crowd there and I was soon amongst them, listening to Rogue Murray tell an unending story of a ship's company wrecked and berserk on the coast of Spain. I had heard it before and it was no good. Long Pole was there, and his brother with the bad eyes, sitting in the corner whispering. They called me over but I didn't go. I saw John Lord Sweet and he bought me a drink and licked my ear like a puppy and wanted me to go with him out the back but I was fine after the woman and said no.

'Will you not Kinnder, no?'

'No John, I'm not right for it tonight.'

'Ah Kinnder do me a favour and I'll be all nice.'

'No John, I won't, so leave it now.'

He sulked then and went off to sit with Long Pole and his brother and he tried his luck with the boy but the boy is nearly blind and assumes everyone is as ugly as Long Pole and keeps his mouth shut and looks after himself.

Maud came to me and told me that I had blood and writing on my hands and winked and slapped my arse. She's fat and smells of burning, but her face is friendly and I've never heard her say a bad word about anyone. She sells apples from a cart and stolen watches and small knives from inside her coat, down around The Blind Quay and the Custom House. She has a room somewhere filthy where she keeps cats.

'Will you be seeing Ross tonight?' Maud asked me.

'I don't know. Maybe. Why?'

Maud just shook her head and shrugged and moved off towards the fire where her sister stood swaying. Why had she asked me that? I knew I would not be seeing him. He would not risk it.

Outside in the gloom I found the pump and scrubbed at my hands, holding them up to the moon then to see what progress I'd made. I scrubbed them again and dried them in my handkerchief and held that up to the moon and saw a pink glow and a few dark smudges of ink.

'Will you touch me?' said a voice from the shadows, and I peered but couldn't make out who was there, and he or she didn't speak again and I went back inside.

Maud smiled at me as I came through the door and nodded and I didn't like it. It made me nervous. She drank with her sister and John Lord Sweet was with them as well, and Biggs and Royo and Mary. Long Pole and his brother were still in their corner, talking now to a gent who hovered uneasily beside them and then turned suddenly and laid eyes on Billy Coyle and grabbed him by the elbow and dragged him out to the street, Billy laughing, Long Pole shaking his head and making faces at his brother.

I stayed until the landlord took the stick out, and then left with Royo and stumbled down to Copper Alley where we chased a dog. Then he turned up towards the Castle and I turned towards the river and made my way home, spitting in the water and laughing to myself and throwing stones at any carriages that passed me. I got home and fell into my bed and stared at my hands and saw a smudge of things with only one word left that I could properly read. *Fleece*.

My head in the morning was like a wound.

I couldn't eat and my stomach fell out of me and I took until late afternoon before I was fit for a thing. I washed myself then and walked out as the sun was getting low, passing children playing on Queen Street and a dead horse by the markets. I followed the riverbank to the last bridge and stood for a while looking down at the Custom House, and the line of ships tied to the quay two deep all the way along, with four big ships tied together there by the bridge like they were one huge ship, and men and boys shifting cargo from the last one onto the others towards the quay. They flung crates and barrels like they weighed nothing, while sailors clung to ropes and hung above the decks like madmen, sorting through the sails as if they were looking for something lost.

I strolled like a gentleman along Parliament Street to the Royal Exchange, and on then up towards St Stephen's Green, taking long ways around and stopping at shops and tipping my hat. On King Street I met Crowley and he stopped me and asked had I heard that Mrs Millington was dead, murdered in her bed, her throat cut and her heart ripped out.

'Her heart ripped out?'

'Aye, and blood on the ceiling Kinnder, imagine that though, blood on the ceiling.'

'Her heart ripped out?'

'Oh yes, and half eaten.'

'And do they know who did it?'

'I don't know Kinnder. They say though that she was the mistress of some gent.'

'Who?'

'I don't know Kinnder. They say that this gent's wife might

have hired a fellow. Hired a butcher I'd say, by the state of her.'

'Why?'

'Ripped apart she was, in several pieces in several places, like a chop shop the scene was, they say, it's what they say Kinnder, what I've been told anyway. And teeth marks Kinnder. Teeth marks.'

His face was pale and he spoke in a quiet sort of voice, as if afraid that there might be some re-doing in the retelling. But there is not. What's done is done, and what was never done is words only. I did not want to smile, but I was seeing what I always see – that whatever horror takes place in the world, it is never enough. It will be puffed up until it shocks, and so the audience writes the plot, demanding teeth marks.

'I don't see that there's anything funny in it Kinnder.'

'There isn't.'

'It'd be a way of getting at them,' he muttered.

'At who? What for?'

'Nothing Kinnder. Never mind. I'm assessing only and it makes you smile. I will leave you to your pleasantries.'

And off he trotted, his hips swishing sideways and his lips pursed up and his coat swinging hard behind him. I laughed. But I wondered.

They were lighting the lamps. All along the Green, carriages were lined up, horses stamping and steaming and drivers busy with shovels and brushes. I saw one I knew but avoided him well and made my way to the corner and stood beneath the new tree and paced and tried not to look up at the house. I saw the lights lit in the windows nonetheless, and a maid come up from the basement and run off with a basket, returning later with it full of flowers. Where she got them I did not know.

It took an hour for him to appear, swinging his cane and dressed no different than he would usually be. He had a smile on him.

'Evening Kinnder,' he said.

'Evening Mr Ross, Sir.'

'Job well done Kinnder. Well done indeed. The talk of the town.'

'Thank you, Sir.'

'Hold out your hands.'

I held them out and he stuck his cane under his arm and took my hands in his and pored over them like a seer reading my lines, turning them over and staring at them and touching them gently, feeling for something.

'Good man,' he said and let go, and turned and began to stroll.

'It's a beautiful evening Kinnder.'

'Yes Sir, it is.'

'The quality of the colour. See that sky Kinnder? That's the skin of God, stretched over us. It is the skin of God.'

'Yes Sir.'

'Did you use her?'

'I did Sir, yes.'

'How?'

I glanced at him. He smiled but did not look at me.

'How, Kinnder?'

'In the usual way Sir.'

He nodded and looked at the ground and continued strolling.

'Are you evil do you think Kinnder?'

'I wouldn't know Sir.'

He laughed and slapped my back.

'Well said, Kinnder. Well said indeed.'

'I know I'm not good Sir,' I said.

'No, indeed. Not good. You are not at all good. But then . . .'

He stopped and looked around. Behind us there was no one but an elderly couple some yards distant, strolling like us, deep in conversation.

'Who could be good beneath the skin of God?'

43

'Yes Sir.'

He took up strolling again.

'What age are you Kinnder?'

I didn't know, not really. I had to guess, and then I added to my guess.

'Twenty Sir, or so.'

He was quiet for some time and we walked on together slowly until we came to the corner. Ross stopped and looked up and then turned and we started back the way we had come. He held his cane behind his back now and his steps were lazy enough to make him sway a little.

'We will die in this world Kinnder.'

'Yes Sir.'

'And awake in another. Beneath the skin of this life is the skin of another. Beneath the skin of God is the skin of Kinnder. And the skin of the world. And the skin of Mrs Millington. Do you see?'

'Yes Sir.'

'Beneath the skin.'

He paused and touched his hat as we passed the elderly couple. The man nodded but the woman seemed not to see.

'I will pay you what I said.'

He handed me an envelope and I put it into my pocket and remembered the purse with the key and took it out and handed it to him. He looked at it, puzzled for a moment, and then found a place for it somewhere in his coat.

'Come now Kinnder,' he said, and he led me to a bench in the shadow of a tree where there was little light. We sat down and he looked around and then for several minutes he looked at me, carefully, unblinking, like he was counting.

'Give me your hands.'

He took them in his own and from his coat he took a pen of some kind, and in the darkness, where I could see nothing, he wrote in his small neat lines all the words that he could not say.

*

Leo Redmond could not understand it.

'It is beyond reason,' he said. 'The poor woman. God have mercy on her.'

'Indeed Sir,' I said, and nodded.

I stood in his office watching him eat soup. I was never sure whether he watched me or not, as his eyes were independent of each other and seemed to circle in his head and rotate in their sockets and be everywhere at once like walnuts in a cup.

'Did you know the lady Sir?'

'Lightly. I had met her at functions and so on, in Gardiner's house most recently I think – he supported her, I believe he gave her the house, bought it for her, some such arrangement. She was a friend of his sister's, lost her husband to a riding accident some years ago, was a quiet, gentle woman, contained, sensible. Why this should have happened I do not know.'

'Might it be political Sir?'

Redmond looked up at me, or I believe he did. He raised his head and his eyes swirled and settled somewhere within range of my own.

'What makes you say that Kinnder?'

I shrugged.

'I cannot think of how. I don't believe so. I would not know where to fit it in, how to weigh it up, give it motive, so on, but certainly, she was not unconnected. Architecture I would say Kinnder, more than politics.'

He resumed his soup.

'I do not follow you Sir.'

'I do not lead you Kinnder.'

He sucked at his spoon, and I fancied that his eyes made the noise of bearings, a grind and rattle, that his eyes needed oiling and his belly needed filling, and that in time he would come to me for these things and I would gently give them, and that then he would be all right.

'Will I go Sir?'

'Do not sulk Kinnder, you are foolish with it, it does not suit you.'

He scraped his bowl, and finished it, and took a sip or more of his claret, and leaned back in his chair. Over his shoulder I could see the river, and Essex Bridge, busy still, and beside the bridge the Custom House with the sun glancing off it from the west, and the ships that sat there, a clump of rope and sail and timber, and the lighters that came and went, and the small boats that passed beneath the bridge with their sails put down.

'It is what you are looking at Kinnder. Follow that. Perhaps it is nothing. Indeed, I would be appalled if there were to be any connection, but it is what happens if you try to move the heart of a man half way down his arm, or indeed, the heart of a woman, or perfectly put, so on, the heart of a city, this city or any other, it bleeds to death, and us with it. Her heart was relocated they tell me.'

'I had heard something of that Sir, though I do not believe it. The telling exaggerates.'

'I had it from a medical man who visited the scene, so you may well believe it Kinnder. So it echoes the plans of some to relocate that.'

He jerked his thumb over his shoulder, and I did not know what he meant. The river or the boats or the bridge or the Custom House or the winches or cranes or the cargoes or the bustle or the cries or the money in the air.

'And that, as you can plainly see, is a heart.'

He stood and went to a cupboard to find his pipe, and I stared through the window and was angry that I did not fully understand what he was saying, and I knew that he would not be plain unless I came at it another way, so I dropped back and I waited, and as he resumed his seat and fell, finicky, his eyes clicking in their little tumblers, to the task of lighting the tobacco, I came at him again.

'May I ask you a question Sir?'

'What is it Kinnder?'

'Mr Ross Sir. Do you know him?'

Leo Redmond closed an eye and scratched his cheek.

'Which Ross, Kinnder? Billy Ross?'

'No Sir, I believe he's called Thomas Ross. Of Stephen's Green.'

Redmond coughed.

'Thom Ross. Yes. I do. Why?'

'No reason Sir. A friend has started working for him.'

He nodded, his pipe flaring, and seemed to stare at me. I waited for the thing to take light to his satisfaction, expecting to hear more, but when his hands were down he simply smoked, and contemplated me, or the view to each side of me, or above and below, his eyes being coins in a walking pocket.

'Would he be a good employer Sir?'

He said nothing for a long moment, and I had to resist the temptation to follow the direction of his apparent gaze, as so doing may have brought on in me a fit. I wanted to laugh. How can a man with loose eyes expect to stare out another? Eventually he stirred himself.

'What are you up to Kinnder?'

'Nothing Sir.'

'Thom Ross has connections. He might be said to be on the side of the relocators, the heart surgeons, the butchers. I believe he has a friend in Beresford and hopes to win himself a seat in the Commons. So I do not like him. But aside from the business of the Custom House, if all else were equal and not in issue, I would say still that he is not a man to mix with. It is my opinion. No more than that.'

He sat up.

'Now Kinnder. I have a gross of cases due on Tuesday from Liverpool and I will need to have some men to move half to the Castle and half to Kildare Street. And I do not want that fool you fetched me last time, I cannot spare that level of breakage. To ship a thing across a continent and then have it smashed on the doorstep is not to be tolerated.'

'No Sir. I will see to it.'

'And you will see to it also that you mark all the cases as they are unloaded and that you keep a careful inventory from there to the end, and that not a single one is relocated, you hear?'

'Yes Sir.'

'Relocation is all in all a bad thing Kinnder. I will have the documents for you tomorrow. Call to me at the end of the day.'

He closed his eyes, and I wondered if the dance changed behind the lids, whether it slowed or quickened or ceased altogether.

'I'll tell you a story Kinnder,' he said, in a quiet voice. 'About Thom Ross. A strange little story I heard from a man who's sober and sane and no liar. And even still it is hard to give it credence. Heard from anyone else I would not suffer it a moment. But my source is intriguing, and his telling of it compelling, and I am forced to think that it may be true, or close to true.'

He puffed his pipe but kept his eyes closed. Behind him, the sun's light had left the Custom House, and the shadows were coming up out of the water and the ground.

'It all happened when Ross was at the University, fifteen years ago or so, while Francis Andrews was Provost. Easy times then, more or less. I knew Andrews a little. For a scholar he was a no bad drinker. In any case, young Ross was by all accounts a clever fellow, though quiet and not very popular. He drank little, and did not gamble, but it was said of him, and widely, that he was a regular with the whores, and that his vices were not of the standard student variety, that they were a little more mature, by which I mean corrupted, a little more adult, a little more alarming. He was generous with his father's money, and seemed to enjoy the most those taverns, you know them I'm sure Kinnder, where all of life is bought and sold for the cost of a half-decent meal and some liquor. I remember that it was said that he would go to these places alone and seek out the worst kind of company, and that on occasion this brought him trouble, and there was at least one instance in which he was robbed and wounded.'

Redmond shook his head slowly.

'I knew his father, Arthur, land in Offaly I think, dead now. A sloppy man, easily confused, alert only to whatever inconvenience or offence he himself might be causing. You could not shake his hand without his apologising for his grip being too tight or too loose. A good heart and a bad head becomes tiresome. But his son was a worry to him, more than a worry, he was all that he could not understand: careless of others, devoid of pity, of sympathy, empathy, or any feeling for that matter. Arthur became angry, which was not anger as you or I would understand it, but a flustered, female thing, of wailing and hopelessness.

'Young Ross had rooms at the University, and a brutish manservant who would follow him where he was not needed, and be missing in those places where you might think a gentleman would like some muscle at his side. Rumours were rife. Ridiculous, sordid rumours which Arthur could not believe in, but the consistency and regularity of which alarmed him. He determined to discover what truth there was in them.

'At one point the young man took a trip down to the estate in Offaly, to do a spot of hunting I imagine. While gone, his father set off to visit his rooms. He had trouble gaining entry apparently, having to physically remove his son's servant from the doorway. Once inside he began his examination, slowly, with an open mind, with some hope I imagine, and some trepidation too. I did not hear it from him, so I do not know how he took it, and I do not know the details of this first search, but I know that he did not have far to look for a first indication. In the main room, the sitting room, upon the table, there were drawings of an obscene nature, detailed, skilled drawings, but of subjects not fit for any civilised sketchbook that I can imagine, and writings, in his son's hand, that were sordid, depraved, internal.'

Redmond laughed suddenly, and it seemed his eyes were out again.

'I can see Kinnder that you are shocked at the innocence of it all. What else, you rightly ask, would one expect to find in the rooms of a student these days. Well we are men of the world, and for all his weaknesses, so was Arthur Ross, yet he was deeply troubled by these first discoveries. And in any case, I have not finished, this is not all.'

He stood and turned his back to me and looked out of the window as the light failed. I stared at his shadow as he spoke quickly, quietly.

'In the bedroom, in the bed, tucked up as if sleeping, was the body of a child, a little girl of no more than seven or eight whose throat had been cut and her blood drained, or had bled out, I don't know, in any case there was no blood on the sheets or anywhere else. Poor Arthur was violently ill. He left, and contacted a friend, the man who told me the tale, and they returned and discovered another body, again that of a child, in a trunk. This time there was much evidence of blood having been spilled. The servant had fled. He was not seen again. They debated it for a while and decided that the scandal would be too great. The children appeared urchins, skinny and unclean. They buried the bodies themselves that night in ground owned by the second man, near the river, and they searched the rooms further, removing all drawings and writings that Thom had made, fearing that there would be something in them to give him away. They removed also a quantity of opium and a large collection of children's clothing.'

He turned and seemed for a moment startled at how dark the room had become. He peered at me, as if making sure that I was still there. Then he fumbled in a drawer and lit a match, lighting two tallow candles that sat on the table.

'Thom Ross went to America almost immediately, and there he stayed until after his father died, though Arthur was ill for a long time. He waited until his father was dead and

50

his mother had gone to live in London with her sister before he returned. He had a brother I think, I don't know where he is, and there was a younger daughter whom I assume is in London also. He came back to the house in Stephen's Green, dismissed nearly all the staff and then hired only a basic household with I think only one maid. And he has changed all the furniture and fittings, paid a great deal for new plaster-work and artefacts of all sorts – imported from Italy and the Americas through Mr Donovan. Donovan tells me he has spent a small fortune.'

He sat down and poured himself some claret from a crystal jug.

'Do you believe the story Sir?'

His head was down and he did not answer for a moment. The light of the sky was gone.

'I don't know if I believe it. I don't want to. But the man who told me is an honest man, and I watched his face as he spoke the words. He seemed like a man who had buried mur-dered children in the darkness.'

'Why did he tell you Sir?'

'I don't know Kinnder. Perhaps such a thing needs telling. For sanity's sake. After all, why am I telling you? You may have a need to tell another Kinnder, after a while. Choose well, that's all I say. Choose well. And once only, I beg you.'

'I'll tell no one Sir.'

Redmond drank and looked at me.

'Then you have a stronger heart than I Kinnder.'

I had seen her often. I would collect her at odd hours and she would slip into the house on Stephen's Green by the back way once Ross had confined the servants to their quarters. He would meet her in the kitchens and they would go upstairs and stay there, for hours sometimes, while I paced the cold rooms downstairs and peered out at the street and drank his liquor. She was pretty. Black-haired and pale, and everything about her delicate and light. Her skin would shine.

I think it was because of her that Ross found me. I do not think she wanted to be collected by his carriage man or have to see his maids. I believe she asked him to find someone they could trust. So he found me in The Lost Child and paid me and talked to me and gave me his trust and his money in return for the nod of my head and the look in my eye.

When they came down she would go to the sitting room and he'd have me make tea and bring it in. I would get the sedan then and take it around the back and she would emerge and ignore me and climb in, obscured by the black veil and the shadow, pressed into the corner like a hiding child. I would take her across the city as far as Thomas Street where I would turn then down Twatling Street to the Barrack Bridge and across through Smithfield and by that way through the back streets to her house in Great Britain Street where she would not wait for my hand but jump from her seat and disappear quietly into the house. Sometimes the old man would come out to me for a word. It was horses he loved he told me. As mad as women, some of them, but more beautiful, he said.

Ross never spoke of her.

Mr Ross has never murdered children. I know him. I have read what he writes on me. I have seen the way his mouth is, and the way his voice falters sometimes. I have felt the way he touches me. There are questions that he always asks, and others that he never asks. It is the way he skirts around my work that tells me. He could not do it. That is why he pays me. That is why he writes on my hands, and sends my hands to murder, and touches my hands then when the thing is done. My hands.

I spent an hour in The Broken Pony after leaving Redmond. Royo was there and he was full of himself. He talked at me and I did not listen. Instead I thought of what Redmond had told me, and I thought him a fool to believe it, as foolish as Crowley and all the others for whom simple killing was not enough, for whom the story had to grow in the dark parts of their heads, casting shadows on the places there where they did not want to look.

Billy Coyle approached me and wanted to know if Ross would be out that night. I told him no, and he seemed disappointed. I asked Billy if Ross had ever hurt him, or threatened him, or been odd or rough.

'Mr Ross is a lamb. He drinks milk and talks in pictures and falls asleep.'

I was home early and ate a meal with Mary that I found I needed.

After midnight I removed my gloves.

In Ship Street they had knocked down the tower and rubble was strewn across the dark road and I stumbled twice and hurt my knee and cursed. I made my way forward nervously, looking out for lights and moving shadows. There was not a soul.

Leo Redmond paid me double, I do not know why. I think perhaps he made himself nervous with telling me the story of Thomas Ross. As for Ross himself, this is the third time this month that he has sent me out. I am flush. I will stay away from him for a while though, once I have collected the money. Three times in one month is too much. There is such noise about Mrs Millington that anything similar, even if it is only a whore or a beggar, will be noticed. And it is the first time ever that he has sent me out so quickly after one job to do another. Perhaps he is madder now than before. For I have no doubt that he is mad. How else could this be undertaken?

There was good light. I read my hands and saw the small picture Ross had made on my left palm, of Golden Lane and Friar Street meeting, and the figure in the gateway by the trough. In the mouth of Ship Street I stood in the shadow and peered at the little traffic of drunks and late men. A coach rattled by one way, and a sedan the other, drawing apart a

silence from the point where they crossed, like curtains opening on a stage, revealing Long Pole in the gloom, hugging
himself, shuffling.

I walked ahead and allowed my boots to make noise so
that Long Pole looked up and smiled as I took out my security blade and held it beneath my coat and smiled back at him.

'Kinnder dear, what brings you up this place?'

'I was lonely Long Pole.'

He lost his smile a little and was about to tell me not to
joke with him, I'm sure, when I pushed him sideways into
the shadows of a yard where timber was stacked and covered
against rain. I pressed him up against the wood, and pressed
myself up against him.

'Easy Kinnder, be gentle now. We'll soon have you sorted.'

His hands were somewhere beneath my coat, the same
place as my security blade, and they met a little and Long
Pole cried out and jerked away.

'God Kinnder, careful with that bloody thing. I'm cut.'

I took out the blade and moved to him, a great embrace.

'You are,' I said.

Ladies wore their hair huge above them and some had their
sedans altered to take the height. Others crouched and others
rode like turkeys with their necks pushed out and their hair
cutting the air before them. I sat on the bench and waited for
Ross, my hands crisp now with Long Pole's blood, unwashed
as they were, both of the blood and of Ross's writing, by
order of Ross's writing. I kept them beneath my coat.

A servant girl smiled at me and I nodded. I must know her.
I think I saw John Beresford on my way across the city, a
slope-nosed man in conversation with a lady outside Lord
Northland's house on Dawson Street. He was richly dressed
and loud voiced and gestured quickly and I liked the look of
him. I may leave Redmond and move down river with the
Custom House – he will need men like me. Leo Redmond can
go hang.

It was getting on for ten o'clock, and too hot for me, especially with my hands covered, before I saw him saunter down his steps and cross to where I was, wigged and frock coated, his skin very pale, perhaps powdered. He nodded, and regarded me for a moment, and again I was nervous that we would be seen there together. But what was written on my hands had to be obeyed, or I would have no money.

'Kinnder, good fellow. All done?'

He sat beside me and glanced at the sky.

'Yes Sir.'

'Did you know him?'

'Yes Sir.'

'Was he a friend of yours?'

'I don't know Sir. No, I wouldn't call him a friend exactly.'

'That's good Kinnder, I'm glad of that.'

He ran a finger along his brow. He was sweating.

'Did you do as I asked?'

'Yes Sir.'

'Let's go in then.'

He stood and walked off towards the house and I had to trot to keep up. He led me up the front steps and I kept my head down. Inside, the temperature was cool and I breathed in the air and was glad of it for once. Ross peeled off his wig and his jacket and threw them on a table. He led me to the sitting room where I had brought tea for Mrs Millington. Simple chairs surrounded a fireplace, and two tables held papers and bottles and a pipe. The room smelled sweet to me, of sweat and opium.

'Sit down Kinnder.'

I sat on a hard chair, and after a moment with his face turned up as if looking towards a blemish on the ceiling, Ross dropped to his knees in front of me.

'Your hands Kinnder.'

I held them out and he stared at them for a while, before gently stroking them, his head swaying from side to side. Then he took my right hand in his cupped palms and seemed to read his own writing, breathing sharply and gasping a little, as if astonished. Then he bent forward and breathed once deeply, and exhaled a warm breath on my skin. I could see only the back of his head then, but I felt his tongue begin to lick my fingers and my knuckles and my palm, becoming stronger until he was kissing and feasting on my whole hand, sucking from it the blood of Long Pole and the words that he had written that had drawn the blood of Long Pole and put it there. I moaned and closed my eyes and leaned back upon the chair and rested my hand as gently as I could upon my thigh. But he stopped then and picked up my left hand and started upon it with the same care and the same wildness. I could not help my moaning, but it was as if he did not hear me or notice my state. He carried on in a rapture of his own, cut off from all calling, all attention to the world, until he took both hands at once and tried to cram them into his mouth, and could not, and half screamed then, a ragged scream like a child in pain, and fell lifeless onto the floor, as if every strength had left his body, even the strength for thought and the strength for sending blood about the veins, and the strength for breathing.

I stared at my hands. They were as clean as though I had scrubbed them. All trace of Long Pole and of the instructions was gone. My skin glowed and throbbed and shone and I thought of Mrs Millington.

Ross did not move. I thought he might have fainted. But his voice came then, thin and shaking.

'You may go now Kinnder. Thank you.'

I touched my hands and stood, unsteadily.

'I'm sorry Sir, but the money . . .'

Ross stood slowly, as if in pain. On his feet he wiped at his mouth and looked at me.

'Of course,' he said, but he did not move. He put a finger to one eye and coughed. I felt sorry for him then. He looked pale and unhealthy, and ruined by himself, and bewildered.

'I'll get it Sir, if you'll tell me.'

'My jacket Kinnder. In the pocket of my jacket. An envelope.'

I went and found the money and thought of leaving directly by the back door, but changed my mind, returning instead to the sitting room where Ross sat on a chair, his head in his hand.

'Sir?'

'What is it Kinnder?'

'I heard a story.'

'Yes?'

'About you Sir.'

He shrugged and looked at me. His eyes were wet.

'What about me Kinnder?'

'I didn't believe it Sir.'

'Why not?'

'You are not that kind.'

'What kind am I?'

'I do not know that Sir, I'm sorry.'

'And what kind am I not?'

I went further towards him and sat where I had sat before. My hands still hummed to me, and I stared at them.

'It was said that you had killed children, pauper children, while you were a student, and kept the corpses in your room.'

He looked at me and his eyes changed a little, widened and dried. He sniffed and rubbed his chin.

'It is not true.'

'I did not think it was.'

'It is one of many things said about me Kinnder. That I am a devil. That I eat living things. That I live in a cellar and copulate with wild dogs and demons from the dead world. That I murder children. I do not murder children Kinnder. It's you who does that.'

He did not smile. The room was cold again. My hands hummed. I have said that. The cleanest hands in the city. Long Pole dead by them, split open in a timber yard. For the first time then I thought of his brother.

'Don't say that Sir.'

'Why Kinnder, not saying it will not silence it. I have known you to be the murderer of men and women and children. I have seen the blood on your hands. I have touched your hands. They are your hands.'

I was silent, and I did not like the silence.

'How did we start this Kinnder?'

'I do not know Sir.'

'Neither do I Kinnder. I have forgotten. Have you forgotten?'

'Yes Sir.'

'Was it you who thought of it, or was it I?'

'I believe you hired me Sir.'

'I believe I did. But what made me do that?'

I could not think. He had talked me into a trance and I had been sent out, written upon, and I had continued.

'I have the money Kinnder, that is all. The hands are yours. I have never killed a soul. I would not do it. I am afraid of hell.'

He stood and left the room.

By the river I saw the ships tied down, their masts slung only with rope and the afternoon sky. On the Custom House quay a crowd had gathered by the crushed shape of a boy, held dying by a cage of corn sacks. I went to look, and knelt by him as his sweat and blood ran on the cobbles and the screaming left him for a soft muttering that filled me with fear.

'You are dying now,' I whispered to him, and stroked his hair.

He gripped my hands.

The Dreams of Mary Cleary

The first one was this:

A hand on her shoulder, as might scare her had she seen it on a screen, with suitable music, making her jump. A long-fingered hand, bitten nails, tree knot knuckles, the wicked witch from Snow White that had terrified her little sister when they were young and Disney-going. But she had not jumped. Rather she had calmly turned, a slow rotation of a dark world to a bright world, as if dreamless sleep was a stroll in a lightless place, and dreams a populating of the void, a bloom of colour and detail and sound and scent. She saw a city in the palm of some hills. She saw the sea. A river to it. Streets that trickled here and there. Buildings with the morning sun upon them. Low city. Summer haze. Oh lovely. She saw the scurrying shapes of vehicles and people, but there was a silence, and the absence of familiar things, and she knew she saw some altered world. And then she saw the face that owned the arm that turned her. A kindly face, old, wrinkled, womanly, but only in the eyes, as if that was where the beginning had fled in the end. She smiled, her head in a blue scarf. Bad teeth. The scent of peeled potatoes.

Then Mary Cleary woke.

At work, a break-in. Three PCs gone, a filing cabinet battered open, paper everywhere, Mary's three canisters untouched. But Pat's slides were all over the place, most of them walked on, most of them ruined. Small smudges on the pale floor, grease spots, tiny shards. Pat sniffed and sipped coffee and scratched his head.

'Maybe they'll catch something,' Mary told him, wanting to rub his arm, or tousle his hair or somehow bring him succour.

'The police?'

'No. The burglars. I mean maybe they'll catch something from the samples. You know. Dutch elm. I was making a joke.'

He didn't look at her. She pulled on her lab coat. Stepped on something.

'Oh. Oh God Pat look what I've done. It was intact. I've broken it.'

'Let's see.'

He stepped over and crouched and Mary sighed above his thinning red hair and wished she could forget the woman she had dreamed of. The woman. The woman. He held a slide cracked sideways as if folded, held together by a tiny label running along its length.

'Blue atlas cedar,' said Pat. 'From the Phoenix Park. 1989. It might be all right.' He carried it to a table, placed it gingerly down, peered at it. 'It might be all right.'

Mary looked carefully for undamaged others. She picked them up.

'I'll put Stephen's Green here, Phoenix Park by you.'

'Liffey by the sink,' said Pat and Mary laughed, a little too loudly.

'There'll be streets as well,' he said. 'Put them together. Fairview. St Anne's. Merrion Square is unopened. So is Milltown. God. I don't know. There's ones missing from everywhere. Most of Howth is smashed. They go back sixty years they do.'

He named the city to her by its green spaces. He named trees. Oak, elm, lime. Beech, sycamore, birch. Lawson cypress. Horse chestnut. Ash.

'Ash from Malahide, Mary. I can find none left.'

He became pale, and for a moment Mary saw the future, when it would not be slide samples of bark and leaf and sap, but the trees themselves that had been lost to us, and she closed her eyes, and whispered a prayer for the work they did and the children of her sister.

*

The second was this:

The same city, stones thrown down and lived in. But this time a storm raged. The sea heaved in the bracket of the bay, splashing the land with its foam, thrumming the air, putting a knife in the cold wind. And the wind. A howl of soaked air funnelled down through the low hills, a mouth-filling punch, all unseen and screaming, as if a great ghost, the ghost of a different city, moved through its taken place, raging at the living places, pushing what was pushable, groaning what was not. Mary stood first where she had stood before, but seemed then to be in a different place, lower, the storm engulfing her, her hands on the stone of deserted streets and small alleys. Crying. Why crying? Why? She felt a childish fear, scared of the high wind, the solid rain, the sea she had seen. All will fall. And then her fear seeping out of her as if the storm was abating. It was not, but she felt a calm come into her, and looked around and saw again the woman in the blue scarf. Younger now. Mary's age. She spoke.

'Island.'

'Pardon?'

'Island in the salty sea, the island in the salty sea.'

Maybe it was that. Maybe not. Mary adjusted her head in the rushing air.

'Say again?'

The woman, she was not beautiful, she was from the pages of a book, as if dreamed. Dreamed. Dream. Mary Cleary woke with a jolt.

In the car park of the church, two teenage boys were discussing the resurrection. Historical fact or no. Not documented said one, not witnessed, second-hand accounts only, and they of the aftermath, (his fine hips, brittle as a thin cheese), and they only written by others, later, sixty years or so later. Consistency of report said the other, documented by proxy, truth through perseverance, the clarity of the notion, (he stroked his own neck, palmed the short hairs, sending pale sparks to

61

heaven), the consistency, always, over several versions, the consistency of rising. As easily proof of a well-worked recipe said the first, not at all said the second. Mary stood blessing herself by the font, waving her wet fingertips up to her forehead and down to her breast and brushing her shoulders with her damp prayer.

'Mary.'

'Father Devoy.'

He came from behind her, out of the cold air and the shadow. The boys glanced at him and moved away. Mary watched their arses, pistoning their pale blue engines across the black world, as the priest took her arm.

'You wanted a word?'

'Yes. I won't keep you. Are they yours?'

He looked. Seemed to squint, suspiciously, at the side of her give-away head.

'They are. Nice lads. Paul there on the left has the stirrings of a vocation. Smart too. His friend is, ah I don't have his name right, something vaguely continental, his father Swiss or Italian, airline man. Good looking boy. Plays soccer day and night. Good at it too they say though it's not my game and I wouldn't know. I'm a hurler born and raised.'

He made an awkward swinging motion and hit her on the hip. She smiled and he blushed. Coughed into his hand.

'What can I do for you Mary?'

The boys went out the gate and parted with outstretched arms, as if, tilted, one was falling from the other, clutching awful air, unable to touch, unable to reach that far. Had they sorted out the resurrection then she wondered? Put it to rest. Laid the ghost. Laid.

'I am having bad dreams.'

'Bad dreams?'

They sauntered through an arboreal archway, into the warm air of the garden, the other silence, the greenery.

'Yes. They concern a city. This city, I believe. I find myself in it, or above it, sometimes below it, around it, beside it,

THE DREAMS OF MARY CLEARY

whatever. I find myself there. In the company of The Virgin. She tells me things about time.'

He looked at her, all his usual pallor returned.

'The Virgin?'

'Yes.'

'The Virgin Mary? Our Lady? The Mother of Our Lord?'

'The same.'

'Christ.'

'I know.'

He stalled in his stroll and sought out the bench. They sat. Mary breathed deep the fragrant heat. She spied out the coxcomb, pinched her eyes at a yellow rose, weighed the chrysanthemums, thought of cooling. Thought of her frozen soil.

'I'd be wary.'

'Of course.'

'Why are you telling me?'

She shrugged, dislodging the buzz of a creature from a point somewhere starboard of her left shoulder.

'Priest. Mary. Fear.'

He hummed, swatted at his deserted knee, seemed at a loss.

Mary sighed, searched the blue sky for a face.

'What does she say?'

'That the city is going up.'

'Is . . .'

'Going up. Ascending. Entire. In the year after, something. Abu Simple. Shifting upwards. Due to flooding. I believe this is metaphor.'

'Abu . . .'

'Yes. Simple. Symbol. Something such as. But this is also the past. *Neither shall there any more be a flood to destroy the earth.* A qualifier there you'll notice. Destroy. This is also the future. The city will go up. Raise itself I gather. Be gathered. Then down below I suppose, there'll be some rainfall.'

'You're Noah are you?'

She gave him a look. He gave her a smile. Oh indulge the Lord.

'No. I am not. All the world is for the bin except here. Except the bit of the river, the length of the river and the width of the river's length across the river.'

He let his breathing be heard. Pushed his feet across the grass, cracked a small bone into place, embraced his self.

'How many dreams?'

'Seventy-four.'

'Nightly?'

'Not at first. Then regular as sleeping. All entirely remembered. All as clear as day. And they do not fade over time. I could close my eyes and tell you start to finish any one of them as if I dreamed it now.'

He shifted his black seat, waved at his face as if sending it away somewhere and clutched the edge of the bench.

'Do so.'

She shut out the light and the heat went with it. Number thirty-three came to mind. A loop.

'We're sitting in the, what will I say, parlour, is that right?, I don't know, of a suburban house in the 1930s.'

'Parlour?'

'She uses the word. A small sitting room, chilly. On the wall there is a wide painting, dark browns and deep greys and shadows on the faces. It is Christ feeding the five thousand. He has his eyes turned up as if in pain, but serene, and baskets of fish at his feet, and his hands out, all palms, and loaves in the folds of his robe. Mary sips tea. Clears her throat. She tells me that there will be a fire. A fire? A fire. Not a flood? A fire first she says, across the sea, and the water will fall before it rises – an ebbing preceding the great foaming rush. She says that before the fire there will be not enough prayer and after the fire there will be too much.'

'Too much prayer?' snaps the priest. His face, Mary senses, a bit like a jumping horse, though she keeps her eyes shut.

'It's what she says. She sips tea. Then she tells me that as the city rises, the length of the river and the river's width etc. there will be sundering. Along the line of the going up there will be the line of the staying put. Families split she says. Farms in two. People driving, safe one second, drowned the next. Houses where the kitchen will split from the parlour. The parlour. Such as this, she tells me, and with that I feel a lift-off, and I cannot help but think of astronauts, and the whole room goes up but for the one wall which is ripped, masonry falling, crumbles of brickwork, flakes of plaster, and is left behind, and the sky appears where it has been and we shoot up into the sky like a fucking rocket.'

The priest inhaled a high squeak.

'Sorry father.'

She opened her eyes. The light was like a liquid. Thick and clinging. The real world.

'Is that it? It stops there?'

'Yes father. We're left in mid-air. Except that it repeats. It's a repeating dream. A loop. Three times.'

'No differences?'

'Yes. The second time it's not the feeding of the five thousand but the wedding feast at Cana, and the third time it's the Last Supper. All food and drink based affairs you'll notice. Other dreams repeat before I wake, some as many as a dozen times. Those tend to involve the apostles.'

'Tell me those.'

She briefly let her eyelids fall. Oh God. There is a touching. She opened wide the world. She did that too. Which was it, James or John with the mole beside his navel, a black eye by a pale gaze, a rock by a pool? Which one was it whispered from the Book Of Daniel, *and he changeth the times and the seasons: he removeth kings and setteth up kings: he giveth wisdom unto the wise, and knowledge . . .* and oh, and oh. That was her last. And Judas was the gentlest but Philip was the best. His chest a drum of wilderness. A pillar of words.

'Thus were the visions of mine head in my bed.'

The priest coughed. Mary rubbed her eyes.

'I'm sorry father. Some dreams are . . .'

'Too upsetting.'

'Private.'

He coughed again. Closed that part. His squinty eyes. Mary stood and he followed. She walked a circle of the garden, feeling the heat less for the height she had and more for moving. A tear of sweat meandered down her back. She cupped a bell lily in her damp hand.

'Do you want them to stop?'

'Yes. No. I want to know what it means. I want to know whether I should hope.'

'You should always hope dear,' he said, without pausing to think. He stopped then, she could hear his uselessness. 'Not of course that it is true. That would be a little dramatic. I think rather that, as you say, this is a metaphor. I would say that it is up to you how you take this, ah, gift, this gift of visions, and up to you how you react, how you yourself interpret it. For after all, I think perhaps we are the only ones who can interpret our own dreams. For we are the only ones who know them fully. Know them all. Know how they are informed by the lives we lead. How they are shaped in that way. Whether they are calls to correction. To prayer.'

No fool he. All of them, he said. Fully, he said. It was her fault then. Her weakness. Her mind.

'You don't believe it is the Virgin?'

'Her name is Mary.'

'What else?'

'Your name is Mary also.'

Mary Cleary straightened her wet back and glanced at her priest. All black to catch the sun. He was smiling.

'Father . . .'

'Yes . . .'

'You're not listening to me.'

Pat folded a sheet of negatives carefully and placed it in an envelope and the envelope in a drawer. He yawned. He turned the small key in the lock in the drawer and pulled the key out, tried the drawer, put the key in his pocket. He had missed a bit shaving, under his chin, giving him a shadow there, as if the sun was above him and he stood in the centre. Mary looked at his shoulders. At his short hair and the way it thinned and disappeared beneath his collar, his skin blotchy there, red. He dressed badly in cheap pastel shirts and shiny-arsed black trousers. She tried to fancy him. She forced herself to look at his crotch when she was sitting and he was walking towards her. There was nothing. No mystery. Flat and black and boring like staring at a flap of road. She wondered what he did with it. Where he put it. In which part of his life. She sniffed at him when he passed. Tumble dryer and soap and a stinging spurt of metallic spray. Man, clamped and clipped. Working man. Naked but for his clothes. Cropped by time. She thought that such men would go neither to heaven nor hell but hover for a while in the light air and form a queue. And re-enter then, reincarnate themselves into middle management. And so on.

'Have a good weekend?'

He hummed. Yawned again. Maybe he'd been up all night fucking a perfume counter girl from Switzer's and didn't know what day it was.

'I went to Cork.'

Well. There are women in Cork. There are long tunnels. Imaginations and staring and adventurous . . .

'I was running in a 5k.'

'What?'

'A 5k road race.'

'Oh.'

He smiled. His body was that of a runner then. An athlete.

'I didn't know you runned. Ran.'

'The odd time. Used to be good. I'm slower now. I might have made something of it one day.'

What did he mean? He was twenty-five, no more. Too late?

Too late already? She pressed her fingers to the wood of her desk. Something shot through her.

'Did you win?'

'Fourth.'

'Will you come to dinner?'

He looked.

'Out I mean. I can't cook. We could go somewhere nice. My treat. We should really. We've worked together long enough. It'd be nice. Do you like Thai?'

His head bobbed, he swallowed a smile, the bastard, brushed at his arm with his other hand, did something with his feet.

'No. No. I mean, I don't think. Thanks anyway. I'm not much for going out anyway. Thanks anyway.'

Anyfuckingway.

Then a dream beyond dreaming:

A pair, more than a pair, of hands, held her ankles, her delicate ankles, and inched her carefully, slowly, out of her bed, pulling, tugging, the length of her, the whole of her, out over the edge, the precipice, the b, br, brink, out, Christ, the cold air rushing, out over the deep black space, out over the abyss, the gap in the world, out from the height, the rise, the going up, the gone up, the push, the haul, out from the high hill of the saved city, and dangled her, dangled her, swung her round and her flat shape cutting the cold night air, and dangled her, dangled her, first by a foot, then by a toe, over the whole sodden world, dammed in a watery pit below her, and she felt her long hair fall and her arms fall also, all akimbo in the high night. And her dizzy eyes picked out the drowning and the spires of swallowed churches. The splashing hands. Mary Cleary screamed and tried to wake. Nothing. The sound of hanging in the brittle future. Again she took a fill of cold wet wind and bellowed out her fear and shook her head to wake it. No. Nothing. She swayed and felt the fingers on her big left toe slip a little. Be still she

68

told herself. Be still. She spat and watched the thin silver traces plummet through the inky distance, disappearing in the small choppy glints of the flood.

'This disjunction,' said a voice, hollowed out by ease and astonishing calm, 'is true in the extreme. Here I am.'

And there she was, Mary in her blue hood, looking a little bored, hovering upside down in front of dangling Mary Cleary, her arms folded, her feet bare, her mouth set in a puckered line, a troubled figure in the earthless world.

'What?'

Not upside down of course. It was Mary Cleary who was upside down, hung head first.

'Your apostate. His mouth is very wide Mary, not that you should have confided in the first place. My son is angry. Wants me to drop you.'

And the fingers let the toe of Mary Cleary go, and the water shot closer like a shift in magnification. Mary Cleary squeaked a scream. Then. A pair of full hands grabbed her arches.

'But I will not. For he's had enough of this world. My touch is subtler.'

Mary Cleary fought for breath. Blinked and swallowed.

'Am I dreaming?'

Silence.

'Am I to understand that there is some dispute between your son and yourself?'

'Yes.'

'Jesus.'

'Indeed. So he's turned his back on us. A certain pique at the balance of devotions. He's elsewhere, trying again.'

'Are you really', asked Mary Cleary, finding it hard now to keep all the blood of her body from the shallow cup of her head, 'who I think you are?'

The hovering holy mother twitched.

'Am I . . .?'

'Who I think you are?'

She made a face then, as if mildly disgusted, as if such a

question was beneath her. Much was beneath her. The world as well. Mary Cleary watched the weight of her question carry the Virgin down a good twenty feet. And pause then, her pale faced raised.

'It is all I am.'

Mary Cleary thought on that, and it hurt her eyes, pounded at her temples. She blinked a long blink and looked for something peaceful. When she opened her eyes again she was no longer dreaming. No longer dreaming. No longer in the same dream.

'Father.'

'Mary.'

He was sitting in a wooden armchair in his ante-chamber, his sacristy, slumped as if exhausted by the mass, the low fumes of wine and dust and altar boys swirling between them.

'You nearly got me killed.'

He was astonished, and shifted a little.

'I . . .?'

'Nearly got me killed.'

He left his mouth open and she looked into it. There was a hollow of darkness with a pale glow and she wondered where the soul was and whether it might be in the mouth.

'How so?'

'You ratted on me.'

'I ratted?'

'Told.'

'Told who? What?'

'Told someone about my dreams.'

He moved his head slightly forward, closed his mouth, raised his eyebrows, looked up at her meekly.

'No,' he said.

'Well actually yes you did, so really I don't mind if you deny it because I know that you did whether you know it or not.'

'I always talk to you in confidence Mary. Always.'

She looked around herself. One of the walls seemed to consist, largely, of little drawers. She liked that – all those tiny hideaway places where it might take an age to locate the simplest of things.

'I swear I have not said a word to anyone about, about what you told me.'

The drawers had small labels on them she thought, with writing which she could not read from where she stood. So she set off on a little amble towards the wall, her hands behind her back, leaving her bag where it was in a heap on the tiled floor.

'Do you pray Father?'

There was writing all right, handwriting, the same hand on each label.

'Of course.'

It was faded, a blue-grey scrawl sloping heavily to the right.

'And when you pray do you tell about your day, relate the incidents thereof, make a little list of all the things that happened, present them as a tally, meditate upon them?'

There were fifteen drawers. Five rows of three; three columns of five.

'Yes, I . . .'

'Bookkeeping is it?'

'Well . . .'

'Debits and credits and bad debts and balances.'

'It is not so cold as that.'

She thought one of the words was *threadbare* or *threaten* or *theosophy*, and another seemed clearly to be *conventions* and a third looked like *fleet* or *foetal* or *fleece*.

'Well that's how it happened then.'

He coughed.

'That's how what happened?'

She wanted to open a drawer and have a peek, but his voice had turned a little impatient and she thought she should give him her full attention. She went back to her bag and looked at him.

71

'You prayed you see. You prayed, I bet, to him, to Christ, rather than to her, his mother, or any random saint.'

He nodded, very uncertainly.

'And tipped him off, inadvertently I know, but nevertheless, and he's gone berserk with the mammy and she's taken it out on me. Nearly frightened me to death she did, never mind about the actual dropping business.'

He looked confused, and made a shrugging, Mediterranean type gesture.

She leaned forward from the hips, spoke quietly.

'They're having a row,' she said.

He nodded, very slowly.

'It seems that he has become jealous, or has always been jealous, or will have become jealous very shortly now in the past, or he was jealous in the next couple of days, he is jealous last week, used to be jealous in the future and is currently oscillating his jealousy over a roughly, in our terms, bifocal, or rather, bi-millennial kind of time frame. Although it is kind of bifocal, or it seems that he is. I'm sorry, I'm not making myself very clear.'

'No.'

He was not buying this at all. He stayed where he was and made slight rotary movements of his lower arms, his hands. His face, though perturbed, was gentle, had assumed again that soft, vaguely stupid humanity which she supposed he felt was required of him. For her own part she felt that it would achieve nothing to shout.

'Basically what it amounts to is that I'm having these dreams.'

'Yes.'

'And that these dreams suggest to me that I know more about your business than you do.'

'Really?'

'Which is very rude of me. I shall not talk to you any further on the matter.'

He formed a church with his hands, which Mary thought

72

very sweet, and looked up at her from roughly the sacristy, thereby seeing her from within a representation which was itself within a representation of what was after all a symbol. There they had it – a little trinity as if by accident. He nodded.

'I have not been very helpful Mary. Please, if you feel that you would like another priest to listen to you, I can make an introduction, without any detail whatsoever of course, and set it up for you. Or if you would like any other form of coun-selling, non-spiritual or spiritual, then please ask me and I'll see what I can do to help. But as for myself, I am really not a dreams and visions man. I play some golf, I raise money, I say mass, I know my lines, what can I tell you?'

'You've been very kind.'

She leant down and opened her bag.

'Have a drink.'

She took out the middle canister, labelled *Island Bridge 1989*, and unscrewed the top.

'What have you got there?'

'Just water,' she said. Just the flowing water rising and the sea will soon meet it, and if she couldn't have one thing she would have the other, and if her dreams were her own they were no worse for all that, and that if they were not she would take what was due her.

She looked around for a cup or a glass and could see only the washed chalice, and immediately liked the idea of that. She fetched it and poured him a mouthful, just a mouthful, just enough to fill his mouth, to bathe his little soul.

'Just take a sip,' she said, and walked towards him and saw the small fear in his eyes, and felt that she might be dreaming and she might not, but that either way there was clearly between them all of the future and all of the past and that if one was to be torn from the other then it may as well be localised, internal, something you might feel from the soul in the mouth to the city in the gut.

He protested but she made him do it. Made him drink.

73

Though the dream here is vague and the distance intervenes and the times are shuffled and the scene is stretched. He drank, he drinks, now, just now, this moment, not before, not after – just as you read this he drinks. The two of them, alone, together, in the room off the cross, in the armpit of the Lord, they sip together, they drink together, their lips together, their lives together.

Some of it spills, and they can sense in the small room, distinct and home-made, shared from the well, gathered from the trough, the smell, the smell, the smell of the river.

The Problem with German

Anger is a box, a shelter, a place to put things for a while, a small container, a quick construction, cobbled together from items close to hand. Such as – your flimsy paranoia, and your rusty, ancient self-doubt, and maybe that inexhaustible low-level terror as well – the one which on good days makes itself known to you as a mild joy at living, and on bad days is simply glue, choking and thick and sometimes, in a way that is a little perverse, a little embarrassing to you, useful. Anger is temporary – it serves a purpose. It's filled with all your huddled fears, your confusion, your failure to understand. It takes in the lost and the damaged – your homeless thoughts and your displaced fears, your abused sense of self and your mass of self pity. It pitches camp in the wide-open spaces of your mind, and gathers in the refugees and gives them the basics, some nourishment, some shelter.

Anger is a place to put the things we do not want.

There is a strange bench at the corner. It is a circular heap of concrete with a flat hollow top where flowers should be, but which is filled instead with dead mud and litter. A ledge in the concrete, lined with wooden slats, serves as a seat. The bench is ugly and the wood is scratched and written on, and cold. Robert sits there, furiously herding, rounding up his damaged notions, his rotten memories, his errors. He is divided, angry.

His legs are stretched out before him and crossed at the ankle, the upper foot twitching quickly, a blur at the edge of his vision. He folds and unfolds his arms, puts his hands in his pockets and takes them out again. Every few moments his head jerks tightly to his right and he stays still. It is a distant corner that interests him. Every time a figure appears there he squints at it for a moment, without moving at all, except for a kind of craning, a barely perceptible stretching. And then he loosens his gaze, and slowly turns back again in an arc, looking up at the sky and down at the hard ground where the grass is losing its colour, and he resumes his twitching, and sets about rearranging his arms once more.

It is dusk now, getting cold. Robert smokes a cigarette and decides what to do. He jumps from one thought to the next, trying to list and register and categorise the contents of his anger. He tries to find the most needy of his pathetic charges, dimly aware that it is a hopeless, impossible task – that he is flooded, that there are too many of them, and that they have come from everywhere, including the most unexpected of places. But his anger rages, his insides teem with voices and clutching hands and cries for attention, retribution, succour, anything, anything but this. He does his best, deciding to go here and there and elsewhere, but in the end staying exactly where he finds himself – sitting on an ugly bench with an overcrowded anger filling his gut. He will do nothing. He will stay where he is and do nothing. It is not up to him to do anything. He will sit here and wait.

Across the street is a bar, its window filling with a watery grey light, a couple of shadows moving about in its gloom. He thinks of going in for a drink, of sitting at the window and watching the distant corner from there. But he does not want a drink. And anyway, Karl would not see him in there. He wants Karl to see him. Karl will stop when he sees him, and then approach him and sit down. And Robert, after a long pause, will allow the wretched inhabitants of his anger to have their say. And the eloquence of the just cause will stop Karl dead. All these pointed voices, so memorable, so loud, will say something so precise and to the point and perfect, that it will cover everything, and that will be that. There will be no need for anything else. And Karl will realise what has been going on, and he will feel in his heart what

Robert feels, and he will apologise, and they will sort it out.

But always, this nagging doubt, this vague presentiment, that his anger will not hold, that it is too weak, that the cause is perhaps not so just after all, that the box will split and its contents spill, and that the eloquence will be dispersed and will lose its cohesion and become silent and will slink away into the crowd of his mind, and that in time this anger will, like all the others, be forgotten.

He thinks about preparing the ground. Of making of the most persistent voices a representative, short speech. He tries several variations, using different starting points, changing the emphasis, bringing certain notions to the fore, tying thoughts together which are not properly linked, losing himself eventually, of course, in the mess of it all. He decides to leave it until the moment. Maybe Karl will speak first. Maybe he will have spent this time on his own considering everything that has happened and not happened, and he will realise what he needs to realise, and he will apologise, and speak about the future and will not need to be told. It should be like that. He should apologise. After all, if he thought for a moment, for even a moment, about why it is he is on his own in the launderette, then he could not possibly fail to realise what the situation is. What the problem is. If he even spent half a minute thinking about what had gone on in the last ten days, about how he had treated Robert, about how he had behaved, about how he had left everything unsaid after all this time, then surely he would realise. Robert had, after all, come all this way. Across Europe. For silence? No. It would not take a lot of figuring out.

A launderette. It was a lowly place from which to launch an exodus.

If Karl did not apologise straight away then there would be something seriously wrong with him. With them. With the whole situation.

Robert will say nothing.

It is not up to him to say anything.

Cars move slowly around the corner where Robert sits. Some drivers look out at him and Robert stares right back. What are you looking at? It pleases him that his aspect, his appearance, his demeanour attract attention. Damn right. He holds the gaze of those who stare at him.

There are passers-by. Some couples, some in threes and fours, some alone. He does not like the couples who walk in silence. He does not understand them. He does not understand the ones who talk either. Robert knows no German. Except for the few phrases and curses that Karl has taught him. Karl teaches the German first, getting Robert to repeat the words over and over until he has it right, without telling him what it means. Then he reveals it with a laugh – that what Robert has learned to say is in fact 'fuck yourself in the knee,' or 'my penis is a little flower'. You would teach a parrot to say stupid things that way. This is part of his anger, and not a small part.

Robert does not like the sound of German. You cannot, he told himself, whisper in German. You can only argue and be adamant and stubborn and precise. He does not believe that a German speaker ever has to search for the right word. Karl wants him to learn the language. He will not. This, too, is contained in his anger – it is a spike in his anger, a high point, a peak.

He looks up the street to the distant corner, and keeps looking. He has to turn his head to do it, and he can feel an ache begin in his neck. He thinks of moving around the bench so that he can face Karl directly. But he stays where he is, so that Karl will be unsure whether or not he has been seen. Every figure looks like Karl now. But Karl will be carrying a bag, so he rules out those who carry nothing. Once or twice he is sure that he sees Karl. But it is not Karl.

From a distance, strangers can look like Karl. They have his shape and his stride. Robert looks at them, and his mind, so taken up as it is by the size of the anger, considers being with them. Sleeping with them, arguing with them. Giving them the bulky, misshapen box of his fury. And also, with that, there is a quieter thought, a tired and weary notion, uncontained, that they might simply go back to the apartment and go to bed and hold each other. Then he realises that the person he looks at is not the person he thinks of. It is some German man who does not know anything about him. What does this mean? To be so easily mistaken.

He glances at his watch occasionally. He tries to work out times and distances. He tries to remember how long it had taken the two of them to walk from the apartment to the launderette. It could not have been more than twenty minutes. He calculates in his mind. He takes into account the time they left the apartment and the distance to the launderette and the distance from there to where he now sits and waits and the length of time they had spent together in the launderette before he had walked out, and the length of time that had passed since then and the length of time it might take to wash clothes and bedclothes and tablecloths and the time it would take to wait for them to dry, taking into account what had been completed while he had been there, and he looks at the sky and sniffs the air and decides that it will be as much as another hour before Karl appears. Anger lends itself to this, to attempts at exactitude, to the careful examination of the facts.

Robert stands up and sighs and feels the muscles stretch in his legs and walks towards the distant corner. He looks again at his watch and stops. Maybe he is wrong. He feels wrong. Maybe they left the apartment earlier than that. Up the street a woman pulls down shutters on a shop. He turns around and walks back to the bench.

Robert lights a cigarette and stretches out again and turns his head to gaze up the street. The light is fading. Shadowy Germans move around against the background of grey walls and buildings like figures in an old film. The only colour is in the sky. He does not like this place. Not the bench on the corner, not the street, not the city. It goes on and on and on as if nothing can stop it or split it or shame it. Or kill it. It spreads like a stain with no centre and no heart. It is all shadows and old films. Here is where this happened, and here is where that happened, and here is where this voice said that and that voice said this and now there has been so much laid down here that it is impossible to take a step without stepping on a shadow. On the long shadows.

He takes care of his anger.

The night before, they had gone to a bar in Kreuzberg, a bar curiously inconspicuous on a quiet street. Karl had sat there watching Robert, waiting for him to be impressed. Robert had not been impressed. He had noticed that all the gay bars which they had visited in the city had about them a kind of grim, bored utilitarian aspect. He did not know if that was the way of things in the city, or whether these kinds of places were to Karl's taste. One was for leather, another for younger gays, another for older, another for young gays who liked older gays. Most had cruising in mind, with dark rooms and videos. Others concentrated on music or drugs or drinking. This one, it seemed to Robert, though now virtually empty, might, when full, be dedicated entirely to bitching. It was a gaudy, depressing place, without atmosphere or imagination. Silver glittered stars and moons and baubles hung from the matt black ceiling, reflecting endlessly in the mirrors which cluttered up the walls. Between and above and below the mirrors hung black and white photos of movie stars and bodybuilders. The bar counter itself was veiled in a bead curtain and lit from below somewhere by a dull red neon, giving the barman the look of an embarrassed corpse. A circular bed with bright pillows and cushions occupied a raised platform by the window. It seemed that nobody was allowed near the bed, surrounded as it was by the kind of red rope which is found holding back the public in museums and galleries. The furniture was wooden and old and painted black. The centre-piece was, of course, a fountain. A rather dazed looking cherub stood holding a large drooping leaf in his outstretched arm, from which the water trickled down into a dirty pool lit pink and blue and studded with coins and bottle-tops.

'What do you think?' asked Karl, adding, after the shortest of pauses, 'It's great isn't it?'

'It is, yeah.'

'It is.'

'Great,' said Robert, as enthusiastically as he could and overdoing it.

Karl frowned at him and drank from his bottle. Robert lit a cigarette.

At a table in the corner two men sat talking animatedly, loudly, laughing with shoulders that went up and down as if they were only pretending to laugh. Robert looked at them and tried to work out what they were talking about, even roughly. But he could not. The words blurred into each other and every barked out sentence sounded like an order to shoot. This way to the showers. Achtung.

The barman leaned on the counter, his head hooded by beads, writing on a postcard, or something. At a small table by the fountain a black man with peroxide blond hair and torn jeans stared into the water. Three men and a woman watched him and whispered to each other. A man coming out of the toilets caught Robert's eye and smiled. Robert smiled back.

'I must ring Elsa,' Karl said.

'What, now?'

'Yeah. Can you see a phone?'

'Why now?'

'I said we'd meet up with her later.'

'Oh.'

He wanted to ask why. He wanted to ask Karl why he had said that they'd meet up later? Why did they have to meet up later? Why Elsa? Why again? Why couldn't they spend just one night together, without meeting anyone? But all he said was 'Oh.'

Karl went to the bar and spoke to the barman with the post-card, who pointed towards the front door. Robert thought that he was directing Karl to a telephone on the street, but then he saw Karl stand into an alcove at the end of the bar near the door and scrunch his shoulder to his neck to grip the receiver and reach into his pocket.

Elsa spoke very little English. She and Karl spoke in German. Then they would turn to Robert and speak in English. Then they spoke in German.

A man came into the bar from the street and the black man by the fountain stood up and they said something to each other and embraced and kissed. The man who had come in went to the bar and bought two bottles of beer and came back and sat down next to the black man. They started talking. Robert thought it strange to hear a black man speak German. It worried him, as earlier that day he had been worried by a playground full of blond kids ordering each other out of the sandpit and into the swings. Onto the swings. Himmel. Gott in himmel.

The man who had just come in suddenly got up and walked over. He stood by the table and looked at Robert and smiled. He opened his mouth and spoke.

'Pllggtgfur?' he seemed to say.

Robert stared at him. He widened his eyes and his head jerked a little.

'Tlugerggtfur?' It was like a spit. An operatic spit.

The man looked at Robert and shrugged and looked around as if for assistance. He was embarrassed. He leaned down, precisely, as if giving a small bow, and in a very loud voice, with his eyes on Robert's eyes, he fired out a string of clipped metallic words as if he thought that Robert was per-haps deaf, or retarded. Or foreign. Robert raised his hands and displayed them, palms outward, and shook his head.

'I don't speak German.'

Then Karl appeared at the man's shoulder, sighing. He leaned over the table and stuck his hand into Robert's shirt pocket and took out his lighter and handed it to the man and said something that sounded apologetic. The man laughed and went back to his table where he lit a cigarette for the black man and for himself. Then he handed the lighter back to Robert and said something else and laughed again.

Karl sat down and drank from his bottle and shook his head slowly.

'What?' said Robert.

'What what?'

'What are you looking at me like that for?'

'He asked you for a light.'

'Well I know that now.'

'But I told you that one. You have that one learned.'

'I have not. I hadn't a clue what he was on about. I thought he wanted to see my papers.'

Karl frowned.

'Is that your only joke?'

'What?'

'Whenever anyone says anything you go on about the fucking war. It's really pathetic. Why don't you try and learn something?'

'You have to understand the way I am Mein Herr.'

'That's your other joke. Cabaret is your other joke.'

'I do what I can – inch by inch – step by step – mile by mile – man by man.'

Robert hummed quietly and lit another cigarette and glanced at the couple by the fountain. The black man spoke and moved his hands and his eyes and the muscles of his face, and the other man nodded and made small noises, 'Ja, ja, ja,' engrossed.

'What did Elsa say?'

'We're meeting her at eleven.'

'Where?'

'Outside the theatre.'

Robert could think of nothing else to ask.

At the airport, they had smiled and fumbled an embrace

and spoken at the same time. They had travelled across the city in a bus. In the first silence Karl had asked how long Robert was going to stay. Two weeks he said. Then the second silence fell. A week or more had passed since then, and the silences had grown and grown.

Robert drank and looked at Karl, at the dark hair that fell over his forehead and which he brushed back with a new gesture, learned in the time he had spent in the city. His city. He had slept with men here. Robert knew that. They had spoken about it, in a way, and Robert had claimed to have slept with men at home, when he had not. He looked now at Karl's hands and felt inside his chest a strange feeling, like a flood of something.

'Diddley de de dee – two ladies,' he hummed.

Karl smiled at him and shook his head again.

'Another beer?'

'Yeah, OK.'

Karl stepped across the floor of the bar with their two empty bottles. He leaned on the counter and spoke to the barman, who smiled as he opened two new bottles, and then put them on the counter and held the bases of the bottles while Karl clutched the necks. They stood like that for a moment, the barman talking, and Robert looked at them and felt the flood inside him rise and felt himself breathless as he saw the back of Karl's body. It was as if he saw it from a great distance, but clearly. It was as if he was not meant to see it. As if it had nothing to do with him. But he had made love to that body only hours before. He had lain down beside it and had matched its length with the shape of his own body, and they had dozed in the sunlight that streamed through the yellow sheet that served as a curtain and was better than any curtain could be. But here, in the bar, the body was different, like a version of Karl that he could not understand because it was not directed towards him, or because he did not know its language. And it was that which was closed to him that caused the flood.

84

He turned away and swallowed and waited to be told what things meant.

'The barman says that it doesn't really get lively here until ten or so.'

'Oh.'

'And we'll be off to meet Elsa by then.'

'We will yes.'

'What's wrong with you?

There was no concern in the question, just impatience.

'Nothing's wrong with me.'

'You're sullen.'

Robert drank.

'Talk to me,' said Karl.

'What?'

'Talk to me.'

'About what?'

'Talk to me. Talk to me.'

'Stop it. I am talking to you.'

'No you're not. Entertain me. Charm me. Make me like you. Talk to me.'

'What do you mean? You don't like me?'

'Not at this very moment, no. You're being very boring.'

Robert frowned as severely as he could and in his head he prepared a sentence about how it should not be necessary for him to entertain Karl. That was not what a relationship like theirs should be about.

'I . . .'

'Talk to me,' interrupted Karl.

'I.'

'Talk to me. Talk to me. Talk to me. Talk to me. Talk to me.'

'I'm your guest,' said Robert quietly. 'I'm the one on holiday. You have to talk to me.'

Karl shook his head.

'I'm fed up talking to you. I do all the talking. Ever since you arrived I don't think you've started a single conversation. So I'm tired and I'm not going to say a thing.'

Robert sipped his beer.

'How's Elsa?' he asked.

'She's fine.'

Robert nodded and drank.

'Talk to me.'

Robert put down the bottle.

'Talk to me.'

He looked around and saw the black man glance at them.

'How far is it from here to the theatre?' he asked.

'I don't know. Talk to me properly.'

'What's properly?'

'Talk to me.'

'About what?

'Talk to me. Talk to me. Talk to me.' His voice was like a clock. There was a look on his face that might have been amusement or might have been hate. Robert could not tell.

'I think you must . . .' he began.

'Talk . . .'

'You must have been a real little fucker of a kid,' Robert said, and Karl smiled. 'Horrible. Nasty. I think you must have caused your parents all kinds of grief. Were you very obnoxious?'

'I was,' laughed Karl.

'A real little brat I'd say. A noisy little monster. Answered back all the time. Annoyed all the adults. Hung out of sleeves moaning about everything.'

'I did.'

'I knew it. You learn some manners young man. Did they ever say that to you – learn some manners? They called you "young man" all the time didn't they? Called you "young man" and told you that if you didn't behave you'd be sent to your room. That shut you up. Being sent to your room was hell. There was no one there to annoy.'

Karl smiled. He leaned across the table and spoke softly.

'You see,' he said, and touched Robert's hand. 'That didn't hurt did it? You can do it when you want to you know.'

86

*

Waiting on the bench at the corner, Robert's anger is restless, or rather, it is not restless enough. Its inhabitants are getting too comfortable. He thinks of it, of his anger, as a balloon, a child's balloon, to which he clings frantically as the string runs through his fingers. But whether a balloon or a refugee camp or a box, his anger is losing its shape, and he knows it, and he knows this is not good.

It is quite dark now, all of the cars have their headlights on, lighting his face briefly from different angles. He peers into the distance and peers at his watch, not at all sure now of his calculations, or of the assumptions he has made. He feels a rising unease. Surrounded by the unfamiliar. Robert on his bench. The cars and their lights seem to threaten him, their engines become louder, their beams fix on his face.

A sudden shouting starts behind him, a rough voice barks out cluttered German, tumbling over itself with aggression and hostility. Robert stiffens. He feels his back like a bow. The voice comes closer and is joined now by another, just as loud, a laugh contained in it like a cough. He thinks of standing up and walking off, but before he can move he is aware of two figures stepping up onto the bench behind him, boots hitting the wood with a thud that he feels in his thighs. They come around the seat in a circle on either side of him, like two arms. Pincer movement, they call it. He is frozen, not knowing what to do, thinking that perhaps it would be best not to look. But he is aware of the boots, like Doc Marten boots, and he is aware of the pause, and of the moment of quiet that comes when they see him, and of the closeness of them, and of their physical shape, distinct as a cut. He feels them near him like a change in the air. Then they jump down and walk ahead where he can see them. They are skinheads. They walk backwards, looking at him, curious. Their jeans are tight against their skinny bodies. They wear short jackets with zips. One has a tattoo of a hammer over an ear. They speak to each other and Robert knows that they are talking about him. One of

87

them nudges the other and turns away. But his friend continues to walk backwards, staring. Robert knows he should look away. But he cannot. They are standing now at the roadside waiting to cross, one facing one way, one the other. Robert does not move. They wait for a gap in the traffic. The one who looks at him is the one with the tattoo. He has a dog collar around his neck and his nose is pierced. He shouts something. At Robert. The other one turns his head. Robert looks at them blankly. The one facing him takes a step forward and shouts the same thing again. He jerks his head. His friend turns back towards the road, sees that it is clear and begins to cross, shouting something impatiently. Robert looks at the man in front of him. He is young. He moves closer to Robert. He is a tall thin creature with eyebrows cut darkly across the surface of his skull. His hands are stuck halfway into his pockets and Robert notices some kind of symbol on the back of one of them. The right. Robert sits stock still, believing that the slightest movement will provoke an attack. He plays dumb. Dead. He does not move or speak because he believes that if he is given away as a foreigner or as a queer he will be beaten. Better to appear stupid, mad. If he keeps his mouth shut and does not move then the skinhead will be uncertain. He might even think that Robert holds some kind of threat. They stare at each other. After a moment there is an impatient shout from across the road. The skinhead mutters something and spits, and then says to Robert the same thing that he has said before. It sounds like contempt, like a dismissal. Robert takes it in and does not move. The skinhead spits again, mutters, and then turns suddenly and runs after his friend, shouting and laughing, disappearing behind the flashing cars.

Robert breathes. He breathes deeply, closing his eyes and shuddering slightly, relief sweating from his body. It is cold on his bench.

With his head back he smiles a little, trying to remember the sound of what the skinhead had shouted at him. He will repeat it to Karl, find out what it means. He says it to himself a few times, then says it out loud. It sounds close. He looks towards the corner. There is no sign. He looks in the direction the skinheads have gone, wondering what they had thought of him, sitting there in the dark. It was lucky that one of them had seemed in a hurry, that they had been on their way some-where. If they had been bored, nothing to do, well . . ..

Karl.

Suddenly he sees Karl and is confused.

Karl is walking past on the other side of the street, directly opposite Robert. He has come the wrong way. He is not look-ing at Robert. He is walking by slowly, one hand in his jacket pocket, the other holding the bag, his head down. The bag is heavy. He has not seen Robert.

Robert watches him for a moment, a little open-mouthed, feeling the slightly ridiculous urge to complain to someone about the way this has worked out. He considers. He will, obviously enough, have to go after him. Fuck. He stands up and walks slowly away from his bench, watching Karl. He quickens his pace suddenly, dramatically, thinking that per-haps he can overtake Karl and wait again somewhere further on, but he can feel the speed he's doing, can see the gaps, knows that the distance to the apartment is too short, that it would involve sprinting and heavy breathing and that Karl would see him as a fast moving blur to his left which would settle then somewhere in front of him again into Robert catch-ing his breath, trying to look casual, waiting at a corner or in a doorway, looking, in other words, like a complete fool. Fuck. He slows down again.

If it was a balloon then it has slipped from his fingers. If it was a box then its sides have torn open and its contents have spilled. If it was a refugee camp then it has been cleared by a dawn raid which has dispersed its population, driven most of them back to where they came from, and left them to fend for themselves, another effort at justice failing dismally in the small hours. In short, Robert, though he remembers being angry, has forgotten his anger, has lost its constituent parts, and feels now nothing more serious than the mild annoyance of a man who has sat for an hour and a half on a cold bench, and feels also, in tribute to his failure, a deep humiliation, and humiliation's close relation, panic – panic that he will be brought to book for this one, that he has done it this time, that he's in trouble now.

He weighs up his options, a little desperately, not really able to see any way out of a climb down, or an admission, an apology of some kind, the whole thing turned on its head. He could call out to Karl, stop him in the street, approach him. Or else follow behind him all the way back to the apartment. But he will have to attract his attention before he disappears inside. Robert, inevitably, has no key.

He can't think.

He watches Karl on the other side of the street, slightly ahead of him. Karl looks at his watch and runs his hand through his hair. He swings around suddenly and Robert stops. But Karl still does not see him. He is checking the traffic. He crosses the road at an angle and arrives on Robert's side, some fifty yards ahead, his back to him. Again, his back.

Robert whistles, surprising himself. He can't whistle. This is stupid. Shit. He whistles again, feebly. Karl does not hear, does not turn around. Robert walks a little faster, comes closer and whistles again. Karl swings around, nothing on his face. He looks at Robert for a moment, and Robert, to his disgust, to his shame, as if his humiliation were not complete already, as if there was still some extra degradation to be wrung from the wet cloth of this mess, as if there were a lower point still to which he might aspire, feels himself start to smile. He tries to stop it, twisting it into a grimace, making god knows what of it, something, he imagines, vaguely subhuman, frothy. He thinks he sees Karl roll his eyes upwards as he turns around again, but he isn't sure. Karl walks on towards the apartment, his head down, and Robert follows, trying to regain control of his face, trying to put one foot in front of the other without stepping in anything else, trying to get close, but not too close, trying still to measure every distance and work out where he is. His heart is flooded.

By the time they turn onto the street where Karl lives, Robert is at his shoulder. He can say nothing. Karl opens the street door and goes in. He holds it open for Robert without looking back. They walk through the front building and into the courtyard, lit only by the light from the windows which face onto it. A woman comes out of the back house and smiles at Karl. He stops to talk to her. Robert feels stupid, standing at Karl's shoulder with his face in some involuntary arrangement which feels like it might be a grin, but a vacant one, entirely void, insensible and perhaps a little scary. The woman looks at him and half smiles, falter smiles. She asks him a question. Before Robert can react, Karl says something to her and they both laugh. She turns towards the front house and walks away, still laughing.

'What did she say to me?' Robert asks as they go up the stairs.

Karl stops and turns, two steps above Robert. He looks down.

'She asked where the fuck you've been.'

He does not wait for a response. He turns and continues up the stairs.

Inside the apartment Karl moves about, putting clothes away, lighting the stove, tidying the kitchen, saying nothing. Robert follows him, talking, making no sense. Karl's silence frightens him. He does not know the edges of it.

'Say something for Christ's sake!'

'I've nothing to say.'

Karl lights a cigarette and sits at the kitchen table. Robert does the same. He has skirted around it, he may as well come straight out and say it now.

'I'm sorry I walked out like that. I needed to. You were treating me very badly you know, like you didn't want me there.'

Karl stubs out the cigarette with a single swift movement and an angry look, and gets up from the table. He goes towards the bathroom.

'I don't know what you expect from me,' says Robert, going after him, flooded and facially not himself.

'Oh don't be ridiculous,' says Karl from behind the door. 'I expected you to stay and help me dry the fucking clothes.'

'That's not what I mean.'

'You don't mean anything,' Karl mutters, but distinctly. 'You mean nothing.'

'What's that supposed to mean?'

'Mean, mean, mean. Everything's meant to mean something with you.'

'I think we should talk.'

'We are talking. I don't want to talk.'

Robert smokes his cigarette, walking back to the kitchen.

'I'm the one who's meant to be angry you know.'

'What?'

He looks around the kitchen, at the cartoons in German stuck up on the wall which he does not understand, at the German magazines which he does not understand. He does not understand the words on the milk carton, or on his packet of cigarettes. He does not understand the titles of the books on the windowsill.

He puts out his cigarette and wanders around Karl's apartment. In the bedroom the bedclothes are lying on the floor, not quite dry. He thinks about putting them back on the bed anyway, but thinks that you need two people to do it – to slip the elasticated corners over the mattress, to smooth it out, to get the cover on the duvet – not realising that it can be done just as well by one. He puts the pillow-cases back on the pillows and sits on the edge of the bed, tired and unsure. He wants to lie down and sleep, wake up somewhere else. He feels that he should make some kind of decision, think things out. He doesn't know how to start. Everything seems vastly complicated and obscure. He thinks suddenly that he can leave, that he will leave. In the morning.

He stands up and walks to the bathroom door.

'I'm going home in the morning,' he shouts. There is no reply.

He goes back to the bedroom and finds his suitcase and begins to pack. He has everything in before he realises that he needs clothes for the morning. He opens the case again and takes out things that are close to hand.

Karl appears in the doorway and watches for a moment.

'You can't go in the morning. You haven't a flight booked.'

'I don't even know why I'm here. Do you?'

Karl is silent for a moment. Then he comes into the room and sits on the bed.

'I asked you.'

'Why?'

'I missed you.'

'You regret it now though don't you?'

'No.'

Robert looks at Karl and does not believe him.

'I'll get a ticket at the airport.'

'It'll cost a fortune.'

'I have credit cards.'

Karl sighed.

'Sleep on it will you?'

Robert looks up at him, wondering.

'I mean, you're overreacting a little,' Karl continues, smiling now. 'You're being a bit dramatic. We've had a fight. It doesn't mean you have to go running to the airport.'

'I'm not running.'

'Well just forget about it. We'll talk tomorrow. I'm tired. We'll fix up the bed and get some sleep, okay?'

Robert is still for a moment and then he nods slowly. He remembers that he has been angry, but he cannot remember why. It is gone from him and he cannot follow it. Karl stands, and as he walks out of the room he trails his hand across

Robert's shoulders. There is forgetfulness in the touch. And a small request. That is always the way. They will sleep. Tomorrow they will go on. In a few days they will have nothing left of each other.

They tidy up the bedroom, put away clothes, fix the bed. Karl makes tea and they drink a mug each and smoke, saying very little. What they do say is gentle, inconsequential. Eventually they climb into bed and lie together in the dark. Robert stares at the ceiling, trying to stop himself from thinking, from going over the evening again and again. He can hear Karl's breathing slowing down, relaxing. He does not want to disturb him, but he cannot help turning on his side and laying his head on Karl's chest. Karl cups him in his arm and breathes.

'I waited for you on the bench at the corner. You didn't see me.'

'No,' replies Karl, sleepily.

'There were these two skinheads . . .'

He tries to remember what they had said.

'What does "Get ess eenen gut" mean?'

'Geht es ihnen gut?'

'Yeah that's it.'

'It means "Are you all right?"'

'Oh.'

Robert closes his eyes. In the darkness as they drift out of the world he holds on to Karl and he does not let him go.

Off Vico

(VERUM ET FACTUM CONVERTUNTUR)

I sat there dozing, perplexed. Autumn is always a shock to me – all that greenery withering where it stands, failing; the dust of the black paths settling on my skin, the grass sickly, the air changing. St Stephen's Green in late September. Awful really.

It is my habit to sit and doze. I buy the paper and stroll from Baggot Street and set myself down and read a little. I have no opinions now; I just wade through the news and feel greatly sorry for myself, rambling as I am in small gentle circles, from home to park to home again, with treats pathetically feeble, such as trips on the train to see my niece, or a game of cards with an old friend in Donnybrook, which entails taking the bus – a great adventure. But the park is my favourite place now. It is easy to be there, because once there it is easy to imagine being elsewhere. I have of course my favourite bench, and regulars to nod to, and all that – the quotidian trivialities of my time of life, my decline, my slinking off. Usually I fall asleep, which is of course not advisable, but I carry a stick now, to help me walk, and I grip it always, ready, as I doze. And I try, in the sighing, resigned way of men my age, to recall the sequence of the seasons, and the months that make them, and the numbers of the days.

This time anyway, this time I'm telling you about, this autumn, I was woken for some reason. A change maybe in the sound of footsteps, eyes on me, I don't know. I woke. And found myself stared at by a man not unlike myself, grey and slightly stooped, of my generation. He'd stopped in the path. He wore a coat like mine. His shoes were scuffed. No stick though. He stood there and looked at me. Pleasantly, with a half smile and a full head of hair.

'Hello.'

'Hello,' I said, squinting, trying to place him. It is a disturb-ing quirk of most people my age that they assume a familiar-ity based on shared decrepitude. This is something I discourage. However I am hampered slightly by my own for-getfulness. I have to trawl, flustered, rushed, through half-remembered faces and lost names searching for a match. I have had so many conversations. He was distinguished look-ing, despite the shoes. The hair was a good shade of silvery grey, very nice, hatless unlike myself. His face was chalky and his eyes clear. He was a handsome man.

'You don't know me,' he said, obviously aware that the chirpy tone of my voice was a thin mask for my discomfort at believing that I might. I was about to become unfriendly when he added, 'Or at least, you won't remember me.'

I was inclined to agree. His tone of voice was far too friendly. I remember people I dislike more clearly than the others. It's one of those gruesome little tricks that old age plays on you. This man rang no bells. Possibly he was a fan. It sometimes happens. Wretched old things that creep up to me and tell me how great I used to be and ask whatever happened?

He sat down, the cheeky bugger.

'It must be forty years,' he said, and laughed a choky laugh. Smoker. He continued to peer at me. I envied his hair.

'Since . . .?'

'Since we met. At least forty. Forty-five maybe. I was about twenty, what, twenty-two. So it's more like fifty. Certainly before the millennium. Mid nineties maybe.'

It was not going to be easy. If I had met him within the pre-vious week, then perhaps, there was a possibility. Even a month. If he was the best of company then I might stretch back as far as a year. But forty? Fifty? He was onto a loser.

'You were days before that prize,' he said.

'Prize?'

'You won some prize for your book. Your first book. About the boy growing up in Tramore.'

96

'Tralee.'

'Tralee, sorry. It was called . . . what was it called? The Blue
Beach. The Light . . ..'

He was not very convincing as a fan.

' "The Bite of the Bright Sea." '

'That was it. A bit of a mouthful. Your titles got better as
you went on. "Shakers", that's snappy. "The Island Square", I
liked that. My favourite though was "The Height Of It".
That's a marvellous book.'

'Thank you.'

Still he looked at me, examining my face.

'You've gotten older.'

It's a blunder I've often made myself. Telling people out
straight the only thing they know for certain, as if it might be
news. Standard rudeness really, I didn't mind, but he seemed
disconcerted by it, embarrassed.

'I'm sorry. I have too. We both have. I was not . . . I was
not accusing you of letting me down or anything.'

What a curious thing to say. Very sweet.

He looked at his shoes, tucked them out of sight. He
sighed, folded his arms. I settled, got comfortable, waited for
the anecdote. How he bought me a drink in the old days and
I said something wonderful. How he used to do a bit of writing himself. Oh I don't mind. It beats sleeping.

'When we met I was just a boy. You had a few years on me.
Seemed a lot then. Now of course you couldn't tell the difference.'

Huh.

'We met where . . .?' I prompted. Less nostalgia I wanted,
more fact. Facts are good, facts are funny. Facts you can argue
about. Not much you can say to cheap little observations,
wise words, sentiments – all that autumnal clutter.

He laughed. Looked at his hands, let them rest in his lap.

'You won't remember.'

Of course I wouldn't remember. That was the whole point.
He wasn't very good at this.

'Try me.'

Go on for God's sake. Get it over with.

'Dun Laoghaire.'

'Yes?'

'I don't know what year. Fifty years ago. Maybe more. Before you won that prize.'

'Where in Dun Laoghaire?'

'Oh well. That'd be saying.'

He sighed again. Shifted a little. I thought he was going to get up and go. Seemed suddenly sad. His eyes lost focus. A woman passed us clicking heels. She coughed. He stared into space. I guessed that he'd realised his mistake, that he'd never met me at all, just knew who I was and thought he'd met me, and was trying now to get out of it.

It was colder than it had been. Is it not strange that your body becomes more sensitive with age and your mind more dulled? There I go, breaking my own rules. What I mean to say is that I was cold, and I wanted distraction. I wanted him to keep going. Who cares? Make it up. It wouldn't matter. Share a harmless piece of time, and part.

'We met by the pier. I wore my sports jacket and carried a bag. It was a Friday. I'd been out drinking with workmates. I told you that and you said, "Well that's always depressing," and I laughed.'

'By the pier?' He was making it up.

'Yes. There were other men there, the usual thing, late Friday night. You passed me and I saw you and I sat down on the bench. You went off down to the shelter and I wandered around and when you came back, going towards the road, I sat down on the bench again. I was shivering. Cold. But it was August I think. Late August. Maybe September. You passed me and looked at me and sat down. It was a bench like this. Just like this. Near the cannon. You said hello, I said hello. I don't know what we said. You moved closer and touched my knee with yours . . .'

Well now. There's making it up and there's making it up.

'I certainly don't remember any such thing.'

'No,' he said quietly, eyes to the ground. 'You probably don't.'

I do believe I stared. Well, it's not the type of thing you expect to be confronted with, is it? Not at my age. Not in St Stephen's Green, out of the blue, one doddery autumn. Oh it was well known that I was queer, I never hid it, not that I needed to – I'd missed all but the tail end of the bad years. Half the bloody books were full of it. I was even notorious for a while, briefly had a lover in politics. We were much discussed. But what was this fellow saying? That I had tried to pick him up in Dun Laoghaire fifty years earlier? Not my idea of a funny story.

'You asked me did I want to go somewhere. I said yes.'

I squinted. Strange to say, I relaxed a little. He didn't fight me off then. Didn't call the police. This was not an accusation.

'Then we discovered that neither of us had a place to go to. I lived with my parents. I don't know why we couldn't have gone to your place, but maybe you were nervous of me or something, I don't know.'

I had lived on the Northside then. Miles away. Fifty years, the nineties, early nineties, mid nineties. I lived on Aughrim Street most of that time, lass of Aughrim, murder town, bus roars. What on earth would I have been doing at Dun Laoghaire pier? I was intrigued now. It was not an accusation. And it was not true. Couldn't be. It was a story, and it would be fun to see how far he took it.

'You said we could go in your car and try and find somewhere discreet. Nice.'

I had to stop him.

'Ah well now there you're wrong you see. I've never had a car. It's someone else you're thinking about.'

I had to stop him. Had to. There's no point if suspension of disbelief is impossible, if it's lost. It's the first rule of storytelling. Believability. He'd have to go back a bit, re-do it.

'No. It was you.'

He was very calm and certain. I frowned. He'd spoil it now, if he insisted on this car nonsense. I sighed. Disappointed.

'Go on.'

'We got into the car. It was . . . It was . . . Oh I don't remember what it was. I'd had a few drinks. We talked while you drove. You didn't know the area at all. I had to give directions. We drove through Sandycove and up into Dalkey and up the hill on the coast road towards Killiney. Wait . . .'

He held up a finger. Good nails.

'I'd forgotten. When we got into the car you held out your hand and told me your name was Ronan. Liar. I lied too – told you I was John or something. Don't know why. We shook hands. You said mine was cold. Every time you changed gear your hand brushed my knee.'

Ronan. Ronan. Ronan. The name ricocheted a little. I closed my eyes. When I was young I split things up. Ronan. Somewhere, in the furthest corner of my mind, I could dimly see, not see, remember, sense, sense a cold hand in a dark car and the sound of the sea. Could I? I was imagining it surely. I could not remember such things. That was a lifetime ago. I opened my eyes. Scratched my nose. He had stopped, was looking at me. His face.

'Did you wear glasses?' I said.

'My God.'

I raised my eyebrows. His mouth opened. Neat mouth, still some life in his lips.

'My God,' he said again, and smiled. 'Yes. Yes I did. God, you remember.'

'No I don't.'

'You do. You remember.' He laughed.

A boy with a beautiful face and a sandy sports jacket and glasses. Cold hand. Coughing. He had coughed a lot. Complained about cigarettes.

'I don't know,' I said. 'I have never owned a car. I do not know Dun Laoghaire. It's highly unlikely.'

He was excited now. He shuffled a little closer, put his arm up on the back of the bench. His smile was generous, happy, delighted.

'We went up those winding roads, you know, and the bay was down below us and the lights all twinkled and you said you'd love to live there and I started telling you all the famous people who had houses there. Rock stars. What was his name . . .'

'It's left me.'

'Me too. And the racing drivers, and the actors. We talked like that. Up we drove, do you remember? Then I got you to stop on Vico Road, where there's that gap in the wall, and you were a little sceptical but you said OK, and I asked you could I leave my bag in the car, do you remember?'

Frank Conway had an old Japanese thing. I'd borrow it sometimes. When he went away. The sound of the sea. I shrugged.

'Fifty years ago?'

'Yes. And you locked the car and we went through the wall and down that sloping path to the bridge over the railway line, and all the time I was terrified that there'd be people there drinking, but there wasn't, there wasn't at all, and anyway, I'd had a few drinks, and I was. . .'

He looked at me, then glanced away, smiling.

I smiled too. I believed him. He had done this. But had I? There was no point, I thought, in gazing at his face, trying to find something that I might recognise. I looked slightly past him, and the out of focus perspective hinted at memory, at recollection, at the face of a boy with beautiful black hair.

Ach no.

The glasses though. I had remembered them. He had been small, or not small particularly, but slim, and younger than me. The face. The hair. A lovely mop of black hair. His smell. I looked at him again, properly. Could I really remember the smell of a boy I was with fifty years before?

No I couldn't.

'We crossed that bridge', he continued, 'remember? It makes an echoing kind of noise as you cross it. And then down steps. Steps and steps and steps. And I think I stumbled once or twice, because it was dark. Stars just, and the sea all the time, lapping the rocks below us. Lapping and rustling. And the grass rustling too. Long grass on each side of us. We went down, and turned a corner where the steps turn, and then I cut away from the path onto the grass where there's a bench. Another bench, just like this one. Do you remember now? Do you?'

I nodded. I did. I didn't. I shrugged. His hair.

'I sat down and you did too. We kissed.'

He stopped. Considered me. I knew what this pause was about. We are very old, past that now, through it and done with it and handed it over, a little shocked that we were ever in the midst of it at all. He looked at his hands. I wanted him to tell me though, to remind me if he could, word by word, for I was hanging on this now more than was healthy, and he must have seen that. Remind me. His eyes receded, lit an inner picture. He smiled.

'We kissed. We kissed and you took off your jacket and the bench was wet. Soaking wet. I could feel it through my trousers. I felt you. I ran my hands over you, over your arms, your chest. You kissed me. We kissed deeply, you ran your hands through my hair. You turned so that you half stood, and I lifted your shirt out of your jeans and I lifted it up over your chest and kissed you there, me and my mouth. You remember?'

'Yes.'

'And we fumbled. Fumbled and kissed.'

I could remember, couldn't I? High above the water. His jacket, light in the gloom. The rest of him black. His shirt black, showing the white of his skin at the neck where it opened. I remembered. Good God, I remembered it all. Didn't I? I fought for some detail of my own. A contribution. The things that came to me were of a sexual nature – my

102

recollections all seemed below the belt. I was hesitant. At my age, at our age, talk is all that's left. Once you go there you can't really go any further. And there is the mundane question of embarrassment, to which we become increasingly susceptible I find, as we are less and less able to do what we say. As if words were ever linked to actions. In any case, I tried to remember something else.

'You were dressed entirely in black,' I ventured. 'Except for the jacket.'

He seemed bemused.

'Really?'

'Yes.'

'Are you sure?'

'Yes. Black. Black trousers, black shoes, black shirt, T-shirt. Underwear.'

He laughed, 'I was not.'

'You were. Black. All black.'

'They must have just looked black in the dark.'

'No. Well, maybe. I remember though. Against your skin, all that black, it was . . .'

I trailed off. I did not know what I was trying to say.

'I can only apologise.'

'No need. Really. Anyway . . .' and I trailed off again. It is damnable, it really is. What I wanted to say to him was that I had slid them right off, that I had stripped him bare in the moonlight, that the colour of the things was not at issue, that it was simply there, a detail, before the import, pre-important, an earlier thing, a symptom of recall, a hook in the myth of it, a toe-hold in legend. I stripped him bare. True or not, it is what I wanted to say. And yet, there I was, staring at my crow hands perched on my stick, mumbling nothing, no blood left for blushing, never mind anything else, and I said nothing, I told him nothing, I communicated nothing. Nearly dead and still this stupidity.

'What is it?' he asked.

'It wasn't me. I wasn't there.'

He paused, and I sensed that he made a movement, but I did not look up. Foul humours take me very suddenly, very completely.

There was silence.

Abstractions by the handful, I grappled with my history for a moment, as one will, must, will, when confronted with a past which one had imagined as a future, and one sees, again, always recurring, that the bulk of things lies behind us, done and dusted, used just once, through in an instant. Abstract regret, abstract sorrow, abstract life. That we discuss anything at all is a wonder to me.

'I sat,' he said, and I closed my eyes and hoped he would go away. 'You stood in front of me. The bay at your back, the water glistening. I could hear the waves and the blood in your veins. I could taste the sea from you. The sea and the stars and the whole world.'

His voice was very light, catering for me it seemed, making allowances. How many decisions is one supposed to make? Either I had been there or I had not. I opened my eyes. My hands were the same. What was the worst that could happen?

'You were naked,' I said.

'No. Was I? Maybe. Dishevelled certainly. Uncovered. I wanted you to lie on me.'

'I wouldn't. I didn't want to cover all of you at once, I wanted to cover you an inch at a time. I explored you.'

'Yes.'

'I remember your chest,' I told him. 'So neat. Your stomach. I remember your hair. Your hair was beautiful. The smell of your hair. So sweet. I wanted to do everything at once. I mean, at the same time.'

'I know. You would kiss my lips, and then you would be off somewhere else kissing, groaning, all that . . .'

Still we hesitated, the two of us. After all this time.

'And all the time I was stretched as if on a rack in the cold air, your hands on me like coals, wanting', he dropped his voice, 'all of you inside me. But there was rustling.'

'Rustling?'

'Yes. We were looking for a condom. I had one. Just one. In my wallet. While I was searching for it you were looking around, being wary. You decided there was rustling in the grass and you didn't like it.'

'I remember. There was rustling.'

'It was probably the wind. The bay to our right. My right. Your left. The sweep of it off to Bray. The twinkling of lights in houses and on roads and by the water. The water. We stood there listening, pale bodies in the starlight. The security lights in a house in the distance kept coming on, and going off again a few minutes later. We watched and I stroked your body. You wanted to move somewhere else to use the condom.'

'I remember. More steps.'

'More steps. Down and down, diagonally, back and forth, until we came to a shelter on the rocks. Not a soul. Dark. The water louder. Wilder. You said, "Maybe this was a bad idea," then I kissed you, I remember that kiss so well, and you said, "Who cares," and we were there again, part of the sea and the air and the night, just the two of us. There was no one else on the planet. You put on the condom and you', he searched for the term, 'made love to me. And I thought I had never been alive before.'

'Hold on.'

'What?'

'I made love to you?'

'Yes.'

'Translate that.'

'What do you mean?'

'I mean who did what to whom?'

'You made love to me.'

'I, pardon me, fucked you?'

'Yes.'

'No no no. You made love to me.'

He stared. Scratched his head.

'No,' he said.

'Yes. I distinctly remember. Everything you said is right, but it was you who . . . I held the stone, a kind of bench, a seat, inside the shelter, and the sea was in my ears and you made love to me. Which does not cover it. You fucked me.'

He seemed concerned.

'And great it was too,' I added, thoughtfully.

He looked at his hands. Frowned. Shook his head slowly.

'No.'

A thought struck me, and perhaps it struck him at the same time, for he looked at me, embarrassed at last, letting it in, suddenly sheepish.

'How', I asked, and carefully, 'do you know it was me?'

'I told you. Two days later, or three, or whatever, you won that prize for "The Bright Blue Sea".'

'"The Bite of the Bright Sea".'

'Whatever. Your picture was in the papers. I saw it, and I recognised you. I thought – thought it was hilarious. You were even on the radio about a week later and I knew your voice. I've kept an eye on you ever since. It was you.'

We had fluffed it. Only words to get wrong and we had got them wrong. Two old men telling each other such things, on a park bench, in autumn, in times like these. I shook my head. Two old vessels leaking fantasy, spilling out private little legends, mixing dreams with the truth, ending in confusion. A mist came down. I am old.

'It was you,' he said again. I shrugged. He was sure. So be it. Good for him. Why should I have any great urge for truth? Why should I feel possessive towards the events of my life? There are versions in every breath. Let him remember me like that if he wants. I'll be remembered worse.

We were silent for a while. He pondered the path. I affected a yawn. I wondered briefly whether we might not, despite the times we live in, despite the blunt doubt, slink off into the bushes and re-enact, reconstruct the supposed sequence of events. Try and jog our memories. Shake them up a bit. Put it to the test. But the bushes looked scrawny – awfully bare. I am past the point in my life where I might be mistaken for the fruit in such shrubbery, and am now much more likely to be confused with the branches. Except to the touch. I rejected the notion. Not in autumn.

In his face though, I could still see something (could I?) of youth. The ghost of it. Is that memory, or can that be seen in any face? And this notion I had, of the smell, the scent, of his hair. Young black fine hair, hair that slipped through my fingers. Clean hair. What was that? And the thought that he'd had glasses, which he had confirmed, as if . . .

'Where are your glasses?' I snapped, eureka-like.

'I had corrective surgery. My eyes are perfect now. It's the rest of me that's knackered.'

He could have made that up. Could have been thinking about it since I'd mentioned the bloody things. I was too slow.

What would it have been, on my part? A random lust, driven south of the city in Frank Conway's car, vented by the sea on the hill of Killiney with a black haired boy in a sandy sports jacket and glasses. Would I not be sure of that? I had never been very good at cruising. Terrified always, half of being beaten up, half of been seen, caught by someone I knew. I was never happy. And I was fussy and slow. Not good with signs, looks, glances. I didn't do it often. I kept myself to pubs, to circles of friends, to socially acceptable predation. Not that I was very predatory. I waited, and had an awful habit of being grateful when someone showed an interest. When I did cruise, in the open air, in dangerous, public places, and got lucky (got lucky!), I would forget about it. Quickly. Why's that? Why?

'Did you . . .,' he started, and coughed. 'Did you go there with others?'

I frowned.

'Where?'

'That place.'

I didn't know that place. I had never been there.

'No.'

Which was why I must have been there with someone. With him, presumably. For I could remember it. I could remember that place. Not that place. That moment. I could recall it, independent of geography or time. That's imagination isn't it?

'Did you?' I asked.

'Yes,' he said. 'Once. I think.'

'With who?'

'I don't know.'

Something went bad inside me. Did mild, but sudden, jealousy prove anything?

'Maybe it was me,' I said.

'What?'

'I mean. Maybe it wasn't. Maybe you were with someone else, who you can't remember, and you think it was me. Maybe I'm not what you recall, I'm just, I don't know, woven in. Whimsy. Later. When you saw me in the paper.'

He smiled at me.

'You think I'd slip you into my fantasies?'

He had a point.

'Anyway,' he said. 'You remember it. You were there.'

'I don't know if I remember or imagine. I don't know.'

He moved closer to me. Out coats touched. He sat slightly sideways, looked at me.

'Imagine it,' he said.

'What?'

'Close your eyes. Let it come back to you. Imagine it. Tell me what you imagine. Tell me what happened.'

'But I can't remember.'

'So dream,' he sighed, sounding terribly like the man who cues in a song in one of those musical films my father loved. The orchestra creeps in.

I snorted, shrugged, demurred, didn't like it. But he leaned close to me, and our coats touched, and he insisted. He insisted.

At first I couldn't get away from where we were. Cold autumn afternoon, near death, but I drifted. I caught a scent and closed my eyes and drifted.

'The car borrowed from Frank Conway. I drove for the sake of it, loving the turning of corners. The long drive across town. I enjoyed going fast along the Merrion Road, taking the Blackrock bypass at speed, on my own in Charlie's car, turning the radio off, turning it on again. Dun Laoghaire. The night and the boats and the water and the pier and the men. I remember all of that, but, I don't know, it's a mess of different nights.'

'Me. See me.'

'You? I can't see you. Him, maybe.'

'Him then.'

'Him. I see him. I imagine him. I saw him. Sandy jacket. Glasses. Shivering. He . . . How strange. Shivering on the bench and I wanted to warm him. I mean that literally. I wanted him to be warm again. I was afraid to breathe, afraid he would disappear. He coughed in the car, told me that he smoked too much. He used his long hand to point the way. The stars played on his skin. I imagine that the stars played on his skin. We went through the gap in the wall, off Vico Road, and we walked into another world, or took another world with us, I don't know. Stepped outside of things. There was only us, and it surprised me. We made love. It was part of the night. We were part of the night. We disappeared. We vanished. No one could see us. No one knew. We were together.'

For a moment I was stuck. His clothes had been smoky, his face pale. I had kissed his neck.

'I recall the afterwards. His coughing. The climb back to the car that he seemed not to notice but which had me breathless. The chill. The fear of meeting someone. I remember driving him as far as the dual carriageway, under his directions, and his insistence that I need not drop him home, that he could walk from there, and I remember the last look I had of him, a retreating figure in my rear view mirror, that jacket, his bag slung on his shoulder. And I remember the regret . . . Am I making this up?'

'No. Go on.'

'Melancholy. It's a young man's thing. It came with the glancing at my watch and knowing that we'd spent little over an hour together. An hour. On the side of a cliff in the cold embrace of the Irish Sea. And that he was beautiful, and that we had been close, and that I would probably never see him again.'

I opened my eyes. I wanted to see him again. But he was not there. Just age and the withered world.

'We were not lovers,' I said.

'We were. For a moment.'

'A moment.'

I cleared my throat.

'Are you sure?'

'Yes.'

'It happened?'

'Yes.'

'It was you?'

'Yes.'

I chose to believe him. Why not? Perhaps he prowled city parks daily, and lit upon the bewildered and filled their heads full of foolish thoughts. Perhaps he was mad. A hypnotist. A subversive. Perhaps he was my boy. Perhaps it is I who am mad. But I think he remembers. I think I knew him, and he me, and I think we had met before, outside the history of our lives, off the standard story, as if we had dreamed the same dream. It pleased me to believe it.

'That night,' I said. 'That night. I kissed you, and I opened my eyes while I kissed you, because I was afraid, and when I opened my eyes I could see nothing but the sea and the lights of passing boats, and the waving grass and the stars, and I closed my eyes again, and there was only you, only you and your body and the sweet sweet smell of you, and then I

looked once more, and I remember being surprised, astonished, that there was no one else but us. It seemed to me that
the hill we were on, the steps, the path, the whole blessed
place, the entire bay, should be covered with couples like us.
Lovers. That the whole world should know the dark night
and the embrace of skin and the taste of the sea and the kiss
that we shared, that closeness, that moment. That moment.
The joy of that. But there was only us. Us alone.'

He didn't move. He looked at me.

'Did you tell anyone?'

'No.'

'Nor did I.' He nodded, as if we had managed to keep
some kind of promise.

He leaned towards me, laid a hand on mine. His hands,
ghosts, were still cold. I dreamed of his shiver. He kissed me
again, gently now, with paper lips, brushing my cheek. My
dying skin. He stood and smiled and bowed a little and
walked away.

I have not seen him since. I think of all the people in my
life. All that love, pain, time. All the places where the people
have been. I can count them and not stop. Year after year of
writing it down, so that in the end, there is nothing of it kept.
Gods, heroes, men. All that living. Telling.

And only one secret.

How to Drown

In the darkness the lake was not silent. It caused a glow in the air above itself and they slipped towards its edge and were lit, at least to each other. The sound was a flapping thing, like a stumbling bird, of tiny ripples that caught the rocks and threw a gentle splash on the grass beyond. In the sky there was nothing, no light, no wind, no noise.

By the water they could see their breath on the air, a lot of it at first as they stopped and waited, and not as much then as they became accustomed to the place where they found themselves and looked more at each other and less at where they were.

He had torn his hand on the bushes coming down from the road, and he put it to his mouth now and had the warm taste of blood.

'Put your hand in the water.'

He moved carefully to the edge, testing the slip of the rocks before each step, and crouched in a way that he had never learned, he just knew, and dropped his hand into the glowing black pattern. It was cold enough to sting him, and he stifled a small gasp and hugged his skinny knees with his free arm.

'It's just a scratch,' he said.

She came towards him, mumbling, and slipping slightly so that she had to put her hand on his head to steady herself.

'Is it cold?'

'It's freezing.'

'Do you wash you hair ever? It's all greasy.'

He sighed and pulled his hand out of the water and poked at the cut and put it under his arm to warm it. He thought he could hear something like a bell somewhere in the distance but was unsure when he thought about it whether it wasn't inside his own head that he heard it.

'Do you hear a bell?'

'No.'

She crouched next to him and they stayed silent for a while and he knew that she was listening, trying to hear what he heard. Her eyes were shadows and he could not tell which way she looked.

'What time is it?'

She fumbled and lifted her hand to her face and moved her head back and forth.

'I can't see. It must be near nine, do you think?'

'Is it?'

'I don't know.'

He found a flat part of the rock and sat down. He bent over to try and get his head level with the surface of the lake, to look out over it and have the same view as he would if he was in the water.

'Billy, what are you doing?'

'Nothing.'

'You look like a dog trying to lick himself.'

She laughed out loud and he did too but they stopped themselves quickly, hearing the strangeness of it in the cold air – afraid of how far it would travel across the waves.

'Mam will hear that,' said Billy quietly.

'How will she?'

'I don't know. She'll be out the back. Over there some-where.'

He gestured vaguely across the lake, but he was not confident of it. It was not that kind of hearing, but he did not know what kind of hearing it was and he was embarrassed. In the darkness he blushed.

'Don't be daft,' said Anna. 'The house is behind us. The road goes the other way. Over there is . . . that's towards town. Massey's farm is that way.'

Billy was feeling the cold of the rock creep up into him,

and he raised himself onto his hunkers and crouched once more like the pictures in his schoolbook of the tall African men who squatted by the fire.

'Do you think we should go home now?' he asked.

'For what?'

He rocked a little back and forth and tried to think of what the tall African men would talk about, squatting by their fire. They would not worry about going home. They were home already – under the sky was their home. But you couldn't live like that in Ireland because it was too cold. And people would not let you anyway. His father had explained it to him. That people would only let you do the things that they did. So that there'd be less crime. If you wanted to do something else you had to go away. You had to emigrate.

'Will you emigrate Anna?' he asked, and listened for a while to the silence, the still air where she thought it over.

'No I won't. I don't want to go anywhere else. I want to stay near Mam and Dad and be able to visit them.'

'I think I will.'

'Where will you go?'

He wanted to say Africa but he knew that Anna would laugh at that.

'England,' he said. 'London.'

'You could go to where Mam is from.'

He frowned in the dark and scratched his ear. He didn't want to go there. His father had told him that where they lived now was better than there. He had made it sound cold and strange.

'Cornwall,' he said.

'That's right,' said his sister, as if she was proud of him for remembering the name. 'Cornwall. It's in England.'

'I know it's in England.'

'We have an aunt there.'

'I know.'

'I'd say it's horrible.'

He agreed with her but he didn't say a word.

He looked out across the lake and imagined that it was the sea. In the middle of the sea there would be a whirlpool. The boats would race around it and be flung the rest of the way like stones skimmed across shallow water. Some boats would not get by. They'd be sucked down into the hollow centre of the world and they would stay there in the darkness and not hear a thing and not see the stars. It would be like this place where they were now, as if Anna and he had been sucked into the centre of a world that was bigger than this one, and that this one itself had at its heart a cold lake beneath a dead sky, where two other children sat and whispered. He thought of all these worlds, one inside the other like the layers of an onion, down to the smallest and the coldest and the darkest.

'We should go home now,' his sister said, and stood up, slapping the backs of her legs. 'We'll be given out to if we're late.'

Billy watched his sister as she made her way carefully over the rocks to the edge of the bushes that rose to the road. Her shadow was like a puppet – all out-stretched arms and crooked legs and joints that jerked this way and that as she explored the ground in front of her with her foot and held out her hands for balance, just in case. He waited for her to fall, but she did not. She kept on going and only looked back when she had reached the foot of the hill and the start of the brambles and the gorse.

'Come on,' she called. 'Hurry up.'

Billy looked out over the lake once more and could not see the other side. He stood up and felt pins and needles in his legs. As he stepped forward he stumbled, and he put out his hands and tried to regain his balance, but his feet were numb and he could not tell whether they touched the ground or not. It was as if he hovered, or walked on air, and he did not trust the sensation of it. He swayed one way and then the other and heard his sister's voice tell him to stop messing, and he tried to lift a foot once more, but he could not tell if he had or not, and he tumbled and pitched backwards as if fall-

ing from a wire and felt the sudden freezing cold of the water
hit his back and his legs and wrap its arms around him like a
dead embrace and run its hands over his face the way his
mother did when she crept up on him and wanted to surprise
him by covering his eyes and calling out 'Guess who?' and he
felt the cold of it inside him like ice cream, and he felt his
shoes fill with it and he felt his body move around beneath
his clothes as if suddenly he was too small for them. He
opened his mouth to call out, and he could taste the cold and
realised that he had better not do that. Then he remembered
that it was only water and that he could swim and that he
would be okay, he would not drown. But for a moment
before he kicked his legs, he allowed himself to drift and he
thought of the whirlpool and the dark world, and of the children inside the starless caves in the hollow centres of all the
earths, and he waited for a second to see if he could hear the
bell, and he waited a little longer and opened his eyes and
tried to find the way in. But all he saw was a black hand still
held over his face, and all he heard was his own heart and the
muffled voice of his sister screaming, as if it were her that
was drowning, and not him at all, held as he was in the stil-
lest of moments, the smallest of times, as if for just a second
he could touch everything.

His father sat him by the fire and helped him take off his
clothes, and his mother fetched towels and blankets and
dried him and wrapped him and boiled the kettle and gave
him tea. Anna sobbed and gave out to him. His father
laughed. His mother looked him in the eyes and he thought
for a while that she knew what he was thinking. But then she
laughed too and told him that he was a little fish.

'You're a fish out of water now,' she laughed, and rubbed
his hair, and he looked back at her and did not smile.

That wasn't what he was thinking at all.

She checked him all over for cuts and bruises and marks,
him standing nearly naked in front of them all, still cold but

the fire getting him warm again, with a towel wrapped around him and the taste of the lake still in his mouth and in his nose. She sorted through his hair and Anna said that it was a miracle he hadn't cracked his head open on a rock. His father laughed again and then there was quiet, and he felt his mother's fingers on his scalp like little creatures exploring him, and he knew that if he had really drowned this was the kind of thing he would feel – the fishes pecking at his head – and he became a little frightened. Except that if he had really drowned he would not feel anything.

He started to cry.

His mother hugged him and told him that it was all right, he was fine, he was safe and well and fine, and his father told him that he'd know not to be fooling around in the dark by the lake again, and Anna left the room.

He stopped crying when his father gave him some chocolate.

In his bed as he was falling asleep he thought he could hear the bell again, but he was too tired to listen. He knew something now that not many people knew, and he knew it by himself, had learned it himself. He knew how to drown. He knew what it was about, what it felt like, how the water took you in and you could decide whether or not to let it. He knew that when you were drowning there was no time, that there was only yourself and the water, and that nothing else really mattered even if you cared about it or loved it and would miss it badly, even people like your mother or your family. He knew that you drown by yourself, alone, and that it was all right while it was happening but could be scary afterwards.

In the morning he went out early to the lake by himself and looked into the water. He wanted to say something to it but felt stupid. He went to the place where he had fallen and looked around – looked to all sides and up at the sky and then down, at the water that had taken him in and wrapped

117

him and tried to keep him. He took off his shoes and socks and sat on the rock and put his feet in the water and stayed there for a long time.

He thought that he would like to be always drowning, but never drown.

The Ravages

He drove to the north of the city and turned then and drove south to the southern most point of the city and drove north-west then to the western reaches and turned once more and drove east to the sea and the sun appearing. And that was the city blessed. A great cross etched in the dying night. The lines were not quite straight. The distances awkward. North to the airport, the forehead, the title (in Hebrew, Greek and Latin), the roundabout with the modern sculpture suggesting a wing, then south, a bit higgledy piggledy in the city centre (in some representations his thighs are twisted side on, his knees bent, the ankle outermost), to roughly Ballinteer, the breast, the foot block. There's your upright. Although he was shamefully vague in his own mind on whether the breast touched by the right hand in the personal sign was representational of the foot block of the actual cross. He resolved to check, though wasn't clear how. Then the blur north-west, the always unsatisfactory link from breast to left shoulder, that smudge. He had sometimes tried going back up the upright, but it had never felt right. Felt he might be tracing something else, a twist on things, such as a swastika or a device of contrary intention. Took the M50 in a quick sweep, pressing his head to the headrest, straightening his arms, feeling the forces in his blood, as far as, where else, Palmerstown, then cutting across the transverse beam, from that curled and rigid hand, along the sinewy limb back to the heart, the centre, the nexus at the shoulder blades, where the bridges cut the day's first huge shadows on the river. He paused at the Custom House, pulled in and looked at the water. Verd-antique, flashing. Hard, even when he closed his eyes, to see it seep from a human wound. No. On then out the other axis, with just the one deviation (as if avoiding a nail), past the car ferry terminal to his place in the shelter of containers stacked like building blocks. There to linger. Tingling.

He watched a ferry set off for Wales and wondered whether his car knew. Whether it had ingested something from him, from his breath. It might be aware, in the way that buildings are aware, of its use. From regularity and persistence and the shape of the air it moved through. He thought of the cars in films he had taken his kids to see. Chitty Chitty Bang Bang. Herbie. The Love Bug. That yellow Rolls Royce. And in a dusty desert, a killer car, driven by a shadow, possessed by the devil.

Cathal sighed at himself. Blew that dark thought from him. Banished it. Out to sea.

The ferry passed a smaller boat and the water drawn out between them was white and caught the sunlight. He stared at that stretching point and sniffed and felt chill. It was only when he looked at the sea like this that he realised how fixed the place was, how settled. With the aid only of charts and electronics they would find the bay again. Here, in this place, this part of the coast, of this island, here, just here, nestled in the little hills, the mouth of this river. Unmoved. It would never surprise a sailor, never vanish in the night, never alter its aspect, never shift its position, never glimmer in the low sky and disappear, not until the last day, the one that came of all the others, when his hands would be finally empty. Cathal sighed again. He needed to watch himself sometimes. Words are useless.

He turned on the engine and left that place. He drove home to his family, taking his time, watching the streets slowly become florid. People with strange employments hunched and proceeded, trying to stamp out the dawn. Others went the other way, delicately, eyes to the sky, bewildered by the connection: their late night and this early morning. Men swept and delivered. Newspapers and milk lay stacked in the doorways of small shops. Men in thick gloves threw black sacks in the air. There was yawning. Pocketed hands. A youth on Clanbrassil Street got in to a car. Over the Dodder a small knot of women waited together at the side of the road, quiet, smoking, all their heads turned towards the city. There was a man and woman jogging, talking as they ran, sweating. The car chugged through it all and the morning rose and the clock continued and his head was clear.

At home, as soon as he opened the front door, he heard his wife's voice. She called his name. He closed the door, took off his coat. She called again. 'Cathal! Cathal! Is that you?' She would wake everyone. He climbed the stairs.

'God Cathal why don't you answer me?'

'The kids are still in bed.'

So was she, a shape beneath the duvet, her unleashed hair spilled on the pillow. She squinted at him.

'Dan is gone to Ethel's. Why he goes at this hour I've no idea. He said he wants to be back before the others are up. I told him she could have breakfast with us.'

'Why has he gone so early?'

'I have no idea I just said.'

'She won't be up.'

'He's probably excited. Come here.'

'No.'

'Come here.' She yawned. 'Cathal.'

'I have to see the dog.'

He left the room and heard her cough. The other doors were closed. A jumper lay on the floor outside the bathroom. He held the banister. Descended.

They were all up in an hour, their mother's voice having woken them. They bustled in the kitchen, only Brian dressed, the girls all dressing gowned, yawning, not fresh.

'You up early Dad?' said Brian.

'Yes.'

'Heard you go out. Couldn't really sleep. Still on Toronto time. It was before dawn wasn't it?'

Sandra looked at him.

'It wasn't,' she said, incredulous.

'Well, nearly.'

'Where'd you go?' She struggled with cold toast that folded in her hand.

'I had to . . .'

'Him and his drives,' said his wife.

Elizabeth squealed and snatched her hand from the grill. She hopped and clutched her fingers and her face reddened and stretched. A commotion ensued. Brian doused her in cold water while her mother rummaged in the press for a burns spray. Sandra flustered, crumby, her arms in a wind-mill. Paula tore off a huge length of kitchen paper and stood by the sink with it flapping around her, waiting for a gap to open somewhere. The dog barked once, twice, then sniffed seriousness in the air and sat by the door, alert, worried that it might be his fault.

'Cathal! Cathal, call a doctor.'

'No you don't need a doctor,' said Brian calmly. 'It's all right. It's not bad. The tips of the fingers. It's fine.'

Elizabeth sniffed, moaned, made a stiff face.

'Are you OK pet?'

'Yeah.'

'God,' said Sandra, her whirl diminishing.

Paula murmured, 'What do I do with this?'

'Cathal, Cathal. Where are you?'

'I'm here.'

'Put the bloody dog out.'

'The dog didn't do anything,' moaned Elizabeth bravely. Her mother had found the spray. She hovered, looking for somewhere to fire it.

'Oh that's good,' said Brian, turning off the tap. 'I'll dry it first. Have you got . . .'

'Here!' shrieked Paula.

Brian dabbed at his small sister's fingers.

'Ow ow ow.'

'Sorry.'

He took the spray from his mother, quickly read the label, 'It hurts it hurts,' then held Elizabeth's hand to the window and obscured it briefly and loudly in a thin mist. She sighed. Her mother breathed out after her. Exhalations. Sandra was still. Paula trapped a loose sheet of kitchen paper beneath a slippered foot. The dog tilted his head. From the grill there was the smell of smoke, the ascent of a thick black plume.

'Oh would you look. Cathal!'

It was her index and her middle fingers only. They were bright shining red. Brian looked after her, fixed a dressing, kissed her cheek. Breakfast became cold rashers and hot tea, eaten in the adrenaline of fast voices replaying the whole thirty seconds again and again, and then drifting down into the kitchen history of calamities and mishaps and the *do you remembers*. Always leading to Cathal slipping on the mess one January morning, kicking the milk jug from the table, ruining his suit. Paula claimed to remember it. He remembered her. Sitting in her high chair, her wrinkled nose pointed at him, astonishment in her eyes. She had glanced at the ceiling as if she thought he might somehow have fallen from above. It had been her mother who had called in the others as he struggled to rise, crumpling and pointing with tears on her cheeks, her face a puffed red balloon. They sat now laughing at him all over again with the doors and windows open, the day warming up as if heated by Elizabeth's fingers. She blew everywhere except on her hand. Laughed with a small choke.

Dan arrived with his fiancée. Ethel was short and prim, younger than she looked. Her eyes were green and bell-shaped, as if some suction had been applied to her head. Her hair was scraped upwards, tied in a knot. She wore jeans on her big hips, a white blouse, nodded at everyone, and was like an older woman in her manner, auntish, fussing.

'Oh Lizzie!' she cooed, and knelt and stared at the shiny mutilations of her future sister-in-law. 'You poor thing.'

Brian kissed her cheek, both cheeks, and Ethel hugged him, while Dan went up and down on his toes, clapped his hands behind his back, delighted with himself, or doing an imitation of it, as if for himself, a cod of an uncle, regarding his cod of a wife. Cathal watched them. And saw, mostly, not Ethel and Dan, but Ethel and Brian, nodding at each other, being quiet, smiling.

'Mr Forkin,' she said, clearing her throat. 'How are you?'

'Fine,' said Cathal.

His wife set the children at clearing the table, all except Elizabeth who described to her brother and his girl, his gal, the horror of the fiery grill, and Brian, who was greatly commended for his heroics, his quick thinking. There would be a second breakfast, announced Mrs Forkin, a new feast. Ethel must be starved. They swarmed around the cooker, his wife a beam of pink and soft corners, telling them all to be careful, careful for God's sake, tearing at bacon, cutting the tiny umbilicals of butcher's sausages, slicing a watery blood from tomatoes, cracking egg shells on the kerbs of black pans. The boys were made to watch the sizzling, while the girls ('We girls,' said Mrs Forkin) reconstructed the table settings.

'Put Ethel there Paula. There, there.'

They used the good service, the one that had come from France, with fleurs-de-lis in gold on a royal blue band. Cathal moved his elbows for it, and rose then after Dan had brushed his thigh leaning across him, wearing aftershave that had come from Brian, a gift from Toronto. Cathal went to the sink and washed cutlery, feeling his wife's little glances, hearing the hum of young voices. Ethel made a joke and they all laughed. Cathal had missed the start of it. Brian still sat at the table, quiet now, since Ethel's arrival, listening. Ethel's voice ran on, filling all the gaps. Cathal sang a song.

> 'He said you can drive him from your mind,
> For another young man you surely will find.
> Love turns aside and it soon grows cold

Like a winter's morning,
Like a winter's morning,
The hills are white with snow.'

His voice was weak and whispered and no one heard him, or if they did they thought he was only humming. He glanced at his wife. She would know, but her mouth was set in a wild smile and her eyes were fixed on Ethel, who was still telling jokes, or maybe the same joke. Perhaps it was a story. Brian had stood, had dried some of the cutlery, was adjusting knives and forks on the table with the tip of his tongue sticking out. An architect in Canada, making straight lines for a living, and still perplexed by this. He caught his father looking.

'In Toronto we have them all in a kind of tumbler in the middle and people just take what they need.'

'Do that so,' his father told him, but Brian shook his head.

'When in Rome . . .'

The telephone rang.

'Cathal!'

He went to it, out into the hall where there was still a bit of gloom, where the light had not yet found its way, and there was still something of the cold he remembered from the waterfront. He paused. Breathed. Settled.

'Hello?'

'Cathal. Sam.'

'Hello Sam.'

'Is she there?'

'Ethel? Yes.'

'She all right?'

'Yes. Why? Do you want to speak to her?'

'No no no.'

He was clipped, agitated. Ethel's father Sam.

'Well?'

'What?'

'What do you want?'

'She woke up this morning Cathal, very upset. Perhaps she didn't sleep. I'm not sure. She might have been out. I thought I heard the door. Very late. But I don't know. When Dan called she brushed it all aside, but, but she'd been sitting here with her mother and myself, here in the kitchen, bawling crying for about an hour. You know me Cathal, never up before about ten these days. But I was woken by the racket. She was on the stairs, just sitting there crying. Her mother went to her but she couldn't talk. She couldn't say a word. Just cried. Eventually we managed to get out of her that she'd had some sort of a row with Dan, but then he arrives and Ethel disappears to the bathroom for twenty minutes and comes back as if she'd just woken from a good night's sleep. I don't understand her.'

'Did you not ask Dan?'

'He was in fine form. Not a bother. The wife asked him, you know, casually. He said there'd been no row. We didn't say anything. Maybe we should have, but Ethel was very insistent that we say nothing to him about it. She'd be angry if she knew we'd even asked him. Which we didn't as such, just hinted, casually, not hinted, questioned, wondered. He wasn't suspicious, which makes me think that he doesn't know a thing about it, and if they've had a row then either he's forgotten or he didn't notice in the first place. Or else she just said that because it came to mind, and it's something else entirely. She came downstairs then all sweetness and light and left with Dan as if nothing had happened.'

'Maybe she's just, you know, not well.'

'No. Well, maybe. But I've never seen her like that before Cathal. It was as if she was hysterical. I was frightened Cathal. I really was. She was racked with it, flung about. Her fists were clenched and her teeth were grinding, and these spasms going through her, tears and mess. It was awful. I wanted to call the doctor.'

'She's fine now. She's perfectly normal.'

Sam hummed. Worried.

'I'll keep an eye on her. They're not going anywhere. I'll

watch her. Don't think about it. Just sentimental probably. They need a good cry now and then.'

'Mmmm.'

'Sam. Don't worry.'

'Mmmm.'

'I'll look after her.'

'OK. Don't say it was me.'

'Who will I say it was?'

'Whoever.'

'Sam.'

'Say anyone. It doesn't matter. Say it was Jack about golf.'

'I can't say that. Jack'll ring then. He's going to.'

'So you make sure that you get it.'

'But I can't be sure.'

'Say someone else then. Say someone from the golf club, checking your slot. I don't know. It doesn't really matter Cathal.'

'I can't lie.'

'It's not a lie.'

'It is.'

'Or just tell them that it was private. None of their business.'

'Everything is their business.'

'Your doctor then.'

'They'll think something is wrong.'

'Our age Cathal, something is always wrong.'

'Not with me Sam. I'm fit as a god.'

'Say nothing then. Don't say who it was.'

'If someone asks I'll have to say.'

'Pretend you don't hear.'

'I can't do that.'

'Just say it was nothing important.'

'That's also a lie.'

Sam sighed.

'Tell them it was an old friend. That is not a lie.'

'It isn't an answer either. They'll want to know who.'

'Tell them you can't say because it's a surprise.'
'A what?'
'This isn't funny.'
'I know.'
'Why can't you lie?'
'I just can't Sam.'
'Not for me?'
'I'm sorry Sam.'
'You sound like that computer in that film, that 2001.
Remember that?'
'Do I?'
'Tell them that it was a good friend of yours but he was
ringing about something private and confidential and you'd
rather not say who exactly it was.'
Cathal thought about that.
'OK,' he said.
'OK?'
'OK.'

The eggs were scrambled. There was black and white pud-
ding, white and brown bread, toasted and not toasted. There
was a pot of tea and a pot of coffee. Orange juice had
appeared. Tomatoes.
'Who was it?'
'Sammy.'
Ethel looked up.
'Sammy who?' asked his wife.
'Sammy from golf.'
'My father?' asked Ethel.
'Are those potato cakes?'
'Cathal! Was it Sam?'
'Yes.'
His evasion had got their attention. Brian chewed and eyed
him. The girls hunched down in their dressing gowns. Dan's
eyebrows were up.
'Well why didn't you say for God's sake?'

'I did.'

Ethel stood. They all looked at her. She did something very odd. She burst into tears. Suddenly, completely. Burst is the word. Her face collapsed, her eyes flooded, her nose blurted, her mouth bawled air. The sound of it was loud and awful. Dan gaped.

'Ethel?'

She shook her hands. Seemed to scream and have it swallowed by the crying. Cathal Forkin touched her elbow.

'Ethel love, what is it?'

His wife put an arm around her and Dan stood and came around the table and moved to embrace her, but she shook her hands again and howled.

'Jesus Ethel, what's wrong?'

She gasped, sucked for air, her face awry as if she was drowning.

'I'm not . . .' she said, her voice squashed. 'I'm not . . .'

'What pet?'

'I'm not . . . I don't . . .'

'Ethel?'

'I DON'T EXIST. I'M NOT ALIVE. I DON'T EXIST I'M NOT ALIVE.'

She stretched the words into a level sound that buckled the air and cooled the food.

Brian had returned from Toronto because his brother Dan was getting married to Ethel Houses. He arrived a week early and would stay a week after, taking two of his four weeks holiday in the city of his birth in the company of his family. Nothing could be nicer. He had packed two new shirts that Hat had bought. Hat with her notion of Ireland as one of the funnier episodes of The X Files.

'There'll be a guy warning you about looking left. Believing your mother. There'll be air magic.'

'What?'

'Fog from nowhere. People in the grass, you know. There'll

be people in a trance, doing that shuffle, what do you call it, that dance, on the streets, comes from too much not screwing, all that. You and your Scully, before you crack the case, you'll be deported because of the way the drinkers can read your mind and can see, they can see, your aberrant sexuality. In all its Canadian winter closeness. Bram Stoker was from Dublin.'

'No.'

'Was.'

He had argued it until she got her copy of 'Dracula' and showed him. He had taken it with him and read it on the plane. It had bored him. He read of the arrival of the Demeter as they came towards London from a strange angle that seemed to miss Ireland completely. He changed planes and came home. Unpacking, between the shirts, he found a taped up matchbox full of soil. A note read, 'From the garden. Sleep sound. H.'

His father was gone strange. He wore something around his neck which Brian noticed when it popped up in the car as they were on the way to see Bohemians play Shamrock Rovers. It was a, what did you call it, a brown thing, a looped string, with a square patch at each end. With a relic or a prayer or something. He knew the name.

'Your thing . . .' he said.

'What?'

'The what do you call it, around your neck, it's sticking out.'

'Scapular.'

'What is it?'

'What day's today?' his father asked.

'Thursday,' said Brian.

'Then it's St Jude.'

'Why is it St Jude on a Thursday?'

'Just this Thursday. Each one gets a day on me. It's all I can give them. There seems to be hundreds.'

Bohs won 3–1.

His mother wanted to know why Hat had not come over. He told her that she was working, but she sent her best wishes and hoped to meet them all before too long. He saw her in his mind, straddled over him in the half-light, her shoulders wet.

'Will we be going to Toronto for your wedding Brian?' Paula had asked.

Dan sniggered and Sandra gave a deep smile into her coffee cup.

'I don't know.'

'Are you getting married?' Elizabeth asked, surprised. All these girls. He was not used to it. He had forgotten. And they had shuffled their personalities since he had last seen them. Sandra had grown up, Elizabeth had taken on her cute teenage noise. Paula was the kid that Elizabeth had been. The baby had disappeared. Dan was still Dan, just bigger, broader. Though only twenty-five he still seemed pitched somewhere between thirty-five and fifty, which was where he had been since he was twelve.

'No plans for it.'

'Leave the boy alone,' his mother told them. 'It's nobody's business.'

She had mellowed. And his Dad had gone strange. Up at all hours, driving. Pacing the back garden while he waited for his tea. Playing less golf. Seemed to be on the edge of something. Dan said that he'd just found religion. But Brian knew that that had always been there, just better hidden. His father had gone to mass every day as long as he could remember. But he had not worn a scapular. Or been so passive, so withdrawn. There were beads in his pocket now. Brian could hear their rattle, see the working of his fingers through the fabric.

'Bohs have it,' said Brian on the terraces.

'Looks that way,' said his father, sniffing, staring at a man in front of them who had cursed a Rovers defender loudly and obscenely.

131

'Take a miracle now,' said Brian.

'Can't do it.'

'No they can't.'

'No I meant, oh, never mind.' He sort of smiled. 'I can't do it.'

And Ethel. Ethel in the grey light, her eyes two thumbtacks that pinned him back to sixteen, seventeen, that night by the castle, tucked into the nettles and the long grass, wound around each other beneath the skin coloured moon.

He had gone to see her in the small hours.

Dan was frantic, amazed. His mother seemed about to join Ethel in her bawling. His father stood there making strange shapes in the air and whispering something that sounded foreign. Brian, good for burns, was hopeless for this. Sandra and Elizabeth were frozen, recognising some young woman thing maybe, some existential grief. Paula wept, as if at a sad film.

'What do you mean? Jesus Ethel. Of course you do. You're alive. Yes you are. Look at me. I'm here. Ethel. Love. Look at me. You do exist. You're here. In the kitchen with all of us. We're all here. Ethel. Ethel. Ethel. Ethel!'

She whirled and withered and drooped into a chair. She was conscious, but there was a vacancy in her eyes, as if in a trance. Her face was a mess and he didn't love her. Not just then. Not at that moment. She was not his. Not at all.

There was silence while they stared at her. Then his mother rallied.

'Right. Someone call a doctor. Someone help me with her. We have to lie her down. Brian and Dan, you lift her. Gentle now. Wait! Cathal, get the car ready. We'll bring her to the hospital. That's what to do. It'll save time. The poor girl. Careful now. Cathal! The car for God's sake. Elizabeth open the doors for them. Sandra you come with us.'

'I'll come too,' said Elizabeth.

'So will I,' said Paula.

'There isn't room for you. I'll go, so will Dan, your father

132

will drive, and Brian will sit in the passenger seat. Sandra will hold the fort.'

'You just said Sandra was going too.'

'Well she's not. You be quiet now. Sandra. Sandra, ring Mrs Houses. Tell her what's happened. Don't worry her though. Tell her Ethel's just taken a turn and we're taking her to, oh God, where are we taking her?'

Dan's shoulder was wet. Ethel's head lolled there and she dribbled. Her eyes were rolled back in her head. He thought that maybe he felt he didn't love her because she was dying, and his mind knew it and was protecting him. Brian it was who carried her. Dan just got wet.

'We'll go to James's.'

'Is the Meath nearer?' asked Brian. 'Or The Coombe?'

'What good is The Coombe for God's sake. She's not pregnant. Oh Lord. Dan, is she?'

'No mother she's not pregnant.'

'Mother, you're in your dressing gown.'

'As if it matters. At a time like this. Doctors and nurses will not mind a woman in her dressing gown. My God.'

'St Luke's,' said Sandra.

'That's for cancer.'

'It has doctors.'

'We'll go to The Meath. Or James's. Depending how the traffic is. How she is. How is she? Dan? Is she OK?'

'She's lifeless.'

'She's OK,' said Brian.

They were out the front by now. Dan and Brian in their shirt-sleeves, Ethel hung between them. Dan shivered. His father stood by the car with the doors open. His lips were moving.

'Gently, mind her head. Cathal, get in will you, you're in the way. Paula get my handbag. Dan you sit in the back, Brian in the front. I'll get in after her. Careful.'

They squeezed Dan's fiancée into the back seat. Dan pushed her head back. She was foaming at the mouth.

'She's foaming at the mouth,' he said.

133

'It's just', said his mother, 'it's just dribble. Here.'

She wiped at Ethel's chin with a tiny handkerchief. Ethel groaned. Her tongue seemed swollen. She was trying to speak. It was the same thing, as far as Dan could make out. She wasn't alive. She didn't exist. But it was blubbered like underwater words and it scared him to see the girl he loved so ugly and so mad.

Cathal Forkin caught himself trying to work miracles by casting spells, and shook his head at it. Vulgar and proud. He was not a magician. His wide mind wished Ethel to be still, purged; it flicked out demons. Nothing happened. He frowned. His wife fluffed his thinking, his prayer, hurried him, harried him outdoors to fiddle with the car. His sons dragged the poor wretch between them and she was like a bag with sticks inside it. They angled her, limp and heavy, into the odd entrance of his car. They had to fold her in half and push her in as if posting an oversize envelope. Cathal meditated ease and a clear road.

They sat in a shimmer. Brian was beside him, his wife and Dan with the girl between them in the back seat. In his rear view mirror he gazed at her and sent for relief. Tried to wish rather than want, pray for rather than demand. A quick rite, a minor ceremony, a nod of his head. She did not move. She groaned.

'I think she's going to be sick,' said Dan, and Cathal glanced at the boy's pale face and sought to make him better by swallowing hard and lifting both his index fingers simultaneously from the arc of the wheel. Dan looked out the window, then looked at the window, then groped for the handle and opened it.

Cathal headed down Rathfarnham Road towards the Dodder. He considered his apparent lack of influence while his wife and Brian discussed hospitals. He concentrated on traffic lights, something that he had never, never done before. Just to see. It worked twice, then didn't, then worked once more.

That was OK. He wrapped his fingers around the steering wheel and fed out the road in front of them. He thought that he might alter the process, put a kink in it so that they made their way more quickly. His driving distracted him. He couldn't concentrate.

'What about Our Lady's?' asked his wife as they came up into Terenure.

'Yes,' he said. 'Yes.'

He turned left down towards Kimmage before Brian had time to finish saying that he still thought The Meath would be better. Cathal wondered suddenly whether there might not be an evil power in the car stronger than he. Then he dismissed the thought as fanciful and silly. He was what he was. No cause for panic. It was just that it was a little previous. That was all. Underdeveloped. It was a touch too soon. It was Cana. Wasn't it? The wedding feast and everything. That was what it was. The similarities, when he thought of it, were quite beautiful. It would be all right. All he needed was to follow himself.

'Cathal! Where are you taking us?'

'To Our Lady's.'

'Oh. God. Oh. All right. Ethel?'

Ethel had woken, it seemed, or emerged. Come to. She looked at the faces on either side of her, and at Brian. She looked long at Brian. Stared at him. He flinched. Cathal watched her in the mirror. She spoke.

'Oh Brian,' she said and her voice was an awful breathy concoction learned from old movies. Cathal winced at it. Cheap seduction voice. Through bubbles and a cracked throat.

'What?' said Dan like a small boy, hopeless with confusion.

Brian shrugged.

'What is it Ethel?' he asked, vaguely North American. Which is far away. 'Are you all right?'

'I have to pee,' she said.

There was a hush. Cathal looked at the road. He could hear Dan give a moan, and Brian turned in his seat and seemed to need to look at the road as well. Ethel looked at Cathal.

'I have to pee,' she said.

His wife coughed.

'We're nearly there love. Just hang on for a minute and we'll soon be there. Cathal!'

Cathal had the road in front of him.

'You've missed the turn,' said his wife behind him. 'Cathal!'

'It was that one on the right you just passed Dad.'

He hesitated, thought of pulling in and trying to do a U-turn. But the traffic was heavy, and no matter what he mumbled he could not seem to clear it. He kept on going.

'Cathal!'

'Next right Dad.'

The next right did not appeal to him. What appealed to him was utter control over situations like this. What appealed to him was the knack of miracles and the light declaring of great truths.

'Trust me,' he said.

'Cathal! For God's sake where are you going?'

'I really need to pee.'

'Dad?'

'You must trust me and fear not.'

'Cathal!'

They passed another right turn. No good. Nor the next. What he needed was a clear space so that he could close his eyes and gather the forces in his blood and do it right. They couldn't rush him.

'Dad, do you know where you're going?'

'Yes. And call me Father, not Dad.'

'Father?'

'Cathal I swear to God I'll . . . Ethel needs . . . Cathal!'

Dan had left them. Cathal saw his face in the mirror grow smaller and smaller as he shrunk into despair. Despair was the same as sin. They were hand in hand. They were. A roundabout.

'Go round the roundabout Dad, Father, and we'll go back that way.'

Cathal went around the roundabout.

'Eh, this turn Da . . . Father, Dad, Jesus, it was that one, go round again.'

'I'm going to divorce you Cathal Forkin.'

'I'm going to pee.'

He sent the car around the circle, turned them around in the one place, held the wheel at the just right angle so that he didn't have to adjust it, could hold it still and keep on going.

'This turn. Dad! That . . . Dad this is crazy. What are you doing?'

'He's gone mad. He's gone mad. Grab the wheel Brian.'

'Dad! Dad!'

'Grab the wheel.'

'I can't grab the wheel.'

Cathal closed his eyes. Kept on going. The circle flowed through his veins, accumulated in his legs, tied him to the task. A small circle. With his car. It was correct. It was what he would have done before. What he did do before. He remembered. The last time.

'Cathal!'

He could feel the spinning, pushing them sideways, Cathal leaning towards his son, who had tensed, he could tell without looking, and was staring ahead. He heard his wife say something about a washing machine. The woman was tied to her time. He hoped they would not hit anything before he got it right.

'Cathal!'

'Dad! Open your eyes for God's sake.'

'I'm going to pee. Really. Right now.'

And he, as though he heard them not, wrote on the ground. Wrote on the ground with his car.

Zero.

Sick as a Dog, Sad as an Angel

A knot of something was lodged beneath her skin, the skin of her stomach. In trying to work out what it felt like, she ran her closed eyes over bumpy things and decided eventually that it felt like she had swallowed an elbow.

'Out,' she mumbled, rubbing it with her fingers. 'Get out.'

'What?' Pip rolled in the sheets, coughed, slid his arm over her thighs. He was low down in the bed, warm in the crisp light, gorgeous. His shoulders, arms. He laid his head on her, flicked his tongue at her navel. She shifted so that he would not feel the bump.

'It's a mystery to me,' said Pip. 'How this happens.'

They had slept well, drunk, she had a headache, she could smell his breath from half a bed away. He was pasty in the face. He talked, then snailed his tongue over her hip, then talked again.

'Sleep I mean. It is, if you think about it, the weirdest fucking thing. It's like you just shut down for eight hours or whatever it is, you just stop working. Every day. It's a major design drawback. You couldn't sell someone something that had to spend half of every day recharging. You just couldn't. It's a bad design, back to the lab God, back to R & D, be real, this is not what people put up with anymore.'

'Don't tickle.'

He coughed louder, pulled away, sat up.

'Christ. And this input output thing is really inefficient.'

He pushed to the edge of the bed and got up, holding his head. She could hear the sound of him pissing, running the tap, taking a drink. He came back with a glass in his hand, stood at the side of the bed and watched her, waiting so that he could take back the glass. She looked at his cock and it looked back at her.

'Okay?'

'Yeah. Head.'

He nodded, rolled her over, massaged her shoulders and her back. She lay on the knobbly growth inside her, pretended that it was just a matchbox fallen in the bed, that it didn't matter.

Pip dressed really quickly, went out and bought a newspaper. He didn't wear socks, felt the breeze about his ankles. When he got back she was throwing up in the bathroom with the door locked. He turned on the television and sifted through a cereal packet for the toy. It was a puzzle, a rectangle of squares that moved around, one place empty, and you had to try and make a picture. It was a picture of a puppet. A puppet of a dog. He winced every time Lill retched.

On the television there was mass, language programmes, Sunday politics. He felt horny. Lill was quiet for a few minutes. Then she opened the door and crept back to bed.

The next day he took her to the doctor and waited on a plastic chair that reminded him of school. Lill came out and told him that she had to go to hospital. That she had to go straight there. Then the doctor appeared and asked Pip to go home and get some things for her, a nightie, a cardigan, slippers. She didn't have any of those things.

The doctor called a taxi and she kissed Pip and he squeezed her hand and off she went. At the flat he sat for a moment. He stared at the blank television. He drank a glass of water. He kept on talking out loud, asking the space beside him questions as if there was someone there.

'I don't believe it,' he said, and his hands kept on opening as if to receive.

He put three pairs of Lill's knickers in a bag, and two T-shirts that she sometimes wore to bed. He put her toothbrush and the toothpaste in a sandwich bag. Her deodorant. A box of tampons and a box of sanitary towels. Moisturiser. He thought about make-up but was unsure. He threw in a lipstick. Socks. A pair of tights. A jumper. Another T-shirt.

The taxi driver took him to the shopping centre first and waited while Pip bought a nightie. The woman in the shop was helpful. Lill was smaller than her said Pip. Thinner he said, and she blushed, and he felt guilty. He bought two nighties, one pale pink, one pale blue. Couldn't believe the price of them.

He paid the taxi driver and thought that she might have died. She might have started to bleed internally. On the inside. In the taxi. On the way there. Internally in the taxi she might have started to bleed. And bled to death on the inside before she'd even got through the door. He made noises in his throat that no one could hear. Found himself checking his pocket for the receipt for the nighties.

He walked inside. Asked a nurse at the reception. She sent him down a corridor to casualty. The first thing he saw when he got there was a small boy with blood on his face being wheeled through curtains. He asked another nurse. She asked who he was. Was he family?

'Boyfriend.'

'Boyfriend?'

'We live together. I have her things. Nighties.'

'She's gone to X-ray. Have a seat. She'll be back in a minute.'

He waited. He sat beside a man who sniffed. A little girl stared at him. He wanted to go to the toilet. Through the doors he caught glimpses of doctors. As young as him they were – some of them.

Lill was dreamy. She was quiet like she was scared, and the nurses kept on reassuring her, but she was not scared. She was dreamy. She liked the pillows and the clean white sheets. She liked the warmth and the hum of voices. She liked the technology – the dials and buttons and the tubes and trays.

She winced at the clack of the X-ray, was sure she felt the radiation in her, passing through her like minor lightning. She could not look at her stomach. When the doctor put his fingers there, she had felt them like additions to the thing inside her, as if it had grown fingers of its own and poked at her from within, trying to find a way out. For a while she pretended she was Sigourney Weaver but it made her feel a little sick and she stopped.

She pushed words out of her mind. Or covered them, hid them. Didn't want to trawl through the mess of them, the way they pointed towards particulars. She flushed them out and filled herself with pictures. Pip in swimming trunks. The carpet in the bathroom. The side of her mother's face. The pointed church. The sky. The sea. Pip in his swimming trunks.

A nurse told him he could see her.

'Is she all right?'

The nursed nodded, grunted something.

She was flat on her back. There was a thin pillow under her head and the bedclothes were straight and neat and her arms lay outside them. She looked like a letter in an envelope, pale as paper. There was a drip beside her, attached to the back of her left hand.

'Are you OK?'

'Yeah. Sorry.'

'For what?'

'Scaring you.'

'You're forgiven.'

He went to her, kissed her on the forehead, put a hand on her hair. Kissed her again. He asked her what the doctor had said but she told him that the doctor hadn't said anything, that he was coming to see her soon, that she would tell him then.

At home he made phone calls. Called Lill's place, sighed relief when her father answered. Her father listened, made small panic noises, but was efficient, sensible, asked good questions, thanked Pip. Told him they'd see him at the hospital.

He called some friends, and was reassured and offered company and help and so forth. He called work and they obviously had some kind of procedure for this kind of thing, some contingency plan for non direct sudden illness necessitating presence of staff at hospital bedsides. They told him it was covered, catered for, it was all in hand.

He smoked cigarettes and worried that he had done it to her with his way of having sex, or that he had mistreated her somehow and she had been too scared to tell him to stop, or that he was the carrier of some disease and had infected her. He was watching a sentimental advert for life assurance or telecommunications or something like that when he burst into tears, and he was very shocked by the thickness of snot and the wetness of cheeks and the whole messy suddenness of it, and it made him think that he must be guilty of something somewhere along the line. And he decided that feeling guilty was a selfish thing, and that he should not admit those thoughts.

He set up the video to tape Brookside for her. He tidied the bathroom, scrubbed the sink and the shower and cried again when he couldn't get the dirt out from between the tiles, which made him hugely angry at how pathetic he was, and he was frightened by how pathetic he was, as well as angry, and all of this internal crap mixed itself into a general selfishness which ran down his face, which he slapped sharply, a brutal little reminder, which as soon as he'd done it seemed entirely indulgent and self-pitying.

He wondered if they would let him stay in the hospital overnight, if they would let him get into the bed beside her, if they would allow him to be like that.

When he got to the hospital, carrying flowers that he thought might be too big, too colourful, might look too expensive, he was told that she had been moved to a private room, and on his way up in the elevator he debated whether that meant she was dying already. Her parents were there, outside the door, her father talking to a doctor, her mother squinting, counting her fingers, and Pip thought it odd that they were standing outside – odd and bad – a bad sign. They didn't see him until he stood amongst them.

'Pip, hi.'

'Oh Pip love are you all right?'

'How is she?'

He said this to the doctor and then thought he shouldn't have, so he half smiled at the parents, and then regretted that too, and looked again at the doctor, and thought that it was ridiculous that everything should be so slow so suddenly.

'She is going to need surgery I'm afraid,' said her father, the doctor's lips not even moving.

'What is the prog, di, the prog-diag, the nosis. What is that?'

'The diagnosis,' said her mother.

'The surgery is exploratory,' said the doctor, confusing Pip with a Scottish accent. 'Lill has a growth, or an obstruction, of some kind. It could be one of many things. We feel that surgery is appropriate, as whatever it is it will need to be removed in any case.'

Pip nodded.

'So rather than keyhole', he said, 'rather than biopting, biopsy, you might as well . . .'

'Exactly.'

'When?' whispered her mother.

'First thing in the morning. So please allow her to get a good night's sleep.'

He nodded and walked away and Pip looked at him go, and watched him pause to say something to a nurse, who smiled, and took a tiny notebook from her pocket and wrote something there and smiled again, the doctor walking off again, down the corridor and through swing doors. Lill's father explained that they had arrived just a moment before Pip, that they had met the doctor as he had left her room, that they had not yet seen her. Pip wanted them to go away. He wanted to see her on his own. He would not be able to kiss her, touch her. He would have to let them do the talking. She wouldn't be able to talk to him, ask him the important questions, be reassured by him. He felt remarkably annoyed – irritated – and he could not bring himself to look at her mother or return her father's watery, worried smile as he held the door for his wife and then for Pip. The room was warm.

She was sitting up, chewing a fingernail, the television remote control in her lap. She smiled at all of them.

'No more bikinis for me,' she said.

They each kissed her cheek, and she sniffed at the flowers and gave him a second kiss for them, and her mother disappeared into a bathroom with a vase and there was noise of water and wrapping paper and little exclamations of delight and mild consternation that she could find nothing with which to cut the stems. With flowers placed on the radiator (where Pip was sure they would dry up and die in no time), looking alarmingly too big for their container, all three of them sat around her, and her parents were so cheerful, so casual, so determined to be relaxed that Pip wanted to scream. They drove him mad with hospital stories of this neighbour or that neighbour, about whose son was a doctor where, who used to be a nurse, how the room was a drab but it was good to have a bit of privacy, and Lill peered at Pip and he could say nothing, could not get close to her, could not make it known to her that he knew, he understood, and that it would be all right, it would all be all right. He went to the bathroom and inhaled his reflection violently and was cross with himself. Then he thought that maybe they were waiting for him to leave so they could be with their daughter, and he thought of things he might say that would politely get the message across to them that it was they who should leave, that they were distressing her with all of this, that they

144

should allow her time to herself, time with him, that it was only right that they should be given some privacy, some solitude, at a time like this. This was important.

He went back out and took his seat and Lill smiled at him, and he shook his head and tried to smile to show that he knew what she was thinking, but his smile was not working and he didn't know what kind of face it was he made but she gave him an odd look.

They gave her a sleeping tablet and as she drifted off she thought of how nice she felt, how safe and warm and painless, and she wanted to bring everyone with her, her mother and Pip and even her father, bring them all along for the sleep.

In the morning she was hungry and mostly thirsty but they wouldn't let her take anything and she was frightened for a while, not feeling cold exactly, but knowing that it was cold outside her bed, and knowing somehow what the cold felt like. Pip had been sweet. In a way. She looked at the flowers, tottering on the windowsill, so bright that they dazzled her. For a while she listened to his Walkman but was afraid that she would miss some real noise related to herself, and switched it off, but left the earphones in so that she looked relaxed. He had stayed too late – the nurse had asked him to leave. It would have been nice if he had made some joke and kissed her, but he had been so serious and teary eyed and had hugged her too long, and he had rushed off then like he was trying to be brave, which annoyed her because it was no help to her to have him freaked out. Her parents had been better, pretending to be casual, leaving her with gentle kisses and a nod and a quiet promise that everything would be all right. Once they had gone Pip stuttered through strange declarations of things she already knew, not making sense, rambling, confusing her with a faulty memory of how they had met, getting the place wrong, and being so apologetic when she corrected him that she was annoyed at him for being stupid. Not stupid for his mistake but for his horror at having made it. He was daft and serious. When she tried to break into him with a suggestion that they have a quick quiet shag, he went pale and seemed to take her seriously, and when he realised that she was joking he went into a long incoherent speech about how much he loved having sex with her and that it was the best sex, and that it would always mean everything to him, although it was not, of course, the main thing, the most important thing, that he loved her for everything, for absolutely everything about her, and that would not stop. She told him to shut up.

A nurse came and got her to change into a smock thing that tied up the back and she could feel the cold through it as the nurse crouched to inject her with something and gave her tablets and a sip of water, 'just a sip now,' and put her back into the bed and tucked her in and told her she would relax and probably doze. Which she did. She dreamed of swimming with Pip, and the air was as blue as the water and Pip's skin was warm and they were perfect swimmers, perfect.

They woke her with their underwater voices and hands piled her on to some kind of trolley and she was heavier than she'd ever been and she didn't care about anything, even thought that the porter sneaking a look at the naked back of her was kind of cute. They went up in a lift and wheeled her trolley to a bed and they asked her to lift herself and they helped her across, giggling, amazingly heavy. A face looked into hers. They did something with her arm, they said hello. It was bright. There were many people. The face smiled at her.

'I'm going to count backwards Lillian, OK? From ten.'

'Lill.'

'What's that?'

'I'm Lill.'

'Lill. Sorry. Ten, nine, eight . . .'

As she went she thought of a joke. I'm Lill. I'm Lill and I'm ill and I need a pill.

*

146

Pip threw up while he was waiting. He threw up twice. The second time someone heard and asked through the door whether he was all right. He thought it was because he hadn't been able to eat the night before so that he was starving when he woke and comfort ate more than he should have and then as soon as he had left the flat the nerves had kicked in and he was in trouble. Mr and Mrs were in the worst of moods for him, for his own state of mind. She sat and counted her fingers and he paced, both of them occasionally staring at each other for brief little desperate moments. But he was desperate too, he knew that. He was more desperate than them. He found himself thinking that they had had her for the whole of her life and he had only just found her and it wasn't fair. Every footstep had one of them panicked, so that there was always one looking up, huge eyed, while the others took turns at head in hands or moving lips. They hardly talked. Pip went to get coffees and had trouble carrying one, never mind three, so ended up doing a trip for each of them, which passed ten minutes, him hurrying down corridors burning his fingers, convinced he was missing something. They drove him mad. He thought that this was maybe a good thing. He even thought that maybe they weren't driving him mad at all but that he had decided they were to distract himself from thinking about Lill. It was when his thoughts formed this particular argument that his stomach heaved for the first time, the coffee not helping, and he trotted to the bathroom with his mouth full of acid and gasses. He felt terrible, which of course made him wonder at how sick Lill must be and made him feel guilty, which he experienced as a nausea slightly beside the one he already had, and a clicking in his head as if his ears had been on a flight.

Lill had once hit him. She had slapped him across the face because he had slagged off a band she liked. It had happened in the Olympia, in the dress circle where the mirrors repeat the crowd. It happened when the lights came up and she asked him what he had thought of them, and he had shrugged and said something he couldn't remember and she had smacked him once, hard, loud, and everyone had looked and he had tried to laugh it off, as if it was nothing, nothing at all, and she had laughed too, as if she had done it because she was happy and it was a physical thing she could do to him without admitting anything, and the two of them had shuffled out of their seats, stared at, his cheek burning, smiling those awful embarrassed smiles of people who don't quite get their own jokes. What he found most startling was his lack of anger. He had told himself afterwards – next time be angry. You can be angry with her and not lose her. That is allowed. But he was never angry with her.

All those mirrors, so that everyone saw that smack a thousand times, from a thousand different angles, hung in the red and gold like puppetry.

When the doctor came it struck Pip that everything was following a very predictable pattern, that this was soap opera formula, that he'd seen it on the TV a hundred times, and so had Lill. And it was just like they'd watched it. Which made him wonder, as the doctor talked, whether the people who wrote these television dramas had done really good research, or whether people who worked in hospitals now knew what was expected of them. Everyone, thought Pip, is comfortable with this.

'Lill is in the recovery room where we'll keep an eye on her for a while and then she'll be going back to her room. You can see her then. We found a growth in the wall of her stomach which we have removed. Obviously this will have to be tested, but I think it's fair to say at this stage that it looks most likely that it's benign and isolated.'

'Oh thank God,' said Lill's mother, and her father held his wife and nodded and nodded and continued to nod.

'How can you say that?' Pip asked him.

'Well, I'm saying it based on what I saw, and the kinds of things I've seen before. There was no evidence of other tumours, or of spreading. The lymphatic system is clear.

148

Obviously I'd caution you all that we have to wait for the results of the biopsy. But I think there's cause for optimism.'

'You can't say that though.'

Lill's father took his elbow.

'We'll wait Pip, for the results, it's OK.'

'Yeah but he shouldn't say that. You shouldn't be allowed to say that kind of thing. It's not helpful you know? To be raising hopes like that and then a few days later apologising to us when you get the results and it's not what you'd told us at all. It's not professional.'

'I wanted to ease your worries a little, that's all.'

'Well it's not helpful.'

The doctor looked at Pip, a little strangely, fixing him for a moment. Then he nodded to Lill's parents.

'Well please get in touch with my office if you want to go over the results with me when I get them. I'll be seeing Lill in the morning. Bye bye.'

And he walked away down the corridor.

'I'll make a complaint.'

The doctor paused briefly but did not turn.

'Oh Pip for God's sake,' said Lill's father. 'The man is trying to be helpful. Most doctors wouldn't tell you a thing.'

'Which is as it should be.'

He went home with them, staying for a while, drinking a gin and tonic with Lill's father, talking about Lill, about how she had been as a child, about the things she liked.

'You should take her on a little holiday Pip,' said her mother. 'When she's better. Take her off to Cliffden maybe, she liked that before, let her do some swimming maybe if she's up to it. She'll need to relax for a bit.'

Pip thought about her sitting on the rocks, about the two of them walking the road out to the headland, chasing midges away, gasping at the ocean, making love in a field and having to stop because of the laughter, and the noises in the hedges, and the snapping in the air.

'Well,' he said. 'One step at a time.'

149

*

They called the hospital twice before they heard that Lill was back in her room. Her father drove, and although Pip thought he shouldn't, after two G & Ts, which had his own head slightly numbed, he said nothing.

She was white. A tube disappeared into her nose, another one went up under the sheets and the blankets halfway down the bed. A device with a huge syringe set into it sat on her bedside table. Her eyes opened when they came in, but she closed them then and did not open them again.

Her mother took her hand and kissed her forehead and whispered things to her that Pip could not hear. Her father stood at the other side of the bed, put a hand on her shoulder, took it away again, sat down.

Pip stood at the door. He looked at the tubes and the syringe. He looked at the flowers he had sent, and the bottle of orange her mother had brought in, and at the half dozen or so cards which lined the windowsill. Only he had sent flowers. Why had her father not got flowers for his daughter? Why had nobody else done that? There was a flower shop at the hospital entrance. Why had nobody else come to visit her? What were they thinking?

He looked lastly at Lill. There was no colour in her – even her hair seemed thinned and diluted and not her own. Her closed eyes were ringed and shocking, as if she was dead or painted dead, and the rise and fall of her chest seemed to him to be irregular and sharp and wrong.

'Jesus,' he hissed.

'Pip, come and sit here. Lill, Pip is here too.'

Nothing in her moved except her heart up and down, pushing to get out, and her hand seemed to tremble, but when he looked at it, it stopped, and his eye caught that of her mother, who looked at him open mouthed, and her father too, staring at him, openly, gawking, fixing him as the doctor had done, and he knew that he was doing this all wrong, that he was incorrectly placed, out of position, and he could not

150

decide whether it was his right to be awkward. It was not clear to him what his role was, whether he was central or sidelined, whether this was hers only or hers and his both, whether he was equal to the parents or allowed only to watch, a friend of the family, not expected to have any investment in this.

'Come and sit down Pip.'

'I'm going to find the doctor. I want to know what's going on.'

Her father stood suddenly, and moved towards him, and nodded, and took his arm, and opened the door and led him gently, firmly, out into the corridor.

'What is your problem?'

'What?'

'Why are you making this so difficult? It's nobody's fault. The doctor has been excellent. He's the best there is. You think I didn't make sure of that? You think I haven't been through everything in my mind, over and over? Do you think I haven't terrified myself with thoughts of what could be going on? But I'm not going to let her down. I'm not going to scare her mother. God knows she has enough to worry about without you behaving like someone's broken your favourite toy.'

'Jesus.'

'So get it together or leave. You're useless here the way you are. You're being neurotic and selfish.'

He turned to go back in, then turned again.

'She is loved by all of us. You don't have exclusive rights here Pip. So stop behaving like you're the only one who cares. It's the stupidest thing I ever saw.'

He glanced towards the nurses' station and then looked at Pip's shoes. Looked at his shoes, pushed the door open with his shoulder and went back into his daughter's room.

Lill dreamed of drowning, over and over again, without being able to wake, and each time she drowned she saw her body laid out naked in the grass beside some fast river in the cold of winter, and she saw Pip crouch over her and stare into her face and hang over her then supported on his arms, and she could feel, dead as she was, the water of him fall on her, tears and spit and cum, all of it washing her, Pip raining on her as if to confirm that she was gone and he was left after, and he was useless in the face of her alteration.

She knew.

When she woke properly, eventually, to a numbness in her belly that she imagined had turned in her dreams into the presence of Pip's body, and to a blurred vision of her parents, and saw that he was not there, she knew.

She could not talk very well, and in any case, after trying once, found that she did not want to talk, that it would be a very dull thing to do. She listened to her mother, and later, to the doctor, who, from what she could gather, was happy with her, and she sipped cold water and heard her father say eventually that Pip would be in later, and she knew.

When he did come, she was beginning to feel the nausea, of which she vaguely remembered having being warned. He was sullen, kissed her, but sat away then, did not pull the chair close.

'How do you feel?'

'Sick as a dog.'

He nodded.

'Can I get you anything?'

He looked terrified of her. She shook her head, which was a mistake, and reached to the bedside table for the metal bowl they had given her.

'I'm meant to throw up in this apparently.'

'OK.'

He leaned forward, rested his elbows on his knees, coughed.

'I'm no good at this.'

'At what?'

'This.'

She nodded, and this time the movement, which he hadn't

even seen, caused her to throw up a spoonful of pale yellow liquid, and she retched painfully and worried for the first time about the dressing and the stitches. Pip stood, placed a light hand on the top of her head.

'Will I call a nurse?'

She couldn't answer him for a moment, and in that time he moved away from her towards the door. She looked up to see him in the middle of the floor, undecided, an arm out-stretched towards the door handle, but his upper body turned back to her, a look on his face that was half disgust and half confusion. For a horrible moment she hated him. She closed her eyes and breathed deeply and wiped her mouth with a tissue.

'It's all right.'

'Sure?'

'Yes.'

He sat down again.

'I want to sleep.'

'Do you want me to go?'

'Yes.'

'OK.'

He waited for a minute, then stood.

'I'll be back in the morning.'

'Go to work.'

'Lunchtime, I'll come at lunchtime.'

'OK.'

He leant down and kissed her forehead.

'I love you,' he said.

'Yes.'

When he had closed the door she threw up again. After a few minutes of it she pressed the button to call the nurse.

Pip went home and drank some cold water, and he looked at the things they owned. He sat by the telephone and made a list of his friends. In his mind he made another list. He could not balance the two.

He touched her clothes in the wardrobe, looked for marks of her, found himself forgetting that she was still in the hospital. He kept on thinking she was further. He waited until it was properly dark and then he made calls, ticking off everyone on his list one by one. In a steady low voice he told them all that Lill was not well, that she was not well at all, that the operation had not gone well, that the doctors were not happy, that she was in intensive care, that she had not regained consciousness, that if they were praying people they might usefully pray. Sometimes he cried at what he was doing, at the trick in his mind that allowed him to do it, and the people on the list tried to comfort him, cried with him sometimes, offered to come over. He declined. He declined it all.

Pip wondered what names could be given him. He thought deeply and for hours about descriptions of himself and he could find none. He waited to wake, he waited all night to wake up, but the sun came and he was still sleeping and he could not shake it off.

Headwound

I took my son to the park while my wife, who is not good with children, went to see her lover in my German car. It is not a particularly new car, but it is very solid, handles very well, and is good for maybe another couple of years. But I don't like my wife driving it. She is not a bad driver, but she is not smooth, does not conduct herself very confidently, is all fits and starts, jerks and tics.

My son is five, just five, having had a very noisy party last month where there was a considerable amount of really very frightening food. Food that is small and seems always to be covered in a primary colour, is, to my mind, rather threatening, in the manner of toys and buttons. There were perhaps a dozen children at this party, and it was difficult for my wife. She prepared a lot of food, by which I mean that she bought a lot of food and put it into bowls, and she distributed a lot of drink – fizzy drink, pop and so forth, usually dark brown to black or orange in colour, though occasionally a very lime green or a sky blue. I was quite surprised by the fact that none of the children were sick, at least not while in our charge, but unfortunately my wife, who is not good with children, was ill in the downstairs bathroom once or twice, out of nerves I think, mostly, leaving me to marshal the children, organise them and keep them quiet. My wife was embarrassed when the children were being collected by their parents, but there was no need really, they could not have known. I sent each child off with a gift, either a ruler or a pencil or pencil sharpener.

So my son is five. He is not a particularly bright child, it seems to me, and I rather worry sometimes that he may suffer from that peculiar defect so evident in his mother – an enormous capacity for self-pity and introspection. Of course the levels of introspection to which a five-year-old may gain access are not particularly profound, but he does display the tendency to examine himself inappropriately at the worst kind of moments, and his questions all revolve around himself. Which is not a healthy inquisition. But it is true to say I think, that he is more like his mother than myself. Which, naturally enough, lets me down a little.

She had, as I've said, taken my car, so that my son and myself, and our very old, very wretched terrier, Ninny, were compelled to walk to the park, which is not far, but is annoying because the best part of the place, the only area where it is actually quite pleasant to stroll, is quite a distance from us, and by the time we got there my son was tired and Ninny was almost dead. Both of them were annoying me considerably, and we stopped at a bench so that they could recover a little.

My son has hair with a tendency to curl when longer than about an inch, so I had taken him to my own barber that morning for a trim, and he was troubled now by ticklish hairs which had found their way under his clothes. So I was obliged, at his insistence, to help him off with his jumper and his shirt, so that he could 'get the wind to blow them away.' It was not especially cold, but it was late September, and I did not like the idea of my son being shirtless in the park at that time of year. But he is like his mother and can feel nothing but his own discomfort. So I sat there, close to the road, while my son ran in a circle half-naked with a dying dog yapping at his heels, and I found it uncomfortable and unsettling and it put me in a bad mood.

I was watching him closely, convinced as I was that he would try to pull down his shorts if I was not sufficiently stern-faced, and he stopped eventually with his back to me and started to fiddle down there somewhere. I had begun to tell him to stop whatever he was doing, when I heard my own name called affably from somewhere to my left, and

turned to see a couple I knew vaguely from the neighbour-
hood. He is in software I believe, and his wife is foreign,
French I think, and their names completely escaped me. He
engaged me for a few moments about inconsequential matters, a new local property development, the weather, the political situation, and I sat and they stood, he looking at me
while she regarded my son, whom I now could not see at all.
She started to laugh, and said something in her own language, and nudged her husband, who turned, allowing me to
look as well. My son had, sure enough, pulled his shorts and
underpants down to his ankles, and was standing, still with
his back to us, waving his arms in the air and swivelling back
and forth on his hips, looking for all the world like a lawn
sprinkler, though thankfully not actually sprinkling, as far as
I could see.

I jumped to my feet, passed my neighbours, and in the one
movement delivered a sharp but not overdone slap to his
behind, and gathered him up, carrying him back to the
bench. The French woman giggled, and scolded me, in a
good-natured kind of way, for slapping my son, while her
husband made some silly comment about park flashers or
something along those lines. I fumbled with the boy's clothing, trying to cover him up, as he started to quietly whimper
in a completely artificial way, feeling nothing more traumatic
than sorry for himself. The couple were by now laughing
openly, and as I was not laughing at all – I think it is fair to
say that they were laughing at me. It was at this moment,
annoyed and embarrassed as I was, that I believe I may have
inadvertently, while trying to do up his shorts, somehow
pinched or otherwise lacerated my son's penis, a difficult
thing to do given its size. In any case, he roared, this time I
admit, genuinely distressed. This screaming of course, predic-
tably, put a stop to the amusement of the by now hugely
unwelcome neighbours, who became immediately solicitous
and syrupy (they do not have children of their own) towards
the boy, the woman uttering a string of baby gibberish in

assorted languages while the man peered at my son's middle and visibly flinched. He thought he saw blood, which I dismissed as ridiculous, and gave me a look that bordered on the accusing. The woman meanwhile knelt beside the bench and soothed the boy's brow. He had at least, due I imagine to a certain preoccupation with his pain, closed his eyes and had his little hands firmly clenched over his groin and would admit no aid of any description, frustrating the efforts of the couple, who fussed for a while and then gave up. I told them of his continuing addiction to tantrums and of his difficult nature, thanked them curtly for their concern and made it plain enough that I thought they should continue on their way.

My wife, I should say, is having an affair with a paediatrician.

They lingered though, offering us a lift home in his new two-seater, also German, which I declined, for obvious reasons.

My son had by now reduced his roar to a fairly level sobbing, and as the couple strolled very slowly away from us, I started the ritual round of apology and promise of reward and general assurances of things being better soon in an attempt to get him fully dressed and on to his feet. Ninny, throughout the entire incident, had been hovering worriedly around the bench, occasionally joining in the whimpering, and I now invoked her name in an effort to uncoil him from his fit of self-absorption. Which seemed, eventually, to work. He looked for her and she came to him, and he reached for her and I glanced at his shorts to see there were indeed a couple of drops of blood, but nothing very remarkable. He saw the same thing and turned a little pale. I was able to assure him with a quick look that everything was still intact and that all that had happened was that he had suffered a little scratch and that it would be something to show his mother. As I sorted out his shirt and jumper he had a look for himself and despite a little sniffling seemed reassured and even a little proud.

158

I finally reunited him with all of his clothing, wiped his nose with my handkerchief, persuaded him to shake my hand as a sign of there being no hard feelings, and got him to his feet, prompting a little celebratory bark from Ninny. I noticed that our neighbours were still within sight, loitering at the edge of a fenced-in lake away from the main road. I gave them a wave and a thumbs up, but they did not respond.

My son by now of course wanted to go home, and Ninny seemed utterly disinterested in any of the usual diversions dogs find in parks. My wife has a theory about Ninny – that she is our marriage, all that remains of it. We got her in the first year, and she is weak now, and my wife insists that when Ninny dies our marriage will be over. It started as a joke, was shared with friends. We used to say, before our son arrived, that we were staying together for the sake of the dog. But it has now become a private thing, melodramatic, often hissed at me in the kitchen after some squabble or other. *As soon as the dog is gone.* I have mentioned that my wife is not good with children. It seems not to have occurred to her to transfer our responsibility, the duty of care that we might have for the dog, on to our child, although perhaps the time frame is a factor. Sometimes I think she is serious about this.

I persuaded my son that there was little point in going home so soon, having come so far. He sighed exaggeratedly and sniffed a lot and tested his ability to walk with his newly earned injury before agreeing to go on a little further, at least to the lake, so that we could throw sticks for Ninny and see if we could get her into the water. So we set off at a slow pace, which actually suited me, as I could still see the bothersome couple up ahead of us, slowly circling the lake, glancing back now and again, talking to each other, no doubt about me. I have no idea how widely known it is that my wife is having an affair. I do not believe she is particularly discreet, although she probably thinks she is. He is single and lives some ten minutes away in a large, rather grotesque new house, probably of his own design, with a red brick front and terracotta roof tiles – the place looks like a bloodshot eye. It has a rolling lawn (he employs a gardener) and a winding gravel drive. He has planted a hedgerow at the front which will eventually provide the public roadway with a little privacy but which for the moment allows him to gape at whoever passes by. When my wife visits him she parks my car sideways on to the house, close behind his own (English) in an apparent attempt at concealment, which does not work. I have met him several times.

My son tried to run, then pulled up suddenly, bent over and looked at his groin. I shooed him along, and anxiously peered ahead, but thankfully the couple seemed to have put the lake between themselves and us. He hobbled a little, and complained of stinging, and Ninny stayed close to his feet and seemed confused. I gave out to the pair of them. I remember before I was married at all, going for walks with my father. They were striding, breathless walks when little was said and after which I always felt refreshed, cleaned up, healthily tired. My father was a quiet, dignified man, not much given to sentiment or nonsense. When I was a boy myself on these walks, he would carry on, even pick up his pace, when I flagged, when I protested or whinged or acted the baby. It taught me a valuable lesson. He is dead now – his heart imploded on the Sugar Loaf in 1987.

I moved ahead of my son – looked ahead and walked on, considering how best to approach the lake in order to avoid once more running into my neighbours. This lake (although to call it a lake is not really accurate, it is more a pond, rather shallow and dank) is ringed by a falling-down metal fence, within which there is a lot of shrubbery, low trees, thick weedy growths and that kind of thing. But there are well-worn paths leading through all of this from almost every gap in the fence. I headed for the obvious one, directly in front of me, and looked around to see if there was any sign of the couple. There was not. They had disappeared. Presumably they had circled the lake and continued on from the other side. This cheered me up a little and I turned to hurry my son along. He was coming anyway, if sulkily, and I restricted myself to a small word of encouragement and a couple of loud clicks of my tongue to get Ninny running, which she did, gamely, prompting my son to attempt something similar, though his gait, bandy-legged and preposterous, and accompanied as it was by a face twisted in self-occupation, made me turn away, a little disgusted by him.

My wife's problems with children manifest themselves in odd ways, such as her inability to have any kind of intelligent conversation with our son, who seems at times to consider her as he might a not unpleasant but rather stupid playmate. She is never cross with him, but does not seem to engage him much either, regarding him from something of a distance, as if puzzled as to where he came from. She can spend long minutes just staring at him – I have seen her do it – and at other times, when I walk into a room where they both are, I often catch her at it again, staring at him with a rather vacuous smile on her face, motioning at me to be quiet or to stand still so that she can continue her contemplation. Which is not proper. Occasionally they whisper together.

I waited at the fence for the two walking wounded to reach me, and noticed as I did so some little sticks at my feet good for throwing. I gathered these up, indulged a couple of moans from my son about his tiredness, and helped him through the fence, having to lift Ninny over the lowest and only intact rung. There was a pleasing coolness under the trees, and a nice damp sensation to the air. We were out of the pale sun and into the shadows and the vegetation. I like such places. My son seems to as well, and he revived now, running towards the water with Ninny after him, without any obvious sign of distress. The dog stopped to mark a tuft of grass and I took this opportunity to throw the first stick, landing it too close to her, rustling the leaves and making her jump. She moved towards my son, who saw what I was at and laughed, calling at the dog and motioning her towards the water. Ninny likes water, but has often to be reminded that she does. It has always been the chief entertainment of these walks (for my son I mean) to see her splash about in the rather rank shallows, disturbing god only knows what kind of spawn and muck and insect life. When we get her home it is necessary to bathe her, which I try to do in the sink of the utility room, but in which I am often pre-empted by my wife, who seems to think that the main bathroom and our own bath is suitable for such a task, much to my own annoyance and the thrilled pleasure of the boy. I threw another stick, further this time, but still not reaching the water. She ran towards it a little but was distracted then by some scent or other and paused to bark at a thick crop of bushes beside the path. I changed my throwing technique from underarm to over and flung a couple more which splashed by the bank and got her back to at least looking in the right direction.

My throwing is quite good. My father encouraged me to play cricket, a game I neither like nor understand, and he was disappointed that I never took to it. He would throw a ball to me for hours, over and over again, to improve my catching, and would set up cans and buckets and so forth for me to aim at. I always threw better than I caught, and enjoyed the noisy clatter of hitting the target. My wife neither throws nor catches very well, as I have noted on several occasions. She is indiscriminate with her hands and simply breaks things. She once broke a favourite mug of mine in an apparent attempt to lob it into the sink. And what annoys me is that she does not seem to see the value of such physical skills. She does not mind that our son can neither play football nor run well nor use his hands to make anything other than a mess. She admires nothing steady or well done, thinks only of her own place in the world, her own pleasures, her own needs.

With my son at the water's edge, calling the dog, and with me throwing sticks into the water itself, encouraging her from behind, Ninny became a little bewildered I think as to

where she was supposed to be going and what she was supposed to be doing. I told my son to get out of her way. I
noticed a duck move slowly past on the far side of the lake,
watching us maybe, and I saw a branch in the water to our
left, a big branch, stuck in the mud and sticking into the air
like a finger. I thought, there in the shadows and the cool air,
hidden from the rest of the world, or as good as, that I should
leave my wife before she left me. That I should withdraw, as
it were, and find my own place, I don't mean literally, but in
the sense of doing what I wanted to do, following my own
path, being who I was instead of allowing her to dictate the
pace and direction of my life.

I picked up some more twigs and aimed them this time
directly at Ninny. I missed, and she scurried a little and
moved towards the water. My son laughed at her and she
wagged her tail. I stooped again to pick up more ammuni-
tion, my eyes on the dog, trying not to lose sight of her in the
greenery. I stood and took aim. As my arm was behind me,
just as it started its forward movement, with my eyes firmly
fixed on Ninny's behind, I was conscious, if that's the word,
perhaps it is, I was conscious of the vaguest of movements, a
small blur to the upper right of my target. I threw.

I am unsure of how it happened. It seems to me in many
ways that it didn't happen at all, that the outcome was not of
my doing, that it simply couldn't be. I am not a careless man.
But what I saw was clear enough. Or rather, to begin with,
what I heard. For it was two curious sounds which came to
me initially and which suggested that something was not
quite right. The first was a hollow kind of knock, as you
might get from certain doors, a small, almost gentle kind of
poc. And the second was a curtailed utterance of surprise, a
gasp or sigh, I'm not sure which, entirely in the mouth, and
very brief, as if it had closed as soon as it had opened, leaving
the merest suggestion of shock in the air. And then silence,
for a moment anyway, while my eyes caught up.

What I saw took a little unravelling. Ninny seemed to have

disappeared completely – to have melted into the general background greens and browns. Instead what I saw was my son, looking, for some reason, considerably taller than he is, standing stiffly upright, his hands held away from his body, his eyes turned upwards, his legs rather crooked, and with a small dark mark on his forehead, just below the hairline. What I saw next perplexed me. He seemed to suddenly shrink, or not shrink exactly, but go down, as if he was standing on a fast downward escalator looking back at me, or as if he were being slid into a slot in the ground. As if his feet and legs were disintegrating. It was a moment before I realised that what he was actually doing was falling. Falling backwards from an upright position. Falling as if, and really this is the only word which comes to me, poleaxed.

You can imagine my surprise.

Next of course was a resumption of sound – a sort of quick rustling, superseded almost immediately by a loud splash, a slap really, like a belly flop noise, as my son hit the water. There was the smallest moment of quiet, and then a rush of things at once – distinct lapping as the lake, pond, realigned itself; the plaintive whimpering of Ninny (who I could still not put my eye to); my own heart; a brawl of voice or voices over to my right; the alarming scurry of shapes through the undergrowth; traffic in the distance; my own heart.

I admit that I paused. I will admit to it freely. I admit openly that for a while I just stood there, while something inside me requested a replay, begged pardon, protested that no, I didn't quite get that, could you say it again? For I had been throwing twigs for my dog, and now there seemed to have been some kind of incident involving my son. It was only when I saw, out of the corner of my eye, but clear nevertheless, the male half of the earlier couple, the software man, the one with the German sports car and the French wife, galloping over the bushes and the grass and the mud towards what I now definitely understood to be my son, unconscious, or at least groggy, with his head under water, that I realised

164

that I had better get a move on. Which I did. And as I ran I tried to work out what had happened, how he had come to be as he was, which, I could now see, was in a perilously unnatural position. He was supine, laid out, on his back, his arms straight and stretched, as if his hands had been trying to get as far away from his shoulders as they could. He had one leg under him and a distinct patch of blood on the front of his shorts. And his head was submerged from the shoulders – his chin slightly protruding from the filmy surface, but his mouth, his nose, his eyes, and a peculiar bloom of blood (more blood), just below his hairline, were all under water.

I did not have to run far, but it took forever, and though my eyes were fixed on the boy, still they took in other things too, such as the position of Ninny, now revealed to be standing rather forlornly beside my son's right hip, edging into the water and out again, flustered and confused and crying. And I could also measure the distance between myself and the other man, sensible as I was of his progress as a soft but furious blur in the extreme right corner of my right eye, and I was able to calculate our comparative distances from our shared target and was relieved to note that I had the upper hand, although he had the benefit of greater momentum and was gaining.

But mostly, while I was running, my mind was occupied with the greatest mystery of all – what had actually happened? I considered several different options, starting with what seemed at first to be the most obvious – that my son had been shot. I had not heard anything like a gunshot, but there is always the possibility of a silencer, which suggests of course a professional job, a *hit* as they say, which brought to mind for some reason my wife and her lover, and I thought maybe that he was hidden somewhere nearby, and might have perhaps been aiming for Ninny in an effort to kill off our marriage, but had missed somehow and murdered the boy instead, which was, I thought while striding over a squalid puddle lined with sexual debris, a bit ironic.

The second theory, and one a lot less likely, to my mind at least, was that my son had somehow banged his head on something. He is forever doing this – concussing himself mildly on presses, doors, door frames, tabletops and corners, banisters, counter tops, chairs, televisions, ceilings, floors, boots and shoes, garden furniture and people. But none of these items, or any others for that matter, were within his reach, unless he had somehow contrived to bang his head off the dog, which one glance at the sad but unscathed Ninny seemed to refute.

Had something banged itself off him then? I thought of several things at once – a giant heron or cormorant or something like that which we had once seen in this very place; a swan, which we had also seen; a falling branch; something Ninny kicked up; something dropped from the foliage; something from the skies, like a little meteorite or a piece of junk – but none of these things made any sense whatsoever. I did consider that I might have accidentally hit him with the twig intended for Ninny, but it was ridiculous that such a flimsy piece of light wood would have had such an effect. So I ruled that out.

Eventually I reached him.

My wife had been having her affair for about a year before I found out about it.

Ninny was in the way. She stood nuzzling his ribcage, her hind legs in the water, her front paws trying to dig him out, her yelping in itself an obstruction. So my first task was to remove her, which I did by lifting her, and then looking around for somewhere to put her down, which was not easy, knowing full well as I did that no matter where I put her she would be back to interfere within seconds. So I hovered for a moment with the dog in mid air, which I fully admit now, with the benefit of hindsight, was a stupid thing to do, given the urgency. I saw bubbles though. I'm sure I saw bubbles in the water above his mouth, which I remember thinking at the time was a good sign, and then thinking that perhaps it

166

wasn't, I couldn't remember, and I decided at this point to jet-
tison the dog and get to the real business at hand. So I let her
go, which again, I admit it, was foolish, but I think that by
this time, the shock of the situation was giving way to a certain unwelcome panic. She fell a little awkwardly, onto my
son's crotch area, where she yelped a bit and scrambled
slightly, her paws struggling for a foothold somewhere in his
shorts. I ignored her, and crouched down on my hunkers to
have a look, to work out how best to proceed, knowing that
the first rule in these situations is to not unnecessarily move
the victim. Or the injured party, however you want to
describe him. I decided however that the presence of the
water was enough to overrule that particular consideration.
So I stretched out my hands and looked for where best to
place them. Given the leverage necessary, and the likely hea-
viness of the water in his clothes, and taking into account my
own centre of gravity, I decided it best to take hold of his
neck and to prise him out as it were, while at the same time
lending sufficient support to his head. So I took hold of his
throat, working to get my hands behind him, having to half
stand and throw one leg over him so that I straddled him and
was in the best position therefore to raise him up.

It was at this moment that the utter stupidity of my fellow
man, so called, was brought home to me, forcibly, in the
shape of my near neighbour, who hit me broadside, with animal strength, either with his arms or his legs, I cannot tell,
sending me sprawling, flailing, sideways into the water, losing my footing completely and landing in the shockingly cold
half muck. From my murky vantage point I watched him
complete the task I had begun, lifting my dripping son and
carrying him to the bank. He did not look at me and I had to
push myself up, my hands sinking into the disgusting sludge,
making sucking noises as I pulled them out, covered in slime
and filth.

As I struggled to my feet and saw the ruin that had been
made of my clothes, I heard the French woman's shrill voice

and looked up to see her shout something at me and move towards her husband, who was crouched over my son with his back to me, apparently administering some form of first aid. She cursed me and seemed to be hysterical, which distracted me, and I stood where I was, dumbfounded. What were these people at? Then there was a fit of coughing, spluttering, retching, and both the woman and I had our attention drawn back to the boy, and moved towards him. I squelched out of the water and onto the grass towards where he lay and saw that he had vomited a little, mostly water, and was convulsing slightly, his eyes closed, his legs jerking for a moment then stopping. It was possible to hear him breathe, urgent gulping breaths. The man had him on his side, with an arm under his head, and he was turned towards me so that I could see, quite plainly, a large bloody gash on his forehead, dead centre, which seemed to start under his hair and creep downwards. It bled profusely, and there were distinct signs of swelling.

Needless to say, I was horrified, as any father would be, and my instinct was to go to him and hold him. But as I moved forward, noisily, feeling a little like a swamp creature, the man turned his head to me and told me, loudly, and with language, to stay where I was, not to come near, or he would (he really did say this) kill me. His wife, by this time, was seeing to the boy, kneeling at his side, next to a rather sedated looking Ninny, and pressing what looked like a handkerchief to his head. I protested, not without anger it must be said, and continued to move forward, but the man stood and turned and faced me, and his face left me in little doubt that he was mad, and would certainly do me some serious injury if I were to persist. So I stopped where I was, feeling increasingly helpless and, if the truth be told, rather pathetic. My son, apparently grievously injured, lay only yards from me, and yet I could not get close.

The man produced a mobile phone from his pocket, which I have to say, I was greatly relieved to see. My wife has one, she got it from an insurance company, but I have eschewed them on the grounds that they are, largely speaking, entirely indulgent and unnecessary. I find their look and their noise vulgar and garish. I object strongly to having to listen to a member of the public, about whom I know nothing, and have no wish to discover any more, arranging their lives or arguing their point or flirting stupidly with someone, simply because I am unlucky enough to be standing beside them in a public place. It is a nuisance, and may, I suspect, be looked upon by future generations as a decidedly antisocial habit, such as smoking has become in our own time. I would gladly see all such devices consigned to the bin, along with many of the other so-called high tech gadgets which have become ubiquitous – filofaxes, electronic organisers, satellite television, this internet thing, wide screen television, disposable cameras, etc.

Anyway, I digress. He flipped this small machine open and pressed various buttons. I half expected it not to work, but was relieved that it did, and he was soon giving directions to the ambulance service, and quite competently describing the injuries. It puzzled me greatly however to hear him say that my son had been struck by a rock. How he knew this I did not know, unless, it suddenly occurred to me, he had thrown it himself. But when I then heard him ask that the police be sent as well, and that the perpetrator (it is not the word he used) was before him and was none other than the boy's father – i.e. me – I have to say that I was astonished. You can imagine my increasing horror as he went on to accuse me, via his telephone, to some complete stranger, of trying first to castrate, then to bludgeon and finally to drown my son. I believe my mouth fell open. I could not quite believe what I was hearing. I have never been a violent man. Even when my wife has been at her most absurd, her most selfish, I have never raised a hand against her. I have never struck my son, never laid a finger on him. To be standing there, sodden, chill, the mud clinging to the skin of my ankles, the stinking pond water clotting my hair and running down my cheeks, and to be accused, like that, of the most hideous of crimes, to be accused, virtually, of attempted murder, the attempted murder of my own flesh and blood, well, it was more than I could stand.

I flew at him. And here, again I admit it, my judgement was flawed. But I cannot believe that there is not a father on earth who would not have done the same. I was enraged at this man, at the cheek of him, at the pure madness of him, his accusation and his lies. I flew at him and tried to grab the phone from his hand. But his wife screamed, and he dodged out of my way, and somehow threw a fist which connected with the side of my head as I went past, and caused me to stumble and fall. The oaf had nearly sent me crashing head-long into the injured child. It was only with a painful and dif-ficult mid-air twist of my body that I managed to avoid him, landing heavily on my shoulder, a sharp jab of pain coursing down the entire right side of my body.

The French woman screeched, and I could hear Ninny yap-ping, and I believe the husband may have aimed a kick at me, for I felt another pain bite into my thigh. I moaned, and heard him talk into his telephone with increased urgency, including now the assertion that I had assaulted him. I was clearly mixed up with deranged people. I thought it politic to stay where I was and not attempt to rise. And in fact, where I found myself was possibly the closest I could hope to get to my son, who was just out of reach, but lying nevertheless about three feet to my left, and facing me, my eyes level with his, which were still closed. He was being administered to by the French woman, who seemed to be trembling, or perhaps it was my son who trembled, or perhaps it was myself. In any case, there was trembling, and a great deal of blood, and the woman was whispering to him, her mouth close to his ear, words which I could not make out. But the very idea of her talking to him was one I found distasteful, and when she looked at me I tried to appear angry, though her own face was so filled with venom and ill-feeling that I was no match for it.

A certain calm descended upon me as I lay there. I cannot explain it, but there is no doubt that I felt a level of resignation and surrender which was not unpleasant. It is odd that I should have felt like that, for I am a man who likes to be in control of a thing, especially if it involves my own family or interests. I like to be upright as it were, and here I was, laid low, my face resting on the ground, my clothes and my hair dripping wet, pain running riot along one entire side of me, usurped from my rightful place as protector to my son by a couple who were plainly insane and might yet prove a danger to either one or both of us – and still, even still, I was filled, with, what can I call it? – ease, I believe. Perhaps it was shock. Perhaps it was that my mind was repeating again and again, reassuringly, that it had been a twig I picked up, or a stick perhaps you could call it, at worst, but certainly not, by any stretch of the imagination, a rock. That was impossible. The hand can tell the difference between wood and stone surely? Even the hand unchecked by the eye, the hand that works itself, surely that hand will not, cannot, pick up a rock when it has been sent to pick up a twig? I am not a doctor, I don't know how these things operate, the mechanics of them, the relationship between the wish and the action – I do not know what the cables and the routers and the junction points and the nodes add up to. I wanted to pick up a twig – there were twigs at my feet – I picked one up – I threw it.

The man stood over me, and continued to talk to the emergency services operator, and I could not understand what use there was in going over the same things again and again. It seemed that he was being given advice, which he passed on to his wife, about putting the boy in a certain position, which they seemed to already have done, and about supporting his head, which I could see that they had not. Ninny was not in my line of sight, but her yelping had become incessant.

I looked at my son, at the wretched state of him, and I

171

willed him to wake. I longed for him to open his eyes and cough a little and say some words. It would take no more than a sentence from him to put these people right – if he could just clarify what exactly had happened. But there was no sign of it. He was deathly pale and slightly blue around the mouth, and although the blood from his head seemed to have slowed considerably, the swelling was really quite something, bulbous and almost visibly growing.

My cheek on the cool ground. The shadows of the place. The pain like a blanket. I closed my eyes.

I do not believe I dozed off. I really don't think I could have. And yet they seemed to arrive without my noticing. Maybe they came quietly, from a direction not visible to me. Whatever the explanation, suddenly I seemed surrounded by what appeared to me, from my position, as boots and voices. Men, and perhaps one woman, were grouped around my son. Odd green bags, like cheap fat briefcases, were laid on the ground and opened, and various materials taken from them, and one voice, definitely I think a woman's, spoke my son's name, loudly, over and over, and made reassuring comments, and asked him to speak, and there was a pause then before the voice resumed, as before, perhaps a little lower, a little quieter. How did she know his name? I had not told her. The noise of Ninny had ceased.

It was impossible for me to see clearly what exactly they were doing to him, as I was myself at the middle of another hive of activity. I was roughly disturbed from my place on the ground by hands which lifted me and turned me, first into a sitting position, and then to my feet, a little unsteadily, while all this time a male voice, not impolite, but not exactly friendly either, gave me directions as to what to do with my feet and my hands and so forth. The last of these directions was to put my hands straight out in front of me, which I did, only to have them handcuffed. I was moved some distance from my son, who was still on the ground, and from the couple, who were talking to a man wearing a suit and wellington boots, who

glanced at me several times. I did not clearly understand what
was going on.

There is much I do not understand.

For some time I was left, not alone, two policemen stood
by my side, but undisturbed, in that nobody attempted to
speak to me, nobody approached me, I seemed superfluous
to things. I watched the activity around my son with an
increasing irritation that he would not snap out of it and clear
this up. I know what he is like. There is nothing more pleasing to him than being the centre of attention. And of course,
obviously attempting to justify their own outrageous actions,
the mad couple were now deep in conversation with the man
in the wellington boots, who was, I noticed for the first time,
taking some notes. He was in charge then. This was another
source of deep irritation to me, as he was obviously getting
one side of the story, and the perverse and ridiculous side of
it at that. On instinct I took a step forward, meaning to go to
them and give my own version, the man in the wellingtons
looking like a reasonable sort of fellow who would soon hear
where the sense lay in this, but I was restrained, and gruffly,
by the policemen at my side, each of whom grabbed an arm,
and held on to me, tightly, painfully, and would not let me
go. One of them said something which was so rude that I
doubted for a moment that I had heard him correctly, but
when I turned my head to look at him there was little doubt
but that he was that rough kind of low life (which the police
force will sadly but inevitably always attract) who was perfectly capable of uttering the words which had so startled me.
I made a mental note of the number on the silver badge
stitched into his epaulette.

After some minutes I caught a glimpse of my son as he was
lifted, extremely gingerly, by about five men, onto a stretcher,
his neck obscured by a large brace, and a large amount of padding on the front of his head. They had opened his shorts as
well, and there seemed to be padding there too. I suppose that
it is their job to be over-cautious, but this level of circumspec-

tion struck me as being over the top. He looked like he had
been pulled from a car wreck.

They manoeuvred the stretcher (which was one of those
ones with collapsible wheels, which were plainly of no use on
this terrain and remained tucked up underneath my son's
body) very slowly and carefully over the bushes and weeds,
back along the path by which we had originally come, and
out through the very same gap in the fence through which I
had helped my son probably only a matter of minutes before,
but which seemed now more like hours. I watched him go,
and of course, I am only human, and I was distressed to see
him in such a state, and perplexed as to how this had
occurred, and I feared for him and I wanted to accompany
him to whatever place he was been taken. Once more, and
once again on instinct, I tried to step forward, and once
again, I was forcibly, roughly, restrained. This time however I
was having none of it. I protested loudly that I wished to go
with my son, that it was my right as his father, and that I
would see to it that the men who now stopped me from
claiming this right would be receiving letters from my solicitor, that I would take this matter further, that these gentlemen
(and I used the word with all the irony I could muster) would
be disciplined, severely so, and that their careers, such as
they might be, would be irrevocably damaged, to say nothing
of the contempt in which their colleagues who were also
fathers would hold them, inevitably, and justly so, for having
treated me thus, I who had never laid a hand on anybody in
my life, I who had been slandered and framed and accused of
the most loathsome of crimes, the most despicable and horrible of acts, by a jumped-up nouveau riche gadget slave of no
character and his foreign wife, his trophy wife, his gadget
wife, his gadget. It was at this point, and perhaps understandably, as I had become quite heated, that the man in the
suit and the wellingtons approached me and made it clear
that I was to cease my tirade, that this was not the place nor
the time, and that I would have the chance to put my side of

the story to him very soon. This was fair. It was, after all, all that I asked for.

My son had disappeared.

So too had the couple who had become the main focus of my anger. It occurred to me that they may have been allowed to go with the boy, but I put it out of my head, so distasteful a notion was it.

There was by now quite a large number of what I took to be policemen gathered around. Not all were uniformed by any means, and as I was led away, in almost the opposite direction to that taken by my son's entourage, I was treated to the slightly disturbing sight of men in white papery over-alls with white gloves, carefully driving stakes into the ground in a wide circle around the place, and linking these stakes with yellow police tape. It seemed that I was being taken, in the policemen's minds, from the scene of a crime. I worried now about the scale of the crime, and asked the detective (for I assumed by this stage that he was indeed a detective) whether my son was alive. Did I use that word? Maybe not. Certainly I made some enquiry as to the state of his health. Which is not, I think, unreasonable. The look he gave me, one of such astonishment and, almost, horror, was quite chilling. He gave no reply, and his demeanour was such that I was discouraged from asking again.

I was taken through the fence. It was uncomfortable to leave the cool air of the lake and to re-enter the full blast of the sun's light and, at this stage of the late evening, not incon-siderable heat. I did not like it, and immediately my head began to throb and my eyes took on an extreme squint. I ducked and was supported by my minders. There seemed to be quite a crowd. I heard a cacophony of voices, could make out a blur of shapes and faces, could sense a hostile, unfriendly atmosphere. I was led to a car which had been dri-ven across the grass to a position near the fence, and I was helped into the back seat, a hand on my head, one of the policemen following behind me, and another appearing through the opposite door, squeezing me in the middle, where there was really not enough room, particularly with my right side still painfully raw. There was already a man in the driver's seat, the engine was already running. The detective climbed into the passenger seat and we moved slowly away, the tyres seeming to me to slip a little on the soft ground.

I do not know where I was taken. I mean that I do not know where the police station was located. For most of the journey I kept my eyes shut and tried to ease the throbbing in my head. They took me through an enclosed courtyard into a warren of corridors and cold rooms, and they led me to one of these rooms and searched me, and asked me basic questions, such as my name and date of birth and my address and telephone number and my place of work, and whether I had ever been arrested before. Then they removed my belt and my shoelaces, which I thought very melodramatic, and left me alone with a table and a chair.

I was tired. I think this is perfectly natural. I was tired and sore and my mind was racing. I thought, of course, about my son, about where he might be and how he might be, and I wondered for the first time how they would find my wife in order to let her know. I was concerned that they would not be able to locate her. That they would try our home, and then perhaps her sister's, or her mother's, and maybe post a man at the house to catch her when she reappeared. But that could be hours. She had warned me that she might very well be late, and it would not be a first for her to telephone in the evening and declare that she would not return until morning. She usually talks to her son when she does that, rather than to me, which I think is cruel of her, and he will chatter to her at length and be none the wiser. Then she will come back in the morning with a gift for him, a little nonsense book, or a T-shirt or some useless knick-knack, and they will hug for long minutes, and she will coo and coddle him and generally behave like a silly teenager. I presume it is guilt.

But whatever her failings as a mother, I felt it my duty to ensure that she was informed of the accident – that she be given the chance to go to her son's bedside and to be with him. To this end, I stood up from my seat and went to the door, and knocked. There was silence. I called out. Nothing, no response. I called for some minutes, but there seemed to be no one there. I thought that unlikely, and it occurred to me that they would have posted a guard, who, through dimwittedness or incompetence (that is, after all, the type of person who would be posted as guard), was ignoring me. So I cleared my throat and gathered my thoughts, and, speaking clearly and loudly, told the blank metal door in front of my face that my wife was having an affair, that she would not be found at our house, that she was at the house of her lover, and I told the door where he lived, and what his name was, that they had been lovers for some considerable time, that they would be together now, in his house, and she should be called, she should be notified, at that address, of what had happened to her son, of the accident that had occurred, of where she might find him, of where she had to go to be with him, if she could tear herself away, and they should send a car for her, or persuade her to call a taxi, or let her lover drive her, that she should certainly not drive herself, that she was not a bad driver exactly, but she was not steady, that she should not take the car, my car, she should find some other way. There was no answer.

I went back to my table and I sat down. I did not know what more I could do. Then, for the first time in what seemed like hours, I missed Ninny. What had they done with her? Who had taken her? Where would they take her? It troubled me. It troubled me greatly. I thought of her left at the lake, abandoned there to fend for herself, confused, lost, ailing, crying. I could not bear that thought. I became a little distressed. She would not be able to survive it – a night out on her own in the cold, bewildered and old and slow.

I tried to remember the last time I had seen her, but I could not. I could not recall her at all. I laid my head on the table. I closed my eyes. I wished to be back at the lake, with my cheek on the cool ground, with my covering of pain and my body stretched on the wet grass, and to have Ninny in front of me, to be able to look her in her gluey eyes, to be able to smell her and hear her breathing and her occasional weak bark, to have her close to me, and safe.

I wanted to see her. See that she was all right. That is what I wanted. Only that. Damn it.

Shame

This is the start of the story, I know. It is the clearness in my head that tells me. My eyes open slick as fish eyes and I see the world sharp and sudden and my mind is strong this morning. I can feel it. It's cold, but a good cold, on the skin only, no deeper, and I dress fast and steady.

The city is squat. There's a section of it pressed to my window, starting with the river and rising then, up the hill towards the Castle. There's a wetness in the morning, and the sun not working right, hidden in a low place somewhere, not touching us. On the hill by St Audon's there was a fire in the night, an orange glow with crackling that woke the child, who woke us, and we stood by the river and stared up at it for a while until the rain came. Now the fire has left a dirty smudge in the middle of the rooftops, a damp patch, with grey timber pointing out of it, shards and black splinters, and a thin smoke still rising, all the colour gone, as if the night has drained it from the day.

By the Custom House I can see two ships that have arrived since last night. They are regular, Liverpool boats, and there are barrel boys running to and from them now, and a bulging crate swinging on the crane a little too wildly, and there are shouts that come to me over the water. The big three-master is gone, though I had seen its shadows and the glow of its watch while we stood staring at the fire only hours since. There is another ship cutting towards the sea now, just passing the lotts.

There is a boat tied to the near bank that I've not seen before. It has a small cabin perched on it like an upturned box and it has a load of wood spilled along its length. There's an ugly man on the deck, drinking from a bottle, talking to my wife who stands with her foot on the hawser, the child at her side, him turned from the river and waving at me. He is five now and curly headed and clever as I am. He does not smile as he waves, but squints an eye at me like he knows something I don't and he's seeing me in a new light. I nod and move from the window and try to find some food.

I have dreamed of eavesdropping now for three nights. I have dreamed of overhearing the noise of the world spun out as a kind of song by a ghost. She was a ghost because I knew her face and the face I knew belonged to my mother. But she was not my mother. She was a ghost with my mother's face. She sang or moaned, I am not sure. She gave off the sound like a scent, a noisome, clicking, pungent wail, and it flowed around me as I hid by a tree in a sunlit field where a silent river winked at me. I choked, and fled, and woke then.

And the next night I listened to my wife, her voice clear and strong and unembarrassed, her words so strange to me that it was a long time before I understood them, understood their meaning, their tight plot. She was discussing my murder with an Englishman. Planning it, working it out. I heard the details that would ensure the rapid decay of my remains, the chemical requirements, what kind of blade, what kind of barrel, a place to place me, a quiet cellar, for three days. Then I would be soup, and they would feed me to the river. The Englishman chuckled, but my wife was businesslike and still, and I awoke as she turned her face and peered into the gloom towards me, and lifted the candle and hissed like a god.

Last night I dreamed of my son. He spoke in his own voice but his words were older, older than I, and though I tried I could not make out their meaning. It was English, of that I'm sure, for there were 'ifs' and 'ands' and 'buts' and once he said 'mother' and once he said 'father' and once he said 'fleece'. He sat on the quay, his legs dangling, and he spat once, and I awoke then, in fright, for as his spit arced towards me I knew where I was, that I was in the water.

She's left a pot of tea still hot for me, and dark strong by now as I like it. There's a loaf cut, and a slice of bacon, and I eat a little and drink the tea, hum, and check the pocket watch she keeps in the drawer. It's after eight already and I curse and pull on my boots with my mouth full of bread, and I take my coat and sling it over my shoulder and fill the mug with tea once more and take it out into the day, out to where my wife and son stand by the river.

'Are you late?'

'I am.'

'This man has wood to sell.'

He looks up at me and his head rises and falls slightly with the water.

'We're not buying wood. We have wood.'

I drain my mug and hand it to my wife, and turn and leave a silence behind me, and I can feel their two pairs of eyes on my back, and my son makes three. She has a liking for ugly men, and foreign men of any kind. She takes them to her bed while I am gone and she leaves the boy to wander the house and hear whatever he might, and see whatever he can. I know this to be true because of the strength with which I know it, and because of the evidence.

I walk along the river, quickly. It is not good to be late, even if there will be little enough to do when I get there. I am hailed by men who know me, and I nod at them and gesture, and call out a greeting sometimes, and it is by that means, as if being handed on from voice to voice, from face to face, that I make my way down to the house where the Englishman is kept. It is for him that I work, although I am paid by his employer, and it is to both of them that I appear to be answerable, which is not to my liking, for their relationship has of late been strained. The Englishman is frustrated at the delays, and he is anxious to begin, and he has had enough of plans and drawings and consultations and wishes to get the thing started. So he tries me for information, of which I have none, and is short with me when I can give him no answer. And on the other side, his employer, and mine, blames me for the

strain, saying that I am not properly occupying the Englishman, which I feel is a nonsense – I am not employed as a
playmate or companion or lady-in-waiting. My job is narrow
and I like it that way, and I think that I will throw it all in if it
continues in this manner for much longer.

I arrive near the quarter hour, to find that my alternate has
left already. I am admitted by a manservant, who smiles at
me and is affable and attempts to start a conversation about
the night's fire. But I cannot linger, and I knock the door of
the gentleman's study and am summoned in, a light sweat on
my brow, brought on by my hurrying.

'Good morning Sir.'

He grunts and stays where he is, at his desk, writing. He is
not genuine in his humours, putting them on and taking them
off again like a coat, with a shrug of his shoulders and a flap of
his arms. So this morning he is wearing his black mood, and
he does not raise his eyes and he writes with a bad tempered
hand, and takes up muttering while I stand in front of him
and stare at the top of his head. The room is cluttered with
books and papers and plans, and instruments of measurement
and calculation, and much more besides which I do not
understand. I believe that he is unproven in his field, which I
do not think bodes well for the project, about which I know
little but that it involves building a new Custom House and a
new bridge and that it is causing upset to a lot of people.

'Are you well Sir?'

'No.'

He is a small-framed man, narrow hands, thin hair, his
eyes are pulsing blue and he takes no notice of his appearance, sitting now this morning in a dirty high-collared shirt
and wrapped in a blue robe as if straight from his bed. I cannot see his feet.

'You'll take this letter to Mr Beresford directly.'

I raise my eyebrows a little but he's not looking at me at
all, he's busy folding and sealing and stamping, and my
silence is not worth much to him.

'And you will wait for an answer.'

'I'll have the boy go Sir.'

He looks at me now.

'You'll go yourself.'

I frown at him, at his angry face. My frown is well shaped and says to him that there is nothing to be gained from snarling at me – I am not the cause of his irritation. Directly he sees it he changes his coat of black humour for a hair shirt, for a cloud grey heavy garment full of weariness and supplication.

'Forgive me, I do not mean to snap at you. But you can understand my frustrations, you can understand my position. It is difficult and tiresome and it does not have a pleasant effect. The letter will read more urgent if it is delivered by you.'

'My job is to stay with you Sir, until the evening.'

'I will not be alone.'

'Nevertheless Sir . . .'

He sighs and lets his head fall back a little. The room is lit from a window onto the garden, and I can see green leaves leaning on the glass, and I think again about the life I lead, and how it is contained within rooms, and takes place through words and directions, and I wonder whether it is a life at all, and whether it might not be just a dreamed thing, and that I might myself, in my essentials, be elsewhere. For what belongs here?

'I feel like a prisoner,' says the gentleman, and I want to smile but do not.

'Indeed Sir.'

'So you will not take the letter?'

'I will see to it that it is delivered, and that a reply is awaited, and I will ensure that the urgency is impressed upon Mr Beresford.'

He sighs again, and ducks his head now, and scratches it, and yawns.

'All right, all right. See to it.'

I take the letter from his hand, and he looks me miserably in the eye, and says nothing, has nothing to say, and I want to test my notion and I glance at the window and the leaves on the glass and I look back at him and I start to say it but I am stopped by the part of myself which does not allow me to test anything.

'What's that?'

'Time Sir . . .'

'What of it?'

I am for a moment at a loss.

'Passes quickly,' I say, lowly, and I feel my cheeks run red, and feel the damp line still on my forehead, and I wish to be asleep so that I can wake.

He nods, or rather, he lowers his head and raises it again, like that.

'Indeed. Not it seems, Mr Beresford's time.'

'Yes Sir.'

He regards me as peculiar, as well he might, and I turn and leave him and I see to it that the letter is sent, and that a reply is received, and I walk in the garden and I count the leaves.

I have given the impression that my wife is not trustworthy, and this is not true. She does not take men to her bed when I am gone. She does not allow the child to wander freely while she does it. And yet, there is the evidence.

I understand the nature of things by the evidence that is presented to me concerning their substance and their place. Evidence is that which I see and hear which allows me to determine whether a thing is as it seems to be. I learned this subject from a man I knew in the Americas who had both curiosity and learning, and who, I think, died, in front of my eyes, as a result of a scuffle with an Indian knifeman in the country of Virginia. But he would have cautioned me to be unsure, as I do not have the evidence that he is for certain dead. He was wounded in the chest, and if he lived it would surprise me, knowing what I know of wounds like those, but what do I know about living and dying? Not enough. Never enough. Circumstances did not allow me to linger and to find out.

But of my wife, there is too much evidence. For I dream of her often, and I think of her more, and these dreams and these thoughts show me more than I know by other means, and I cannot, in truth, separate them out and judge one as weightier than the other. So that there is always doubt, and this doubt infects my life with her, and I know that there is no reason to it, but that does not disperse it.

I am no fool. I have seen men torn apart by jealousy, and rage at imagined slights. I am aware of those dangers. These are not things I take on. It is not jealousy that fills me. It is dreams that fill me. Thoughts. Evidence. I see her in the past and in the future, sometimes with me and sometimes not, sometimes alone and benign and faultless, sometimes rank and foul and eager for others. And I know that she does not dream these dreams. I know that she does not plot my death with Englishmen and barrels. I know that she has no plans other than the plans she should have, and that she has no desire to hurt me or to wrong me or to see me dead. But these things exist. I have seen them.

Where do they come from?

It is past midday and the reply from Mr Beresford has cheered my gentleman considerably. I have instructions to escort him in the evening to the site, and to allow him to survey and take measurements and so forth, though I must take my alternate with me, as well as three of Mr Beresford's own men, in convoy, for protection. This is good news for me. It will break the monotony of these days.

There is caller at the house, a woman who will not give her name. She stands in the reception room and surveys the furniture and the paintings and is haughty and will have no truck with me, though she is not very moneyed or grand or impressive. It is the gentleman she wants to see.

I knock on his door and interrupt him at his soup, which he slurps as I tell him that there is a caller, a lady, who will not tell me her name, but who says she is expected. He is properly dressed now. I can see that already he has grouped together those items he needs for our expedition.

'No. I have no appointments. What does she look like?'

'She is a delicate lady Sir, dark haired, pale skinned.'

'Is she pretty?'

I hesitate. I do not find her handsome, but I wonder if he will.

'Well?'

'She is pleasant Sir.'

'That's no answer.'

I am silent. It is not my job to answer questions like that.

'Oh show her in then.'

I am not entirely easy with this. My instructions are to admit civilised callers and to report their visits, but there have been few, and none before who have not either been expected or known to me. When I summon her she gives me a small shake of her head which is intended to scold me for my foolishness. I lead her to his study, and follow her into the room, remaining at the door, behind the precise, cut out shape of her back. He stands, his soup things pushed to one side, and waits for her to speak. She glances behind herself, at me.

'Good day ma'am. How may I help you?'

'You are Mr Gandon?'

'Indeed,' he says, shrugging a little.

'I am Mrs Millington.'

His face changes. It opens wider, in surprise or shock, I do not know. For a moment he stares at her. And then he becomes solicitous, sympathy floods his features, as if the name has evidence hanging from it like ivy. He moves from behind his desk, walks towards her, all the time saying, 'Mrs Millington, my dear lady, I had no idea you were in Dublin, but of course, how do you do, how do you do, it is an honour . . .'.

And he shoos me away with a flick of his wrist and an irritated look. I hesitate, but if he is content with her then it is none of my business who she is. I leave them, and the last sight I have of them both is like a painting, I view it like I would a painting, so clear is it, so fixed and certain. He stands slightly to her side, with her hands held in his, and his head is at an angle, inclined towards the window, and he smiles, but a sorrowful smile, as if he wishes to commiserate with her, to condole and to comfort. She stands with her head bowed, staring somewhere towards his chest, accepting his wishes, surrendering herself to his sympathy, giving up her shallow indifference for a shallow kind of grace. I do not like her.

Why do I say that it is the last sight I have of them? For I do not mean that it is the last sight I have of them for the moment, but for ever. This is how it presents itself to me. And yet this is unlikely to be the case, unless I die now and am removed from seeing this daily unfolding of my standard life, my routine life, my measured time.

I go to the kitchens and eat some bread and some cheese, and find a jug of claret and help myself to a glass. A maid flirts with me and I am silent in the face of it and she withdraws, a little sullen, her fingertips gone green from polishing. The kitchen is warm, and it has the look of an older place that has not changed in many years, and it puts me in mind of my boyhood, when I was quiet and still and scolded for it. We had dogs who nuzzled me and snapped at strangers, and they would take me sometimes, to strange parts of the city, to streets and lanes which were at odds with the rest of it, and I would want to return home but the dogs were always onward bound, seeking out cracks in the ground, holes in the walls, tears in the blanket of my little mind. I would think us lost, and be ready to bawl and ask a stranger to take care of me, when the dogs would turn a corner and we would be home, suddenly, as if we had never left it. With my mother or my father I knew where I lived. With the dogs I was never sure.

She has left without my knowing, after spending maybe an hour with him, or not much more. He is packing two bags now, with instruments and papers and notebooks, and he worries that I have not left enough time to make all the arrangements necessary, and will not listen when I tell him that all is in hand, that my alternate is on his way, that Mr Beresford's men are due at five, that he is not to concern himself with that side of things. Concern himself he does however, and from upstairs somewhere he produces a short sword in a black scabbard, and he confronts my amusement with hoods on his eyes and a grim look and words about chance and importance. It seems to me at first that he inflates the latter, but I am not sure after all, where all of this is leading.

He is impatient to be gone, but there is nothing else to be done – other than to wait for the hour to approach us. He sits with his bags at his feet, his sword hung from his waist, and glances at the sky in the window, and at his pocket watch. It will not rain. I wonder how he would use the sword, and try to draw him out about it, but he is not keen on conversation, preferring to hum and fret and make occasional notes in a moleskin book he keeps in his pocket, licking his pencil more than he needs to and leaving a black line on his lip.

I find him so ridiculous that he scares me somewhat. What is he doing here? I mean in this life, my life. In my city. What are his plans? He has about him an arrogance and surety of purpose which does not seem to fit here. He is come amongst us to alter things, and I cannot frame the alteration properly in my mind, cannot see its reach or its import. Maybe it is nothing.

It is close to five, and my alternate has arrived – I can hear him complaining to the staff about his rest being disturbed. He is a surly man, hard, well suited to looking after our charge during the night, but without much usefulness otherwise.

Our gentleman now wants to be on his way, and I have to persuade him repeatedly that we cannot meet Beresford's men en route, that there is too much chance in it, that we should follow our directions. But they are late, and he is restless, and my alternate grumbles incessantly, and the house is too warm, and my mind is unsettled here, it edges towards the reckless and the river, towards moving home along the dark water, towards leaving all of this for a different time. I want to be gone.

They arrive, three of them, loudly, and it is just as well, for it gives me a chance to be angry, and my anger fixes me, points me front wise, along the line I'm on, and before long they are chastised and we are organised, one bag on my shoulder, one on that of my alternate and the three heavies around the gentleman like an arrowhead. It occurs to me that this will raise a few eyebrows, and that perhaps just the two of us, early in the morning, might have gone unnoticed – but it is too late now for that. We move down the steps of the house and into the street, and we set a decent pace east, parallel to the river, with my alternate wondering out loud why we do not take a coach, and the heavies casting glances at children, and our gentleman a touch embarrassed, but as excited as a boy, his legs skipping a little on the stones, his sword hung beneath his coat, the bulge of it front and back both comic and grotesque.

I do not know what we look like. I do not know who sees us. Six men in procession through the back streets, making our way to the thin parts of the city, taking the leaking lanes and the cobbled, straw strewn pathways, seeping out of the civilised world with all the waste and the wretched surplus, spilling out into the shallows, into the mud and the stagnant pools and the half swamps, into the sinking part of the island, the nearest to water, where we stand then, as if we have arrived at a centre, and we breathe deep and stand in a circle, and our feet are sudden wet, and our noses tight, and the gentleman amongst us claps his hands in fear and wonder, and exclaims, and I know not where he finds the words –

'By God it's worse than they told me, by God it is, what a wonderful worse it is.'

And indeed it is. It seems to me that in a thousand years of trying you could not build a solid thing here, nothing lasting or secure. This is madness. The river here is invisible, in that it is everywhere, we are standing in it, it is level, it washes my boots with its black mud. My alternate gapes at me. One of the heavies laughs. But our gentleman notices nothing. He is gesturing at me for the bag, and I hand it to him, and he looks for a place to set it down, and has to balance it in the end on a bramble bush bare of leaves, and he rummages and mutters, and mutters and squints, and comes up with a measuring stick of polished wood, and I know that he wants to find a solid surface under us, a layer or rock or some such, and I know by the smell of the place that he'll need a longer stick than that. But he fiddles with it then, and I think for a moment that he is trying to snap it, but I see then that the stick extends – that it has been folded in on itself, and now he unfolds it, and it becomes longer and longer until it is maybe five yards, and thin but solid.

Beresford's men stand together, and I think they probably have a flask to share amongst themselves. My alternate has found a small rock, and has sat himself down upon it, gingerly, holding the tails of his coat out of the dirt, and he pulls up his knees and crosses his arms on them, and lays his head upon his arms, and pays no more attention to anything. I retrieve the second bag from his side, and I go next to the gentleman, and when he looks at me I help him with the measuring stick, which we push down together, using a clever cross wood slotted to its end. He tells me to keep it straight, to watch his hands, to keep my own level with them. He stops a few times, and stands back and squints at the notches in the handle piece and at notches in the stick, and when he is satisfied that they are aligned, he allows us to continue. When we come to a halt, he makes a note in his pocket book. Then he pulls the stick from the ground, making his hands and his coat muddy. He walks some distance, and we repeat the procedure. We do this four times, over a wide area, and he would do it more, but is concerned at what little light we have left and remarks that the whole site will need proper measuring in any case. The pushing is very hard. It makes us grunt and sweat. The heavies simply stare at us, silently, their flask out in the open now, one of them with a pipe lit.

Of all the instruments he uses, and of all the tasks he performs, the measuring stick is the only thing I understand.

He retrieves various devices from the bags, and either puts them to his eye, or lays them on the ground, and makes copious notes. He has me walk through the mud some five hundred yards away from the river, holding another polished stick in my hand, and he peers at me through some complicated instrument which reminds me of those sextants a ship's navigator might use to fix himself against the stars, or the sun, or whatever they do. He waves at me and shouts, and has me move this way and that, and I can see that this is to the great amusement of Mr Beresford's men. My alternate appears to be dozing.

At this distance from him, from my gentleman I mean, I can see him against the city, with the sun going down in the west, and the shadows creeping out across the pools and the weeds and the scattered rocks. He is small. His group is small. I can see the far bank only as low land and the occasional building, and in the distance I can see the hills with their bright peaks, and to my left I can see the widening of the water and the falling away of the land. It has been this way for centuries.

I am baffled by what I do. I cannot grasp it. Something in my chest hangs heavy, like a dead branch, and I cannot lift it. I am unable to explain myself. This place is empty, it has always been so, but I have seen the gentleman's drawings, I have seen his plans, and I know what he intends to do here, and I no longer know where I am, I no longer know what this place is, whether it is barren and useless or whether it is more real in his mind than it is now in the last of the day, with the sun ending at last, leaving at last, giving up its watch. Where does this place belong? When does it belong?

When the light is too little we gather up his things and wake my alternate and set off again across the marshy ground towards the first paths. The gentleman is happy, his face is glowing, his eyes are bright. He sees what we do not, he occupies the future like a child, his plans are everything. So he does not appear to notice that a small crowd follows us from the edge of the lotts, and that the heavies, a little rough now with the liquor, are shouldering him along briskly, while my alternate and I swing the bags and bring up the rear. There is a man amongst them whom I know, I do not recall his name, but he is a well known city man and popular, and I can hear him at the back, his voice loud, crying 'Shame,' the same word, over and over, as if it is sensible, as if there is no need to explain it, as if everyone who hears will understand what he means. His rabble of men and boys call it too, and throw stones and laugh, and we move quickly through the streets, pushing guilt ahead of us, pursued by an anger that has its root in the future, clinging to a sorrow that is always present now.

My wife has prepared a meal for me, and the child is still awake, and I do not talk about my day – I eat and say nothing and I watch them at play. I wish to live with them. I wish to stay here in my home, with my family, to be present when my life comes to its end, to be here amongst the things I know and almost understand. I will not work for Mr Beresford any longer. Tomorrow I will go to him and say that he must find another keeper for his plans.

I am tired but I am afraid of sleeping. I repeat to myself that I am to quit my position, in the hope that it will influence my dreams and that I will not once more spend my night eavesdropping on the future, or on other times that are neither the future nor the past, but cracked views of the time I occupy. I am tired of the chronologies that compete and intertwine and which clutter my mind like weeds.

My son plays with pebbles on a board. He moves them
and lets them roll, and determines where they rest by the tilt
and balance of the wood, moving his hands as if struggling
with a great weight. I can see him deciding in his mind which
way they will go, and I can see what he likes and does not
like, and I can see that he likes to come close to dropping
them, to let them run along the edge until it is almost too late,
and then to save them with the smallest movement of his tiny
hand. He is skilful at it. My wife sees me watching, and she
smiles at me proudly, and I return her smile, and I think that
we are happy here, by the river, the three of us.

I remember the woman who called, I remember the picture
of her that I am left with, of her acceptance, her pride. It
comes to me suddenly, unexpectedly, and I do not welcome
it. There is too much evidence here, my head swims through
it, and I wonder who she is, and I think of saying her name to
my wife, but I do not want to tie one to the other, I do not
want to mix the stories that flow here. I finish my food and I
kiss my wife and my son and I go out of our home and I
stand in the dark and watch the river.

I know that I am not being sensible, that I do not see things
clearly, that my mind worries at loose threads, that I cannot
find room enough for all that I see, all that I hear, all that I
dream. I sit by the trough and look at the river, and I let my
mind run on in the hope that it will tire itself, but it collects
things, gathers them together, and the great mass that results
is too big for me to contain, and I feel that I will burst, and
that all the parts of me will be thrown to the river and there
they will scatter and swim and that they will not – no matter
how I desire it, no matter how I weigh them down – they will
not drown. This is what I feel. That I will always swim the
river. That I will always be there, separated out, made into
essentials, never knowing my time, slipping through the
water, hiding beneath the bridges, never knowing my time,
always in the river, my skinless mind, swimming the river,
trying to find a standard time, a set place, a dry bank, a

stopped city, a place to emerge, a complete place, to emerge again.

My wife comes out to me. She holds my shoulders and kisses my hair. We stand together silent in the dark, and we can hear, without wanting to, without listening for it, we can hear the city breathe, and sigh, and breathe, and continue.

Angelo

Angelo was just this guy I knew a few years ago and there's not much reason for writing about him other than that I liked him and he disappeared in a strange way. That's all. When I met him I was about twenty-four and he said he was thirty, but I never believed him about his age – he looked no older than me really, and he was never very consistent with details about himself, such as where he came from or what his name was or what exactly he was doing in Dublin, or why he kept on turning up in front of me. He would appear on my door-step, stay the night, go again, maybe take me out to dinner, spend money on me, then a week later be looking for a loan, and then he might disappear for a while and then he'd be back with a new haircut and a new coat and all these ridiculous stories which, if you believed him, had him in New York and Naples in the same night, and he'd be dropping in and out of Italian and English and watering down the bits he thought were not suitable for his audience – so that there would be ten different versions of the same story depending on the people he was talking to – and all ten people thought that they were the ones getting the full thing, the complete honest picture, straight from Angelo, just to them.

But you know that there is a limit on the words you can hear in your life, a ration, and you can't take them all in at one go. You know this is true, you just haven't heard it put like that before.

I think Angelo was Italian, in that I think he was probably born there, or lived there for a while at a very young age, because all of his baby and little boy recollections seemed to happen on sunny hills and lithe, sweaty roads where it was always hot and his accent would thicken and he'd cough out names that only made sense to me as things you'd throw in a pot. But he was also possibly American, because he mentioned the states of New York and New Jersey frequently and had that general American brashness, you know, here I am, what you want? Tough sometimes, stupid sometimes, white teeth. His accent was so fluid that I occasionally suspected that he was eastern European, Romanian perhaps. I don't know. Maybe he fooled me. When asked he'd say he was Irish.

'I'm Irish don't you know. I live in Dublin city,' all wide-eyed shock and surprise and most people would be embarrassed and let it drop. I did chase him about it and he admitted to me nothing more than that he had lived in seven different countries and the whole sequence was lost to him and he refused to sort it out.

His skin was sallow, his eyes were brown, his hands were long and thin. He was beautiful actually. He had a scar, horribly pinkish white, on his lower back, ending in his left buttock, which he claimed was from a stabbing in London, which was one of those version stories, it changed over time – from a mugger in Clapham to a lover in Notting Hill to falling on a bottle at a party in Watney or Wimbledon or some such. His face was slightly plump, no cheekbones to speak of, tiny dimple in the chin, his hair tending to curl, either a mop of it or skinned, occasionally peroxide blond, which I liked. He had piercings of various kinds at various times. Always at least the one in the left ear, sometimes two there and one in the other. Once an eyebrow and he talked often of his tongue but never had it done, and talked as well about various genital options, but I never saw any of them done either, though he did get his nipples run through, and I watched them do the left, as he clutched my hand and laughed at me convinced that I had an erection, which I think I didn't, but I remember it as if I did, which confuses me as to whether I actually might have, and makes me wonder in any case about how we remember physical things, which is not just a drippy little aside, but bears some relation to the end of this. Which is coming. You know. The way it does.

And it also clarifies something else, which is that I found Angelo, at the worst of times even, hugely attractive, desirable, sharply so, like a needle, like a needle and all that that evokes. But strangely, and for me this is quite strange, my interest in him was almost entirely carnal. I wanted to have sex with him, complicated, extended, innovative sex; sex in all the rooms of my entire life from start to finish, I wanted to be with him in the corners. But I didn't fall in love with him, not even a little, not in the way of love which gets in the way. I never once felt jealousy or pride or expectation. Which is why, I suppose, he liked me. People were forever falling in love with him.

We met in one of those circumstances which never tell well, never read well, because you wouldn't believe it, and therefore I'll skip it, not tell you, other than to say that it was in the rain, at night, and by the river, I swear, and we had some kind of sex before we were properly introduced, and that he was on a bike. That's all you're getting. Anything else and you'll think I'm making it up. And it was in the city, by the Liffey, not in some shitty cruising park somewhere on some trickle of a thing. Angelo always sliced through his surroundings, as if his presence changed the nature of a place, which it did of course, as is true of all of us, in some small way, but he did it big. Anyway, when we were done with the sex, about which I cannot remember very much other than that I had rain running down my back and kind of liked that, and that he made a lot of noise when coming, which made me a little nervous given that we were in some yard or entrance or some such, behind a shed of some type, perhaps a security guard's hut, something like that, when we were finished, recovered and re-buckled, panting a little, we muttered little civilities, as you do, and I wandered off satisfied, happy little twists in my boxer shorts, heading for home in the hard rain, chasing the taste of him around my mouth, wondering vaguely whether he had been as good looking as he'd seemed in the close up darkness, dreaming I was, already, when I heard the clickety tick of a bike behind me, the idling sound of spokes and thin tyres in puddles, and the low squeak of handlebars gone a little rusty.

'You have far to go,' he said.

I was not interested, really, but the way he left the question mark off it, making it sound in some way like a derogatory comment on my sexual abilities, had me stopped and staring at him. His looks were remarkable. All his hair stuck to his head, his smile a bit cherubic, his body with a bike propped under it, one leg down now, the other crooked in the drizzle, hung over the crossbar, as if he was taking a rest during the climbing on procedure. And he was wearing this mustard yellow windbreaker thing, no hood, and sodden jeans probably blue but gone black now, and boots, black boots, and a jumper, which actually I couldn't see now, but I knew, and a T-shirt under that. Two of the buttons on his jeans were open.

'What?'

'You gonna walk all the way? Where you go to?'

I don't know, I think I felt that he was a cheeky bastard who should disappear now please, not bother me anymore, that it was all right to exchange blow jobs but pleasantries like this were something of an invasion, and of course I also thought, very distantly, that I was in trouble, that here's a weirdo come to stalk me home, he's got a knife, he's racked with guilt, he's going to kill me, which may have had something to do with the accent, I admit it, because we're all a little afraid of foreigners after dark, aren't we? – they're not easily read, the charm of them turns sinister, it all gets very nasty. Does that make me racist? Does it? I'm not sure. Does it make me racist that I wanted to have sex with this guy but didn't want to talk to him? Well in fact when I had sex with him I assumed he was from the East Wall, or Ringsend, or maybe Phibsboro at the most – somewhere within cycling distance anyway, we didn't exactly discuss it. So this was news to me, this accent, pretty much, though we had exchanged some words, but accents in those situations are never reliable, I tend to put one on myself, or acquire one from somewhere, thick slurred with lust, I sound like I'm from a bad Czech porn film.

'Your, um, your fly's open.'

He always understood things first time did Angelo. As if the accent was a fake. He didn't look down, just sent his long fingers fiddling.

'That's your fault,' he said, big smile, and I thought it pretty lame and predictable that he would flirt after the event, betraying an over commitment to the queer ethic of doing everything backwards. I walked on, cool as you like, and he followed, zigzag on his bike, which had drop handle-bars and loads of gears.

'My name is Angelo,' he said loudly, and the rain just stopped. Stopped dead I swear it, and I nodded and said nothing and he followed me all the way home, making me laugh, and then kissed me very casually and drifted away on his wheels, cheerful, and I went in and I thought about him for days, and that was the start of it.

Angelo.

Events become telescoped in your mind, in your memory, so that it becomes difficult sometimes to recall the chronology precisely, and you're left with a flurry of phone calls and meetings and you wonder when you stopped doing one thing and started doing another, so that for example I have no clear notion now of whether I was still a smoker when I met him, which might strike you as incidental, and of course it mostly is, but it is also minimally important in the way of recreating things with accuracy, and accuracy is important, because this is not a little reminiscence, this is a document going towards evidence for the circumstances of his disappearance, which is of course the same as any other disappearance, but is my disappearance, not literally but in the sense that it is the only one I know up close, in which the disappeared was someone I know. You know. Small things are important.

He called to my place on the Sunday afternoon after we had first met. There he was, dry as a bone, his face a little obscured by a wispy lack of shaving, a grin on him which seemed to suggest that he thought himself very clever for turning up. He had his bike with him.

'What kind of coffee have you?'

I let him in and I wanted us to have sex, and he seemed much more interested in the books on my shelves, and the CDs, and the contents of the fridge, and he made himself a pot of coffee and sniffed at some smoked salmon which had come as a gift from my sister, and which I don't really like, and I don't know how long it had been there, but he sniffed at it and made a face and scolded me then for not eating well.

'Where is your fruit? You have no real water, this tap is not healthy. What are all these packets? These packets are not food, these are advertising, so these are. This is television, not food. Where is your fruit?'

I pawed at him. He took me to my own bedroom and allowed me to fuck him, which was very nice, and he told me the first story of his scar, and insisted also that his cock was smaller than mine, although it plainly was not, and again he made a great deal of noise when coming, much louder than anyone else I have ever had sex with, and he was also the only person I ever met who actually did that tying up the condom thing, which made me laugh and think of balloon animals and children's parties, but which he took utterly seriously and insisted was necessary 'to save the environment.'

'It is true because see this condom is full of your come and if it is not tied then all this will seep out and then the condom will not rot away in the earth in the dump, but if all your come is inside it then it will rot away eventually from within after many years, and that flower will grow there, the flower that grows out of come, I do not recall the name.'

He left me on his two wheels and I did not miss him.

*

We saw each other in the bars and the clubs, and we would go together sometimes to a sauna late at night, where we would part and have adventures, and then return to each other to giggle in a manner which is not entirely appropriate in these places and I remember lots of dirty looks and solid shoulders. In the bars he liked to watch people, and he was pass remarkable in a way which was mostly amusing, sometimes cruel, but which was never really bitchy or typical. The comments were quiet asides, and the funnier they were the quieter he said them, and if he was with a group of people he would direct it all to the nearest to him, which I always tried to be, because it was fun to hear him give a little commentary on someone who'd caught his eye.

'This man in the blue shirt now, he is very bored by this friend of his, and this friend is starting to panic, you see that? He is panicking now because he will not have sex with this man so he thinks, but he is wrong, because this man is getting so bored that he will soon be horny and he will think to himself that the only thing he can do with his friend is the sex, and his friend must be careful now not to say anything interesting. One interesting thing he says and he is doomed.'

He did not fit the bill as a gay man really. His clothes were random, occasionally awful, he was lazy about his appearance so that it was not uncommon to see him turn up with greasy hair and unattractive stubble, and it annoyed me greatly that he could often be seen in places like The George or The Front Lounge, carrying an old plastic bag from Dunnes containing his bicycle lamps and lock, a novel, a toothbrush, a clean T-shirt (or a dirty one, depending on which way he was headed) and an apple. Or an orange. Or a banana. He was utterly baffled at the criticism and hilarity which this provoked. When I eventually became so fed up with it that I bought him an expensive and extremely trendy little knapsack, his response was to thank me profusely and then promptly forget it, arriving at our next meeting with a

Quinnsworth bag, as if to say that he had noted the problem and had moved therefore to a better class of supermarket. I refused to talk to him. Our friends howled with laughter. He was puzzled, I sulked, it was explained to him. He nodded, thought about it, took me aside and told me that he was hugely sorry, that it would never happen again, that I was the best friend he had and that he would always love me for it, and that I was not to be cross with him.

'You are so right and I am so wrong. I do not know how to look after myself, I get all ass ways all the time and first my mother and then Mr Duncan and now you are the people most in my life who help me. Come.'

And he dragged me to the bathroom for a reward, and I started to laugh, as he kept me firmly by the arm and waited for a free cubicle, into which he pushed me, uncovered me and promptly dropped to his knees. He was good at this kind of thing. It never took very long.

'Who is Mr Duncan?'

'I didn't tell you?'

'No.'

'I will tell you some time.'

From that point on he took the knapsack with him wherever he went, carried, I thought, a little grudgingly, and always slightly too high or too low, so that at some point it would always need adjusting. It became quite a thing, that. I heard people argue about who would get to adjust Angelo's knapsack on a particular night, and I thought it rather sad.

I can't remember who else there was. Well, I can, but it's not that important, although I suppose it might be. I can't remember now for example, whether it was Angelo who introduced me to Dolores, or whether I had just bumped into her myself, or whether it was at the same time as I met Angelo that I met Brian, who promptly, and for no good reason, fell in love with me, complete with flowers and letters and midnight phone calls. But there was the regular crew – the usual crowd, small and terribly democratic, thrown together – with whom I'd

spent most of the previous couple of years, socially. John
Keane was the oldest, mid-thirties, a very fast talker, very
bold, very funny. He was a heavy drinker from Tipperary
who enjoyed bitchy fights and younger guys, who had property all over the place, too much money and three cell phones.
Angelo was fascinated by all this, but could never understand
a word John was saying, given the accent and the slurring and
the fact that John didn't find Angelo at all interesting and
spent most of his time trying to get me to introduce him to
'eighteen- to twenty-two-year-olds like, with a sense of fun,
you know the kind a thing,' and trying to arrange dodgy parties in empty flats which never really quite came off the way
he'd intended, at least never when I was there.

Then there were the dispirited twins, not twins at all, but a
couple I'd known since they weren't a couple, which was
years and years before and which nobody else could quite
recall, who looked alike, same dour features, same aversion to
cigarettes, alcohol, late nights and sex. Or sex with each other
anyway. Every so often one of them appeared alone because
the other was invariably studying for some exam, slaves as
they were to the night course culture and the accumulation of
testimonials of expertise in things like first aid, t'ai chi, Renais-
sance art, the history of Dublin, how to grow your own
anorak, that kind of thing. Anyway – you knew you were in
trouble, because one of the twins on their own was like a child
let loose in the sweet shop, shameless in the pursuit of a shag,
a one nighter, preferably with someone from abroad who
wouldn't be around to become complicated, and usually for
some reason Scottish, can't quite work out why, with whom
they'd either visit a sauna or a guesthouse or a hotel, and then
spend the next couple of days on the telephone tearfully beg-
ging that their indiscretion would not become known to the
clueless partner. And you were also in trouble if they
appeared out together, caught as they were in a horrible, hateful, domestic little arrangement so close to marriage that you
had to remind yourself sometimes that no, they weren't, and

that this level of bitchiness and squabbling and sheer mutual spite was not necessarily the result of straight people being stupid, but could also spring so easily from the sisterhood, given a few years and a joint house purchase.

Adam was around then I think. Certainly he was at the beginning, which reminds me about names, and the way they work in this little story, but I'll have to come back to that. Adam was my age exactly, in that we shared a birthday, and we had once gone out together, more as a comfort to each other than anything else, when we had first emerged on the scene as really terrifyingly stupid seventeen-year-olds. I don't think we ever had a formal relationship, in the sense of dates and declarations and forward planning, but we certainly shagged a lot when there was no one else to shag, and we were friends without really noticing it, closer than we realised. He left the country with a guy from Seattle about two months after I'd met Angelo I think, and the effect it had on me was something to behold, all public crying and serious drinking and general trauma. Angelo was sweet, telling me that 'love is like a cancer, it will kill you in the end, but before it does that it makes your life better, better in quality, because you can see the horizon, and all is a joy, except for the radio and the chemical therapy.' I think he thought he'd said a beautiful thing, and of course he almost had. About the best kind of love being the one that you never discover until it's too late, which is almost the case with me and Angelo, but is also not the case. I didn't really love him. Not like that.

Mathew, Mattie, Matt, the eternal quarry of John Keane, a beautiful twenty-one-year-old from Larne, just out of UCD, working as a designer in some kind of advertising agency – spending all his time doing websites and hustling for nixers. He was smart was Mathew, and cold with it sometimes, so that he and I argued often, and he blamed me for the fact that he lived in one of John's flats, paying well below the going rate, but having as a result to put up with John's constant attention, making sure the shower was working and the gas was safe and the bedroom maybe needed a lick of paint did it? He blamed me simply because I'd said it mightn't be a bad idea. It had got to the point that he and John had a big falling out, and no one was quite sure what happened, but it ended up with Mathew moving into my place ('well it's your fault so you can just fucking well put me up and stop complaining Jesus') until John had delivered, with me as witness, and with much embarrassment, a solemn promise not to turn up unannounced ever again, and to surrender his key ('there it is, there, take the feckin thing'), and to understand and accept that being a tenant did not involve being anything else.

I think Mathew fell in love with Angelo. I believe that he did. I don't know where I'm coming from in this talking so much about love all the time. It's not the purpose, but if I'm going to talk about that odd little group in which we moved, then I'm going to have to mention the fact that I think Mathew fell in love with Angelo. He adored him. Which made him hate him of course. It was all very predictable. As soon as he worked out that Angelo was not really interested, at least not in a relationship, which was the only way that Mattie could think about, well, relationships – as, you know, RELATIONSHIPS – as soon as he had this figured out, he started to hate him. Then he went through this big thing of seducing him – which was the word he used, it's not my word, it's a Mattie word – a whole big rigmarole of waiting for the right moment, and planning the right words, and the right place and the right music and all that, well, pardon me, but all that straight stuff, and of course all during the preparation to seduce, he's shagging around, and Angelo is shagging around, and they both talk about the fact that they're shagging around, and all the time Mathew is sure that if he can only get Angelo in the right mood, with the right CD playing, that it'll turn into a great big love affair, that Angelo doesn't know what he wants, he needs it pointed out to him.

We think we're so self-contained, and in fact we're spilled down our shirt fronts, we're all dribble and emissions, walking around with our plans hanging out, making noises that we can't hear.

'Mathew,' Angelo told me one day, while we were watching television in my place, an activity of which he disapproved, but tolerated occasionally on the basis that it was my home and he would be a polite guest, 'Mathew wants to do sex with me.'

'Do sex? Like as a subject?'

'Pardon?'

'You mean have sex.'

'That's what I said, he wants sex with me, it's clear, but I don't want to have sex with him unless you want me to.'

'Why would I want you to, not want you to?'

'He is your friend.'

This kind of logic was frequent with Angelo, and always deeply annoying. I couldn't bring myself to believe a word of it.

'I'm not going to tell you who to have sex with, I'm not your boyfriend.'

This seemed to strike him as somehow ridiculous.

'What are you then?'

'I'm your friend.'

'Yes, good, at least there is that at least, thank you.'

'And that's it.'

'You have just this minute had to take a shower due to my friendship,' he said, very sulky.

'I'm your friend and occasional shag.'

'This is a boyfriend.'

'No it's not.'

'What is it? Why not?'

'We're not a couple.'

He shrugged and rolled his eyes and uttered something which I took to be Italian and would talk no more about it. I think he was embarrassed, and I think I had said the right thing really, although perhaps not in the long run. I just don't know.

Whether as a continuation of his sulk or as a result of my argument, or maybe because it would have happened in any case, off the two of them went into Mattie's rosy little sunset, and I suppose he must have done all the things he'd planned to do, and worked his magic and laid on the charm, assuming that this was all new to Angelo, that he would crumble, melt, do all those things that either reduce you to what you are or reduce you from what you are, but either way, reduce you. And of course this whole seduction-reduction routine of Mathew's failed miserably, sadly – went down as sunsets tend to do – and Angelo enjoyed the shag and resumed his life, unreduced, unchanged, uninterested, up and off with the first light.

So then Mathew really hated him. In that forlorn way of scorned lovers who haven't been scorned at all, just put right, and he kept his distance, and bitched about Angelo from that remove, annoying me greatly with his increasingly bizarre ways of going about it. He would, for example, invent things he was doing, people he was seeing or had met, and blather on about them, contradicting himself all over the place, in an apparent effort to inspire some kind of regret on Angelo's part, even jealousy maybe, but he would get it so wrong, so mixed up, that Angelo felt nothing stronger than a mild bafflement and a generous embarrassment.

'What is wrong with Mathew that he is so peculiar?'

'He is in love with you.'

'Oh,' said Angelo, and disappeared for about a week.

His disappearances were perfect. They were complete and sudden and he never said a word about them, acting puzzled if you asked him where he'd been. He had been nowhere. Until ten minutes later when he would tell you a little story which suggested very clearly that not only had he not been nowhere, but he had been somewhere entirely odd.

'Yes in a bar for gays in Glasgow I saw that man we saw

207

last week with the tattoo, and he was the same man but he was dressed like a sailor which was sad, but it is very hard for me to understand what they say. I ask for repetition, repeatedly, and it is embarrassing.'

'You've been to Scotland then?'

'No.'

'You just said . . .'

'Several years have passed since that.'

And he would move on to something else, telling one of the dispirited twins that he still had a bank account in Sicily but they would not give him the money because he did not have the proper identification any more, or telling an incredulous John Keane that he once saw a ghost in New York, a face in a window of a brownstone in Brooklyn, the face of a murdered boy who waved to him every morning as he walked to the subway.

'How do you know it was a ghost?'

'He was just a face. Not a body.'

'Oh right. How do you know he was murdered?'

'I looked into it.'

'Oh right.'

We were an odd group I suppose, the lot of us. Angelo sideswiped us, brushed past, but I thought at the time, honestly, that I had found in him someone slightly perfect. By which I mean, I suppose, that he did not arouse in me any, or many, imperfections of my own. He did not trouble me. I enjoyed him, and it was enjoyment without clutter, without notions of permanence or exclusivity or special treatment. Except of course that I must have had some kind of notion of permanence, or at least one of slightly longer duration, or else I wouldn't be doing this wondering lark. I'd be quite happy to be clueless. Like the others, who seem strangely unaffected, who don't seem to notice that he's gone. But that is maybe the way of groups like ours. If you can call it a group.

Of course there were others, who came and went, but what makes a group of gay men friends is the fact that they're not, despite whatever enjoyable little tensions there are, and even the occasional surrender to temptation or circumstances or too much drink, they're not actually having sex with each other, not really, not like that. Not even the dispirited twins were having sex with each other. And OK, Angelo and I were having quite a bit, but it was different, he was different, and I didn't care, I really didn't. Maybe though if you asked the others, they would count Angelo as one of those who came and went, that he was nothing more than my relatively short term exotic interest item. Maybe they would say that. Whatever. It's not like it matters.

I think I gave up smoking before I met Angelo.

Now there's this silence from them all about Angelo – about where he is or what might have happened, as if they don't care or don't want to discuss it. As if it's somehow, well, embarrassing.

We could never work out what Angelo did for a living. He said he was an artist at first, that he was a painter, but he never spoke about it and I never saw any paintings, not until much later anyway, and even then I'm not sure that they were his. And he also talked about opening a shop, what kind of shop exactly no one quite understood.

'Items,' he would say.

'What kind of items?'

'Beautiful items. Books and paintings and items of love.'

'A sex shop,' was Mathew's suggestion.

'No no no, love of the heart and the soul. But nothing will be ruled out.'

'Where?'

'I'm looking at several premises.'

John laughed at this.

'In Dublin?'

'Of course.'

'You have the money?'

'I have the money.'

He didn't look like he had the money. He did not, as I've

said, dress well, nor did he seem to aspire to any more expensive form of transport than his bike, or ever talk about holidays. He didn't have a television, did not wear aftershave, did not belong to a gym, did not go to the theatre or the cinema or seem to do anything that involved any kind of expenditure at all. He seemed to read only second-hand books, though I bumped into him more than once in places like Waterstones and Hodges Figgis. I remember clearly that on one occasion he was hunkered down in the travel section reading a book called 12 *Great Gay Bars Of Europe*, and on another he was studying a map of Leitrim. Once or twice he would take me out for wildly expensive meals or buy me small but classy gifts, like shirts or jumpers. For my birthday he bought me a Tag Heuer wristwatch, which myself and Dolores later priced at £465 in Weirs, leading Dolores to claim that I now not only had a boyfriend, but had a boyfriend of the officially scary variety.

So I suppose he did have the money. Or maybe he didn't. My watch, though heavy and solid and seeming to be in possession of all the right stamps and marks and so forth, barely worked, would go slow or speed up or skip dates. I once broached this with him, only to have him reply that he had never worn a watch, didn't really understand them, and had no advice to offer.

He didn't have a telephone either, or claimed not to have one. Though he would call at all hours and conduct long and rambling conversations uninterrupted by dropping coins. And as for where he lived, this was perhaps the weirdest thing of all. He told me first that he lived in Baggott Street, and I had no reason not to believe him until I heard him tell Mattie that he lived in Donnybrook, and, later, tell John Keane that he lived in Elgin Road. He never invited anyone over, and it seemed that when he picked a guy up he went to their place, always. I was tempted to follow him sometimes, and did once, and managed to, very successfully I thought, until he disappeared into thin air on Earlsfort Terrace, coming up to

Adelaide Road, as if he had fallen underground, or gone up into the night sky in exchange for the starlight, peculiarly bright as it was just there, that night, I don't know why, maybe the streetlights were faulty. I wandered around for a while, pondering various doors and turnings and directions, but was worried that he had either seen me and was annoyed and hiding, or that he actually lived there somewhere and might be looking at me through a window like his Brooklyn ghost boy.

You have to understand why I'm telling you all of this. All of this background information, all these names and places and half remembered things. It's because I don't know what is important. I no longer know what is important, what matters, what the essentials are, so that I have to cram everything in, I have to build using everything I've got, I have to paint with all the colours and I have to use every single word in the dictionary to do it. And I wish that I could be precise, that I could tell you only the interesting things, the things which would make you sit up and pay attention, the words that would tell you immediately that something was going on here, that this was leading up to something, and that it was something important. But I don't have the time to be brief. You understand me? I don't have the time to sift through it all and distil the moments of importance, and communicate them in a way that would make you care. I am distracted by the debris, by the incidental, by the little bits of minutes and hours and days that stay with me, that have lodged somewhere in my mind as tastes or sounds or inclinations of his head or movements of his hands or words he said. Because I need to show him to you, and I'm not doing it right, I'm not covering it all, I'm all side-on and oblique and I'm too self-conscious and it's not going to work if I try to frame it just so, try to get it perfect. I have to just throw this at you. And you just have to catch it.

We were having dinner once with, I think, Dolores and one of the dispirited twins, in a place on Dame Street, the name of which I just can't remember, and I was having too much to drink, and Angelo was not talking to me because he disapproved of drinking too much, and Dolores and the twin were having a conversation about computers or the internet or some such, and I was drunk and bored and I resented the presence of almost everyone, and I was ready to pick a fight with whoever seemed on for one, and I was heavy in my chair and I was leaning out from the table to try and catch the eye of the waiter for another bottle of wine, and I fell. In a big way. I mean I crashed, sidelong, flailing, all legs and arse, my arms having ceased to work, or having decided all by themselves to try and clutch something overhead rather than do the intelligent thing and try to break my fall. So I managed to kick my chair over, or take it down with me, and to disturb I think one glass of wine, full, red, spilling it all over the table, and I landed hard on my right hip, painfully, so that I uttered some oath, and I sprawled on the terracotta tiles like an insect on its back, and I felt the whole world pause to stare at me and I felt, you can imagine, that it would be a good time to die.

A flock of waiters came to my aid, graciously, worried no doubt about law suits, and they actually had everything cleaned up pretty quickly, with me back in my chair and the standard hubbub of the place gradually resuming. But what are friends for if not to magnify your emotions? Dolores thought it was hilarious, and laughed loudly. The twin was embarrassed, but in an awful, supercilious, almost gleeful kind of way, his view of me as a dirty drunk obviously confirmed. Between the two of them I was getting quite a helping of good old fashioned public mortification. But Angelo. Angelo. Angelo was furious. His face looked like it had been splashed by the wine in large lopsided blotches. He clenched his hands together in front of his mouth and for a good three minutes just stared at me without saying a word, letting the others go through their little routines, letting them get their minor neuroses out of their respective systems. It got to the point where I looked at him and got uneasy and prompted him with –

'What? What?'

He just shook his head. Then he looked down at the table-top, and said in a very low, very slow, very scary voice –

'How much do I owe?'

'What?'

'I want to leave here. What do I pay?'

'Don't be stupid,' I said, still pissed obviously. 'Finish your meal.'

He kept his head down, put his knife and fork together in the middle of his plate, stood up and walked out. Well, he nearly did. If he had done that and that only then I might not remember it like I do. But he didn't just walk out. As he passed me, and I said something incredibly dumb, something about sulks or tantrums or scenes, something slurred and pointless and, I have to say, fucking typical, he, very neatly, with barely a flicker, lifted his right hand, the one nearest me, up to his waist so that his arm was bent, and without moving his body, without seeming to pause in his stride at all, elbowed me, hard, in the head.

And he was gone.

I was in shock really, I think, for a minute, and was embarrassed that it hurt so much, and embarrassed that he had done it, and I laughed, or tried to laugh, my hand to my cheekbone, worried that there was blood, and I looked at the others and raised my eyes and smiled as if it was nothing, just a flick, just a stupid thing, that he had just brushed against me, that it was nothing, that it was not important. But the twin was staring at me with his mouth open, and Dolores, if I had not been in her way, would I'm sure have gone after him, decked him probably, sent him flying, and she shouted something after him, I don't know what, and I remember shushing her, using that 'shussssh' sound, and I remember that making the sound made me feel that I wanted to cry, and of course the last thing I actually wanted was to cry, but it

213

gave me that feeling, you know that one, you remember it from when you were a kid, or from yesterday, I don't know you, when your chest fills and your eyes fill and your mouth fills and everything fills and you want, suddenly, right now, right this instant, to be on your own, somewhere quiet, somewhere dark, so that you can let yourself flood and spill and overflow. That.

After about thirty seconds a waiter plonked the bill down on the table and stood there waiting for us to leave. Which we did, me still with my hand to my face, sure there was blood, I could have sworn I felt the trickle of blood, and we went out into the street and the others kept on asking me was I all right, which of course I was not, but yes, I said, yes, absolutely, he's just annoyed, it's nothing, forget about it, it's not important. They let me get a cab home on my own.

I tried to see blood on my hand, but couldn't, which I didn't understand. And I squinted at my palm, and licked it even, but there was just the salty taste of eye spillage, and the vague mushroom musk of my risotto.

I got home and the telephone was of course ringing, and it was of course Angelo, and I of course hung up. In the mirror I could see a black eye starting, which surprised me because it was my cheek which hurt, not my eye, and my cheek had just this thin graze on the ridge of the bone, and I touched everything gingerly and showered in an attempt to sober up, and let the telephone ring and ring and fell asleep and slept for days. It seemed like days.

I wouldn't talk to him, which I think was only proper, and while he couldn't reach me he apparently went crawling to Dolores and the twin and apologised to them and got an earful from Dolores and an irritated absolution from the twin, him being much more interested in an apology from me I think. Then he sent me flowers, and a letter with them, which I read several times trying to make out his handwriting. He told me basically that he was sorry, that he was ashamed, that his father had been an alcoholic, that he would do anything to make it up to me, that his anger was unjustified, that I was the nicest person he knew and all that kind of bollocks. His father was an alcoholic though. This struck me. Firstly as a pretty lame excuse for his behaviour, and secondly, as the first purely personal, historical, informational, you know, *actual*, bit of detail about himself that he'd ever volunteered.

I agreed to meet him after about two days, partly because he was annoying me with his guilt, partly because I'd gotten over it and I believed that he was genuinely sorry, partly because I wanted a reconciliation, but mainly, mainly because my eye looked so spectacularly gruesome by then – black and yellow with a nice line of dark blue along my cheekbone – and I wanted him to take one look at me and burst into tears. Which of course he did.

It was quite a scene, that. We met in Dolores's place, with her acting as chaperone, and I was decently late, and wrapped in my good leather jacket and a scarf, with my face stuck out in front of me like a banner. I remember taking off my watch and sticking it in my pocket before I went in. And he stood up, and looked at me, and one hand went to his mouth, and then the other, like he was going to be sick, and then he let out this great moan, and sobbed, and seemed so completely ashamed and distraught that I just crumbled, and I sobbed too, and I opened my arms and went to him and the two of us just stood there wrapped up in each other for ages, crying like eejits, and I don't know who was comforting who, or which way the apologies were flowing, but there was a river full of them, and we just went with it, all soaked and baffled and surrendered, gone with the current, pulled right under, utterly drowned. While Dolores sat disgusted, and snorted and fumed.

After that he was different. But in a way that I don't know how to explain. It was as if he had been slightly damaged by it, as if he had lost some of his confidence, some of his nerve. Or maybe he assumed that these things had happened to me, and he wanted to reflect them, to empathise, to be with me.

But I don't think so. Because I was properly healed as soon as we'd embraced, and if anything I felt better about things, as if I'd been through something difficult, something awful, and had come out the other side, stronger. I thought that I was closer to him, because he'd hit me. And I know there'll be people who'll think that's kind of sick – that it's the worst kind of self-delusion, that it's a classic case. Why is it a classic case then? Maybe because it has some truth in it? Maybe because I felt that he could sleep with half the planet and there'd be nothing I could do about it, but that the fact that he had hurt me, and then felt such shame, such sorrow that he had done it – that he could ever have allowed it to happen – maybe I felt that it tied us together in a way that sex, or anything else, never could, ever. No? Really? What then?

Anyway, all this is beside the point. The point being that it happened, and then it was resolved, and it's really nobody's business what either of us thought about it. It was private. And it's not like he threw me down the stairs or anything. It was a knock, a sideways knock with the butt of his elbow, it wasn't kitchen knives or clenched fists or screwdrivers. It wasn't serious. And it never happened again. Ever.

He was quieter though, afterwards. I think maybe he was embarrassed. Everyone knew about it. John Keane avoided him for a while. Mattie of course just ate it up. Told me all kinds of nonsense – that I should report him, that I could have him 'seen to' which I think was Mattie's way of suggesting that he knew some serious people. The twins just disappeared, having had their fill of all of us probably, off to re-decorate their bathroom. Angelo and I went out on our own for a while, until John Keane drifted back, having forgotten probably, why he had stayed away, and then Mattie, afraid he might be missing something, and Dolores, and the whole thing slowly got going again, the same rhythm, the same routine. Except Angelo stayed closer to me now, he sought out a space beside me all the time, he kept an eye on me, he always made sure I was all right, it was as if he had made some kind

216

of promise to himself. Which was nice, but also altered things slightly in my mind, made him a little less perfect, made him appear slightly clingy and occasionally annoying. But I couldn't raise it with him, at least I didn't get the chance to. I was indulging in it for a while, letting it happen, enjoying it mostly, but knowing that at some point up ahead I would have to put a stop to it. But not now, not just yet. Then everything went kind of haywire. Everything went weird.

It was a Tuesday night. I was staying in after a weekend spent with Angelo that had involved much sex and much sleep, all in my big bed with the street noise barely noticed, with occasional trips to the shops and one long walk, with funny little rows about what music to play. He was interested in traditional Irish stuff, mostly instrumental, jigs and reels and what have you. All of which leaves me cold I have to say. Particularly when the only real effect it has on me is to remind me of my father, and one of the main effects it had on Angelo was to make him horny. He said it was very sexy music. Which it is not. But he was mad about it. I wanted to make love to the sound of Air if I was feeling mellow, or of Suede or old Red Hot Chilli Peppers stuff if mellow wasn't where it was at, and all he wanted was to get naked to 1970s Planxty and the new De Dannan.

'You must know this is in your soul.'

'It is not.'

'If only you would listen to your country. You import everything you Irish. You export people and you import your dreams. You are a very strange people. It is explained to me now how it is you do sex like an American boy.'

'I do what?'

'Like McDonald's sex.'

'Fuck off.'

'I will say what I like. I am well travelled.'

That kind of weekend, sweet and close, all the loose ends left hanging, everything else forgotten. One of those weekends when you drop out of your life, you drop out of time, and you spend a while in your own universe, and you remember it like a dream, or like something you stole from the day to day grind, something you weren't meant to take but you took it anyway. We made love all day and we laughed at the world, and we got up and we made a meal, our bare feet on the lino, our hips touching. Nothing else. You either know what I'm talking about or you don't.

On the Tuesday I got a phone call. It was a strange voice, with an accent I couldn't place, maybe English, maybe American, but posh, wealthy, clear and business-like. He said my phone number to me, and I said yes, and he paused, and then said my name, and I said yes, and then he paused again, and then he asked if Angelo was there. And it was an odd thing – maybe it was the accent, and the fact that nobody had ever called for him before – but for a moment I hadn't a clue who he was talking about. You use a name every day, you have it in your head all the time, it's part of your world, and you stop thinking about it, and you forget what it sounds like. I told him that no, Angelo wasn't there, who was this, could I pass on a message, and he was very polite, but wouldn't give his name, wouldn't leave a message, apologised for disturbing me and hung up.

I'm not sure that I gave it much thought on the level that I should have. I mean I don't remember being particularly intrigued about who it might have been, or where he had got my number, but I do remember thinking, maybe for the first time, about the oddness of Angelo's name. Angelo. What the hell kind of name is that? And it struck me that there was no reason on earth why it should be his real name. I didn't know what his surname was – he would never tell me – and I didn't know anything about him other than that his father was an alcoholic and that he was very sweet and that we had a lot of great sex. Angelo. Angelo. It was too close to 'angel' and I found myself wondering whether he was a kind of gay boy's fantasy Mary Poppins type figure, whether he was real at all, whether I hadn't just imagined him, whether he might tell me one day that his work here was done and it was time he was off to show some other boy with a McDonald's sex life how to live a little.

And while all this is vaguely amusing and so forth, it does bring me to something else that has bothered me about all this. The names. Generally speaking, the names. Angelo. Angel – temporary, translucent, or trans something, imprecise, flighty, hard to pin down. Adam – there at the beginning (though that makes me Eve, which is a bit scary), tempted out of paradise by a man from Seattle (get that hissing sound?), exiled now, lost from the garden. Dolores, which is like dolorous, which my dictionary tells me is sorrow or distress, from the Latin for pain, and it is her who has been the chief witness to all my own dolour, horrible word, from the cracking elbow to the stuff that follows. And Mr Duncan, which at first makes me think of doughnuts, but when you consider it a bit it is not a million miles away from dungeon, and is also Shakespearean, isn't it?, though what that signifies I have no idea (I did it in school but I don't know, you know, I don't know how to use it). But I'm getting ahead of myself here. Am I? Have I mentioned Duncan before? I don't know. Probably not. And I'm not sure of the timing here either. I have no idea how long after the phone call I saw Angelo. I know I spoke to him, I know he called me at least once, and I know I forgot to say it to him. Because it didn't seem that important. Or not as important as the things we actually discussed, not that I can remember what we did discuss, probably something to do with the lack of action in Vortex or where we could go to avoid the crowds on Saturday night, apart from Vortex that is. Or maybe we talked about my ongoing problems with this Brian character, whose love for me was unflagging, even though I had been plain rude to him. Maybe it was that week, still on his McDonald's theme, that he told me to let Brian shag me – that would put an end to it.

But. Stick to the facts.

At some point, at some time, some days, at least, after the strange phone call, I told Angelo about it. And I know I told him face to face because it is his face I remember most of all. Not just generally, but specifically too, at this moment, on being told of the telephone call. It froze. His face I mean. It stopped where it was, head stuck out a little, eyebrows up, eyes in mine, on mine maybe, mouth a little open. And it just stayed like that. For ages. And it didn't move. All it did was get a little paler. Just a degree.

I think we were in a bar, possibly The Front Lounge, because we were certainly sitting down, and it was quiet enough not to have to shout. It may have been during the day, Saturday afternoon probably, when Angelo liked to go for a drink, thinking it 'civilised'. Though maybe I'm getting it completely mixed up. Maybe it was earlier in the week. Maybe it was the next week. Maybe I told him over dinner in Dish or Odessa. Maybe I even told him on the phone. But I remember his face. Maybe I imagined his face. I don't know.

'What man?'

'I don't know. English? American? Posh accent?'

'What did he ask?'

'For you.'

'But how did he ask that?'

'What?'

'What words did he say?'

'Is Angelo there? Can I speak to Angelo?'

'Which?'

'What?'

'Which of those questions did he ask?'

'Jesus. I can't remember.'

I'm not sure that he actually needed to know the exact form of words used. I think now that maybe he was just talking so that he could think. Of course now I remember it clearly, distinctly, as 'May I speak to Angelo please?' but I don't really know where that's coming from.

'What age?'

'What?'

'What age was he would you say?'

'I don't know. Grown up.'

It must have been face to face because I remember pale, a lot of pale – pallor, pallid – a general whitening out of his features. A kind of cheese melt thing, nothing left to read, everything just collapsed a little, sunken down and formless, messed up, ruined.

'Are you all right?'

'He left no message?'

'No.'

'What exact time please did this happen?'

'Tuesday night. I don't know. After nine maybe, before eleven. After nine before eleven.'

He snapped a little sigh at me for being so forgetful, but I was looking at him oddly now I'd imagine, a bit worried, and he probably saw that, and he smiled, very weak, very white, like someone buried in snow, and I'm sure it took an effort, and it looked genuinely awful, and just made me more curious, and he patted my knee and shook his head like it was nothing, but I could see immediately that he wanted to go home, or wherever, and that he was shaken, disturbed, anxious, scared, all those things I never associated with him very much.

Not sure now. Well. We must have been out somewhere. Because he wanted to come home with me. Or, to be more precise, he wanted to meet me there. So we left wherever we must have been, and Angelo, being very peculiar and intriguing, kissed me goodbye on the street, and walked off, as did I, towards home, and I got there, and let myself in, and about ten minutes later he's at the door, very sleight of hand, very third man, very daft really.

'What the hell has got into you?'

'I'm sorry I don't understand the question.'

He was behaving like Malcolm X at the curtain.

'What is wrong?'

'Mr Duncan,' he said, and gave me a look, as if he had explained it all.

'Who's Mr Duncan?'

'I told you this.'

'You didn't.'

'Are you sure?'

'Yes. And get away from there you're making me nervous.'

You have to understand that this was not entirely out of the ordinary behaviour from Angelo. Well, it was in the sense that this was a different variety of oddness, a new variation, but the theme had been pretty much established by then. That he was secretive, that he was furtive and intensely private, that he was occasionally duplicitous and more than occasionally just told barefaced, baby-faced, out and out lies – all this must be clear to you by now. But he was fun with it. It was entertaining. Maybe you wouldn't think so, but I did. He told me once that he had been in Peru, and had slept with a boy he liked, whose father found out and had chased him then for three days and three nights across the foothills of the Andes, trying to force Angelo higher and higher 'so that I would drown in the thin air' and that he had escaped by clinging to a log and hurtling downstream, almost frozen to death, down to the river and on towards the sea, half dead, splintered and whipped and his skin a powder blue in the sun. And I asked him what had happened to the boy and he said that he had been exiled from his village and was now an ornithologist in Lima, studying the legendary Gorrión de Jesús, the bird which flew too high and burst its heart and fell sometimes like small rain in the autumn months.

You either like that kind of stuff or you don't.

So when all this pallor started, and this curtain flicking and the talk of Mr Duncan, I didn't immediately feel that we were on entirely new ground, that this was utterly strange. And when I made tea for us both, and got him sitting down and asked him to tell me about this Mr Duncan, I was quite looking forward to it really – not too troubled, not too concerned. This after all, was Angelo.

'I don't want to tell you.'

'Why not?'

'Because it is not funny.'

'That's OK.'

He sighed, and rubbed his hand over his chest, and winced a little, and looked at me, and nodded slowly.

'I will tell you because you never ask me things and I am happy about this and you are easy to be with for me.'

It wasn't exactly a ringing endorsement, but I shrugged, said nothing.

'Mr Duncan is my enemy.'

And he seemed to want to stop there, as if that explained everything.

'Yes?'

He sighed again, winced again.

'I met him in another country, that does not matter, some other time, and he was very nice to me, and he was quite rich, and he looked after me for a while and then I hurt him I think, or something, and since that time he hates me.'

It was really not easy dragging it out of him. It turned into a question and answer session, Angelo being by turns evasive, embarrassed, and blunt, and contradicting himself all over the place, altering details as he went on, going over something again and again that seemed completely unimportant, skipping past things that seemed like they really might matter. Basically, from what I could work out, Angelo had met this guy in either London or Rome, or perhaps neither of those places, but certainly they were, at different times, in both cities for long periods. And Angelo had been quite young, and, it seemed to me – though he did not say so – quite stupid, and he had been taken under the wing of this older, very rich, very odd queen called, simply, Mr Duncan, who had treated him to expensive living, nice clothes, exotic holidays, that kind of thing. But there was some evasion on the question of who benefited most. And there was even a little hesitation in confirming that it had been a sexual relationship, and even when that was eventually confirmed, it was 'not important really, not the big thing,' and Angelo seemed to regret, not that he had become mixed up with Mr Duncan, but that Mr Duncan had become mixed up with him, if you see what I mean. And he talked of an incident, in London, involving a large amount of missing money, and of the police becoming involved, and of Mr Duncan being angry, very angry, to the point of violence, and then Angelo backtracked and said that no, there had never been any violence, not really, that the money had been his in any case, and that he thought it was stolen by another boy, Mr Duncan being quite the collector, and that the police had not done anything other than poke around a little bit and check everyone's age, and that anyway, that was not important. Then there was a woman, who was maybe Mr Duncan's sister, who had appeared in Rome and had argued with him, with Mr Duncan that is, and after that Mr Duncan told Angelo that he could no longer support him, that he would have to go, that he could no longer look after him, and that Angelo had been quite relieved, glad to move on. But then, when Angelo had moved to somewhere else, before Dublin, but he would not say where, Mr Duncan had come looking for him, and had said that he wanted Angelo back as before, but Angelo was not interested, and Mr Duncan then was involved in an accident, which to me sounded like he'd tried to do himself in, but which Angelo insisted was definitely an accident, and he spent some time in a hospital.

At this stage I'm thinking that what is going on here is that Angelo is being tracked down by a jealous former sugar daddy who wants him back and who would be harmless if he wasn't so rich. But Angelo looks at me as if I'm mad and tells me I've got it completely 'ass ways up your arse.' So he goes on.

Mr Duncan is not, apparently, Scottish, but he goes to

Scotland to recover from his mysterious accident, and Angelo, out of sympathy or friendship, or loyalty, or some such quality which he is unable to name, goes with him. So the two of them are living in an old Scottish castle ('it is not a castle you understand, but it is called this because of the Americans') where they seem to have a staff, and are visited several times by the woman who was Mr Duncan's sister, but who has been edited now in Angelo's mind into his wife. She and Angelo have a frosty relationship, understandably enough I suppose, and when she is there he tends to head off somewhere else, to Glasgow or Edinburgh, where he books himself into big hotels and ruminates. He didn't use that word. I can't remember what word he used. You're getting this second-hand, at least, at best.

He became embarrassed here. Very red faced and slow. And this was the point where I decided that he was making this up as he went along, that none of this happened at all, that he was searching for a reason, a rationale, to explain why the sugar daddy story wasn't true. I thought he was so embarrassed by the sugar daddy theory that he reached out for something more embarrassing still in order to cover it up. So he told me, stuttering, shame faced, that he had an affair with the wife. Or the sister. Take your pick.

I laughed.

'You did what?'

'She and I became lovers.'

'Lovers?'

'Yes.'

'You just said that you went away whenever she arrived.'

'At first yes. And then she wanted me to stay, so I stayed. And it happened there, in the castle, that we became lovers. And then we would go away together.'

He had lost me by now. He was, I decided, spinning out any old nonsense to avoid telling me a boring, pedestrian truth.

'You're gay though.'

He fixed me with a very cross look.

'That is a not intelligent thing to say. I am alive. Anything else is only words.'

Which was fair enough I suppose. But I still didn't believe this story, this part of the story – that the affair continued, very clandestine, very passionate, very intense, and that the intensity was because of the secrecy, and the secrecy was because of the passion, and that they were lovers only until they were discovered, and once they were discovered it had run its course, it was over and useless. You may say that I don't believe this bit because of jealousy, because of my queer prejudices, because of my fear of things that I know nothing about. Which is also fair enough, I suppose, if you think of me as being subordinate to all those things, which I do not think I am. I can take all of them into account and still honestly say that I didn't believe him. Honestly.

Anyway, this spoof was spun out, interminably, with lots of really quite unnecessary sexual detail, until it got to the point where Mr Duncan, still poorly, propelling himself on crutches with velvet rests and rubber feet, stumbles, literally, upon the two of them having it off in what Angelo first said was the chapel, and then corrected to the pantry, if you don't mind. There was a scene. The wife, sister, whatever, flees. Angelo gets a smack from a crutch, and defends himself, causing Mr Duncan to fall and crack his head, and Angelo thinks he's killed him, is sure that he's killed him, and leaves, deserts the place, takes all traces of himself with him, and travels the back roads and the minor routes, and ends up, eventually, in Dublin.

It's a pot-boiler isn't it?

I sat there and stared at him. He shrugged. He seemed almost apologetic. As if he knew it wasn't very good.

'I'm tired,' he said.

And we went to bed. And in bed, in the darkness, not having had any sex at all, he turned to me, and put his hand on my chest and said a very strange thing.

'We will not need each other always.'

'What do you mean?'

'Just that.'

And he would say no more, not that I asked him. I'm not sure I wanted to know. It sounded too much like a warning, not that I heeded it. It suggested a future which I did not want to think about, which I am now in the middle of, which has proven to be only half true.

I didn't see him for a few days I think. He called me a couple of times, wondering if there had been any more phone calls, or anything strange or out of the ordinary at all. Which there hadn't. And he seemed to calm down eventually, and get back to something like his usual self, a bit dizzy, a bit confused, but happy enough.

We saw plenty of each other, and of everyone else. Things went on as they always had. John Keane found a boy he liked. Mattie broke his wrist in a dance related incident at HAM and spent a week talking about suing. One of the twins reappeared one night in The George and ended up going to The Boilerhouse with Angelo and myself and disappeared into a cubicle with two Germans and was not seen again. Dolores changed jobs and started talking seriously about buying a house, so we knew she was loaded. I got a raise, but was still far from loaded. Brian seemed finally to give up on me, settling instead for a late-thirties, fully bearded minor writer, much to my annoyance and Angelo's amusement.

I don't know how much time passed like that. I don't know if we knew John was sick before or afterwards. I don't know when the twins had their punch up in Out On The Liffey. I don't know when my father died or when Dolores got engaged. I don't know the chronology. I really don't. I'm just not good at that. But all of that stuff happened in an about six month period, and sometime in the middle of that six months, or maybe at the beginning of it, or maybe at the end, I don't know, Angelo disappeared.

First though, there was the fucking taxi driver.

I was going home, late, about three in the morning, and I had walked all the way down from The Pod to Dame Street, and I still hadn't got a cab, and I was thinking of walking all the way, though it was starting to rain, and then this taxi pulled in beside me to let people out, and I grabbed it. Which was pretty good going, because there was a crowd around, all looking for a taxi, just outside the Olympia, at the pedestrian crossing. So I got in the back and told him where to go, and there were people on the street shouting at me for having taken their cab, and the rain was getting heavy, and the driver looked over his shoulder and did a U-turn around the little traffic light island and headed up towards Christ Church.

It actually wasn't Angelo I saw first. I think the first thing that caught my eye was the other guy. He was late-forties maybe, sandy haired, wearing a pale raincoat and holding a folded umbrella in his hand, and maybe it was that, the unused umbrella, and the rain really coming down now, that I saw first. He was having a pointed finger conversation with someone, leaning forward a little from the waist, his finger bobbing up and down, and it was only as the taxi accelerated past them, up the hill past the Castle, that I saw that the other guy was Angelo. His arms folded, his bike propped up against his hip, wearing the yellow windbreaker, and with the knapsack I had bought him strapped to his back. He was shaking his head.

We had been together earlier in the evening, we had gone for a drink in The Bailey, which he hated, which always put him in a bad mood, and he had not wanted to come to The Pod with me, he had said he was tired, that he wanted to go home, that he would call me over the weekend. So I think my first reaction on seeing him was to think, the bastard! Out cruising around on his bike at all hours when he was meant to be tucked up in bed, all faithful and alone. I remember laughing out loud, and the taxi driver saying something, I

don't know what, and me turned around in the seat, looking
out the back window, having a chuckle, and then seeing, or
thinking I saw, through the condensation and the rain and
the darkness, something, a blur, a movement, something. It
looked like a scuffle. It looked, and this is only something
seen in an instant, in the smallest of seconds, barely seen at
all, it looked like the older guy had raised the umbrella and
had brought it down hard on Angelo's head, or on where I
imagined Angelo's head to be, and there had been a flurry
then, of punches, kicks, I don't know what, both ways, and I
thought I saw the bike fall over, and I thought I saw Angelo's
face, clenched, drawn, struggling for something in the dark,
the rain on his hair, trouble all over it, and some panic too,
and I shouted, loudly I think, for the driver to stop.

And of course this is the fucking taxi driver from hell.

'What do you mean stop?'

'You can leave me here.'

'What do you mean I can leave you here?'

'Just stop the car will you?'

'Sure you only got into it.'

'And I want to get out of it.'

'I thought you wanted Island Bridge.'

'I did. Just stop the fucking car will you?'

'No need for language. You don't want Island Bridge?'

'No. Jesus. Will you pull in for Christ's sake?'

'OK OK. What's your problem?'

'I saw someone, a friend. In a fight.'

'Where?'

'Well you've driven so fucking far now that I can't fucking
see where.'

'I'm not a bleeding bus service you know. You can't hop on
and hop off you know.'

'What do I owe you?'

'You hired me to Island Bridge. There were other people
waiting you know.'

'What do I owe you?'

'Some of them were big fares probably, going southside, Dalkey some of them probably. They'll be gone now.'

I opened the door.

'Where are you going?'

'How much do I fucking owe you?'

'Island Bridge is about seven quid.'

'That's bollocks,' I said, threw a tenner at him and was gone, out of it, back down the sliding pavements, down Lord Edward Street like a maniac, sprinting down to the corner of Parliament Street with my legs threatening to buckle and my lungs to burst.

There was no one there.

I did what you'd expect. I looked all four ways. I ran a little way down Parliament Street, nothing. I peered towards the bridge. I came back up, crossed the road and had a look in Castle Street. There was a couple snogging in a wet doorway. There was a rent boy wandering back towards Dame Street. There was no Angelo. I walked for a while, past The Olympia, up to the all night shop opposite George's Street, down Dame Lane past where Incognito used to be, back to the Castle gates, back to the corner of Parliament Street. They were nowhere. He was nowhere.

Of course I then began to doubt that I'd seen anything at all, and while I was pretty sure that I'd seen Angelo, might I not simply have misconstrued an umbrella waved in parting for a full scale assault, and the contortions of Angelo climbing onto a wet bike for a scuffle in the dark? I might have. The truth is I still don't know what I saw. I never found out. But I stood there in the heavy rain, rivers of it running down my face and my back, blinking at the lights, turning in circles in the darkness, peering into faces and doorways and examining the ground for torn buttons or splashes of blood, and I felt, very deeply, very soberly, that something was very wrong.

I had to walk home.

I have to apologise about the whole time thing. I'm just no

good at it. And I become more and more aware of its importance, and I know that if I was ever a witness, in a court, that
I'd be pretty useless. I couldn't tell you if something happened last week or last year. I wasn't always this bad. I used
to be quite well organised actually, and at work I'm still
mostly on the ball. Of course at work I have this big desk
diary that everything goes into, and I have Lotus Organiser
and Microsoft Outlook and e-mail coming and going and a
whole room full of people who seem to exist simply to
remind me of what I've forgotten. So if I wanted to I could
reconstruct my entire last working year, tell you day by day
what I was doing, where I went, who I met, what I was working on. But that's, you know, not where I live. It's completely
unconnected. And while I know there's scrawls in my desk
diary about meeting Angelo or John or Dolores somewhere
that night, scribbled during a telephone call, I can't relate that
date, that time of year even, to the chronology of my actual,
real, important life. Which is the one squeezed into the gaps
between working.

So I don't know. I've tried to work it out. I've thought of
definite dates, like the death of my father (I had to ask my
mother, she was sort of pissed off about it), or the June bank
holiday, or the August bank holiday, and have tried to
remember where Angelo was. I think he was gone by the
time my father died. But I remember going swimming with
him down in Brittas Bay in August, so you figure that one
out. And I've asked various other people, like Dolores, but
she's even more hopeless than I am – claimed Angelo was
around for about six months, when it was at least three times
that; and Mattie, who probably knows but won't help on the
basis that I'm 'obsessing'; and John, who is not well, and is
not really interested in thinking about time at all; and the
twins, who have their entirely own calendar anyway, based
around things like pre-painting the downstairs loo and post-
painting the downstairs loo. Before double glazing – after
double glazing. There is no standard time.

So apologies, but again I have to guess. After the fight in the rain, or whatever it was, there was a gap, I don't know how long, before I heard from him. From Angelo I mean. I don't think it was a long gap, a couple of days. And I think that in that couple of days I must have asked absolutely everybody if they had seen him, or when was the last time they had seen him, and it turned out that nobody had seen him, that I was the last, that night, in The Bailey, when he left at about ten, not wearing the yellow windbreaker, not on his bike. So he must have gone home before coming back into town. I tried to remember what kind of mood he'd been in. Not a good one. But I had just assumed that he didn't like the venue. He was quiet. Glum. Tired. I tried to remember if he'd said anything unusual, out of the ordinary, strange. And I couldn't.

Then he called me. And this time it was definitely from a payphone. I could hear traffic – quite a lot of traffic, and general street noise, and I thought he must be in one of those non-boxes, just the kind of phone on a pole with a hood over it, maybe in College Green, or by O'Connell Bridge.

'Where are you?'

'In town. Can you come?'

'Are you all right?'

'Yes, can you meet me?'

'Sure. I saw you . . .'

'I cannot talk.'

'I saw you the other night. On Dame Street, with someone. Are you OK?'

'Yes yes. I will meet you in that hotel, you know . . .'

I didn't know.

'What hotel?'

'Where you want to stay.'

'What?'

'That fine hotel you like. You want to stay there.'

It's true that sometimes I think it'd be kind of cool to take a week off work and everything else and book into The Shelbourne and spend a fortune not doing very much.

'The Shelbourne?'

'Yes.'

I didn't know that I'd ever mentioned it to Angelo though.

'OK. When?'

'Now now.'

'Are you OK? Angelo?'

There was a bit of a pause, and I thought I heard him say something to someone else, like 'Yes, in a minute, in a minute,' quieter, as if he held his hand over the mouthpiece, or maybe he said it to me, and just had his head turned, and maybe he was saying to me that he would be OK in a minute, that in a minute everything would be fine. I don't know.

'Come now,' he said, clearer, and he hung up.

It was early evening, it was fine weather, it must have been September, or maybe it was early October. I don't know what it was. I called a cab, thinking it would be quicker, because there are no buses that go straight from my place to St Stephen's Green, not really, and I had to wait then, for the taxi to arrive, and I stood out on the street, and I remember smoking, though I thought I had given up, I clearly remember smoking, and eventually it arrived, the taxi did, and once we got going it was quick enough, and it must have been no more than half an hour, forty minutes at the most, between the phone call and me walking into The Shelbourne – it wasn't any more than that – but it seems I was too late, that 'now' had meant 'then' and that whatever had prompted him to call me, whatever he had needed to see me about, had either passed, or I had missed it and had let him down, because he wasn't there, not in the lobby or either of the two bars, and I walked in circles around The Shelbourne, and I cursed myself, and I probably cursed him as well, and I could not find him, anywhere, because he was not there, I could not see him, he was gone.

I stared for a while at the reception desk. Then I asked the man there if they had a guest staying called Angelo. And he looked at me, paused, and asked, 'Would that be a surname

Sir?' and I said no, but that I didn't know what the surname was, it could be anything, and could he please check whether there was anyone staying there with the first name Angelo, and he did sort of glance down at his desk, but not for very long, and then told me that no, there was not, and I asked him to look again, that it was very important, and to be fair, he did look again, and this time he did make a little show of running the end of his pencil over a list in a book, but he had two computer screens there as well, and he never looked at them, and then he told me, still very polite, that no, there were no Angelos staying at the hotel, he was very sorry.

I did another tour of the place. There were businessmen, there were American tourists, there were nice elderly ladies having tea, there was a politician I recognised in The Horse Shoe Bar, but there was no Angelo. Looking at all the suits I thought that he would have hated this place anyway. I went back to the reception desk.

'Is there a Mr Duncan staying here?'

'A Mr . . .?'

'Duncan.'

'No Sir.'

'You didn't even look.'

'There's no such guest here at the moment Sir, I'm sorry.'

And he turned to someone else who wanted to change their room to a non-smoking floor. I tried to look at the book on the desk, but he had closed it. The computer screens were blank.

'Excuse me?'

'Sir?'

'Sorry, but when you said there was no Mr Duncan here at the moment, did you mean that there had been one here, previously?'

'I'm sorry Sir, I'm dealing with this gentleman.'

Then he leaned a little closer to me.

'And in any case Sir, guest information is strictly private, as you can imagine.'

He turned away again and that was it. Which was not very much. And there I was, left standing in a bustling hotel with the dusk settling down, uncertain as to whether a man, who might or might not exist, may or may not have been a guest, at some time, and whether this, about which I was merely guessing, might have anything to do with my missing friend, about whom I knew nothing other than an extremely suspicious first name, an alleged alcoholic father, and a fondness for making up stories and tying up condoms.

One thing I think now that I could have done, at some stage, which would have been really useful, especially at this point, was to have bought Angelo, as a gift, as a toy, a mobile phone. And I know that he would have hated the idea, but he may have humoured me if I had told him that he need never use it, just let me know the number, so that, if I needed to, I could reach him. But I never did. I'm not sure I ever thought of it.

I stood on the steps of The Shelbourne, and then paced up and down outside, until it got properly dark, and I went back in a couple of times too, and had a look around, though the doorman began to eye me suspiciously, and the last time I went in he followed me, which was a pain, because I wanted to go to the bathroom, but couldn't really. So I waited outside until I couldn't wait anymore, and then ran up the road to Foley's and used their bathroom, and then ran back, positive that he would have turned up in the meantime, which meant going back in, this time to be confronted by the doorman with a 'Can I help you Sir,' to which I replied, truthfully, all smiles and in my posh voice, that I was meant to be meeting a friend and I thought I'd been stood up and wanted to check the bars again before calling it quits. Which he seemed to think was fair enough.

It must have been two hours or more since the phone call. I had given up really, and thought I might as well have a drink, hang around for a while, given that the doorman seemed not to have followed me this time, and so I ordered a pint in the bar that isn't The Horse Shoe, which was too packed, and I stood at the counter and sipped, and I'm sure I lit a cigarette, but, you know, I wouldn't swear on it.

'You're a friend of Angelo's aren't you?'

It was a woman, at my shoulder, late-thirties, maybe forty, quite glamorous, tanned, straight fair hair, long, wearing a charcoal top and black jeans, Prada shoes I think, and smelling of something vaguely tangerine and expensive.

'Who are you?'

She had a thick link gold necklace, and a matching bracelet, and a single diamond wedding ring that caught the eye. She had put her drink down beside mine, and stood there with her hands on the bar top and a smile on her face. She was quite beautiful. She ignored my question.

'I'm here with friends,' she said. 'I saw you come in and out, I thought I recognised you. But I don't know your name.'

So I ignored hers.

'Have you seen Angelo?'

'No. Was he supposed to meet you? He is very unreliable sometimes. Have you known him for long?'

I couldn't place her accent. It seemed definitely foreign, but her English was so faultless that it didn't carry anything – she may have been German, but she looked French maybe, or Italian.

'Yes. Are you Mrs Duncan?'

She smiled. She looked like she was sorry for me.

'I don't think so,' she said, and shook her head a little. 'I hope not.'

'I'm a bit worried about Angelo actually. Have you seen him recently?'

She frowned now, considered me, and didn't say anything for a moment. A man, suited, dark haired, Dublin accent, put a hand on her shoulder and I heard him say 'We're going now,' and she didn't look at him, just nodded, and leaned towards me, and said, so that the man couldn't hear –

'Is he not at his home?'

'I don't know where Angelo lives.'

She looked startled, almost worried. She scratched beside her eye, looked down, muttered something, then slowly, clearly, told me an address.

'I thought you were his friend,' she said, and put a peculiar emphasis on the word *friend*.

'I am.'

She sighed.

'Well. Go there. Maybe he is there. But if he is not, well, I don't know then. Maybe he is gone.'

And she smiled, and nodded with pursed lips as if to reassure me.

'He is not reliable. But don't worry. He does not mean it.'

And she left me with a little wave.

I know, I know. It's mad. It's like a bad movie. It's like one of those old Hitchcock mysteries full of missing men and glamorous women and conversations that don't make any sense. I had a headache. I thought the whole thing was a pain. I thought that as soon as I found him I'd give Angelo a good kicking and sulk properly for about a month. And I decided that I'd had enough of him anyway, that this was ridiculous, that this was playacting and it was getting boring and I could really do without it.

The address was close to where I'd lost him that night. Close to Earlsfort Terrace and about ten minutes' walk from where I was. I didn't finish my drink. I waited for a while to let Mata Hari make her getaway, and then I went out through the side door, and scurried my way around the front keeping my head down, and crossed the road where I shouldn't, causing at least two cars to blow horns at me.

It's strange, that as I'm getting towards the end of this, as I'm moving forward, I don't want to go on. I want to stop right here, or maybe somewhere before here, and just let it stand. I think it's because I don't want him to just be missing, just traces and theories and odd, well dressed clues. As if he was not worth mentioning until he was gone. That isn't fair. I want to leave you with the picture of him sitting up in my bed in the early morning, his body sucking in the sunlight, his hair a mess, reading one of his battered novels, and seeing that I was awake, and smiling at me, and leaning down to kiss me, his eyes honest and clear and with nothing to hide, just Angelo, just Angelo, here and now, not divided into before and after or past and future or what I did know and what I didn't know. Just Angelo. You understand me.

But I started this. It was the first thing I told you, that he'd gone. So I'm left with that. Picking up pieces. Chasing around the streets of Dublin after his odd little ghosts.

So on we go.

I found the place easily enough, but it took me a while to convince myself that I'd got it right. It was a house. I mean it was a stand alone, front gardened, single doorbell, proper, grown up, house. Not flats. So then I just assumed that me and Miss Penelope had been talking about different Angelos. He rode a bike for God's sake, and he borrowed money. From me.

I rang the bell, expecting to be confronted by maybe a retired chip shop owner. But there was no answer. I rang three times. Nothing.

Property in Dublin is expensive. I mean it's crazy expensive. This looked like a three or four bedroom place, with a front, and probably a back, garden, double garage, Harcourt Terrace, beside the canal, five minutes from St Stephen's Green. This was probably a couple of million, easy, these days. So I had misheard the address, the number at least. I walked up and down the road. Most of the places were offices, old converted houses with plush modern extensions added at the side or the back. There were only two other places that looked like private houses, one of them with locked gates and two great big Dobermans roaming around inside, and the other with a guy and his two kids in the front driveway unloading a station wagon. So I went back to the first place.

I couldn't tell anything by staring at it. All the windows were dark. I could see nothing inside. It was maybe a little shabby, needed a paint job, and the garden was a bit of a mess, overgrown, slightly chaotic, and though the grass was cut, it was cut badly, all stubble patches and untrimmed borders. Which was, I thought, a little bit like Angelo. Maybe. At a stretch.

I had a quick look out on the road, making sure there was no one around, and I wandered as coolly as I could up to the garage and tried one of the doors. Sure enough, it opened. I don't know what I was thinking I'd do next. I don't think I had thought. I expected them to be locked. Once the thing was halfway up I was left with little choice really, other than to stoop and step inside and pull the door down after me. Which seemed to make an awful racket.

I stood there in the dark for a couple of minutes, trying to breathe quietly and listen. I could hear nothing. Not a sound. I couldn't see a thing either. I felt my way to the wall, and bumped into something, which a bit of a feel suggested was the lawnmower. A little further on I found a light switch. I had a long debate with myself as to whether it was a good idea or not to turn it on. My eyes had adjusted, but I could still see only vague shapes and I was afraid that if I went any further I'd break my neck. So I flicked the switch, and immediately flicked it off again.

I had seen only one thing really, with any great certainty. Leaning against the back wall, unmistakable, was Angelo's bike.

I think I just stood there for a long while. Just being confused in the dark. Where the hell was I? Where the hell was Angelo? Who the hell was that woman? And I think I was angry too. That he could have kept this from me. Not because it looked like a nice house, a good place to hang out in maybe, and not because it was so close to town, and would have saved me countless long walks home, but because it was so, what, straightforward? What was the big fucking deal? So it was in that frame of mind that I put the light back on, and left it on. If someone came and accused me of something, at least now I knew I was in the right house, and I could say that I was worried about my friend, afraid that he might have disappeared up his own arse, the bastard.

The garage had all the typical clutter you'd expect – garden things, including a set of furniture, two chairs and a table with a parasol, which were set out in the middle of the place as if he might actually sit there. With whoever. And there was an ancient washing machine and what appeared to be a kind of workbench, with a vice, and a drill hanging from a nail in the wall, and some short planks lying there, but with no evidence of any work having been done at all. And bits and pieces, I can't remember, nothing exceptional. Garage stuff.

There was a door of course, on the left, leading presumably into the house proper. It had small square panes of frosted glass, and was locked. But you know, I had come this far, and I was so annoyed with the whole thing, and I had my story ready if I needed it. So I found, sure enough, a hammer on the workbench, and an old cloth too, and I wrapped the hammer head and went to the door, and after about five minutes of psyching myself up for it, thinking first that I should wait until it was really quiet, then thinking that no, that was stupid, I should wait until a car roars by, and then getting bored waiting, and I gave it the lightest of taps, and nothing happened. So I hit it harder and it sort of rattled. So I hit it again, thinking that someone trying to rescue his friend who he thinks might have drowned in the bath or fallen down the stairs or been done to death in the kitchen, doesn't worry about making noise. So I walloped the thing, and it smashed, incredibly loudly, glass shattering everywhere, and the whole door frame shaking, and I just stood there looking at the mess and thinking, for the very first time, maybe there's a fucking burglar alarm, what the hell are you doing? But there was nothing. No alarm. Just the tinkle of falling glass, very delicate, very polite.

I wrapped the cloth around my hand and stuck it through
the broken pane and found a key, which I tried to turn but
couldn't, so I took it out, very nearly dropped it, and brought
it back to my side. Thirty seconds later I was standing in a
large, clean-smelling kitchen, having another debate about
lighting.

I went through the house, not slowly exactly, but not rushing, and I looked in every room, turning lights on and then
off as I went, and I looked for evidence, I suppose, not only of
where Angelo was, but of who he was. The whole place hyp-
notised me. To move through spaces that I knew were his,
that he had occupied, lived in, was very odd. I felt as though
I was visiting a museum, a place left to look as it might have
looked when its famous, long dead resident had last lived
there. It was like a time capsule. But still. No museum would
have looked like this. There were dirty dishes piled up in the
kitchen. There were bread crusts on the sideboard which
were not completely hard. I looked in the fridge. Fresh vege-
tables, yoghurt, some milk, which smelled all right, grated
parmesan, a bowl of grapes. Mineral water, apple juice and
two unopened bottles of poppers were stored in the door.
Angelo had never used poppers with me. There were newspapers on the table, one of them from the day before. On the
windowsill was the last novel I had seen him reading. In a
corner, in front of a brand new washing machine, was a pair
of his shoes.

There was a narrow hall with nothing in it. I looked for letters. There was some junk mail on the doormat, but nothing
with an address label. The carpet was worn, the wallpaper
very 1970s, there was no furniture, there was nothing on the
walls. There were two doors on the right and another on the
left at the bottom of the stairs.

I opened one of the doors on the right, and even before I
turned on the light I knew that this was a large room that
stretched from the front to the back of the house, and I could
tell that it was empty. With the light on I could see that the

walls had been whitewashed, and that large white sheets splattered with paint covered the floor. Propped against the opposite wall there was a large almost blank canvas. It was white, with a single black line which started straight and bold at the top, and which seemed to waver and loose direction as it came down, and which then petered out hopelessly into dots and traces and thin splashes at the bottom. In a corner by the front window there were more canvases leaning against the wall in one large group. The outermost one was turned away from the room. There was nothing else. No paint, no brushes, nothing. I closed the door.

The room to the left at the bottom of the stairs was full of packing cases, most of them overflowing with books. Again there was no furniture. I couldn't decide whether he lived like this or he was moving out.

The staircase was narrow and it creaked, and I climbed it very slowly, and wished that I had never met him.

The landing was nothing. I don't even remember the landing. There were five doors though, and I realised that the garage was taking up half the downstairs, that upstairs the place was huge. There was a bathroom, and it was newer than the rest of the house, with a great big circular tub, and a separate shower unit, and directional spotlights and a pair of Angelo's jeans on the floor. There were three toothbrushes, and another two new ones, still in their packing, and I didn't think that this proved anything – he was always buying new toothbrushes. There was only one razor, and standard bathroom stuff, nothing out of the ordinary. There was a bottle of Issey Miyake aftershave still in its box. There were two glasses with desiccated slices of lemon in them beside the bath, along with a well-thumbed copy of Spartacus, 1999/2000.

The other rooms were meant to be bedrooms, I assume, though three of them were completely empty. The last was obviously Angelo's. And not just because it was the only one in use. It was not the biggest, and it was at the front, which perhaps meant it was not the quietest either. But it had a huge double bed, and a spill of books, and a small stereo, with CDs and tapes, of Planxty, Sharon Shannon, Davy Spillane, stuff like that – some Christy Moore as well, and even a Dubliners tape. There were French and Italian things too, and a Woody Guthrie collection. On the bedside table there was an English dictionary, and two things that made me sit on the bed and feel hollow. One was a photograph of me. It was not a very good one, but I recognised it. My father took it, on holiday somewhere, years ago, and I am wearing a baseball cap and a T-shirt and I am smiling a little goofily, and I remembered Angelo seeing it in my place, and loving it, and I don't remember giving it to him, but there it was, given or not, beside his bed.

The other thing was a telephone.

It's amazing how you'd think regret was a creeping thing, but it's not. It hits you as suddenly as fear or anger. I was filled with it, and I could not move for a while. I wanted to lie down on his sheets, just close my eyes and stay there for a minute and try to get him to materialise. But I didn't. I thought it'd be kind of stupid.

There was a wardrobe filled with his clothes. There was a small stash of porn under the bed. There were scattered mugs and glasses and plates. There were little sketches, mostly nudes, pinned to the wall. There was a postcard from London with a signature I couldn't make out.

And there was a computer.

This was the one odd thing, the one thing that I thought didn't fit. Angelo had never shown any interest in computers, even though it was the generally the chief conversation topic of at least one of the twins. And he just didn't seem the type. At first I thought that it was an old thing, unused, but then I saw cables, including one that went to the telephone socket, and when I went over to it I saw a Pentium badge and it looked new. I turned it on.

I'm not really the type either. I have one at work, and it

does what it's meant to, and I like the e-mail thing, and I know basically how to find my way around Windows, but it doesn't exactly, well, enthuse me.

This was at least Windows, and it had Word on it, so I opened that up, only to find that it had never been run before and wanted to know my name. So I closed that. There were other bits and pieces like Excel, and Outlook, but they hadn't been run before either. So I was beginning to think that he had just bought it maybe when I started Internet Explorer, and before I knew where I was it was dialling.

His username was Angelo, and his password was saved, and it connected straightaway, I didn't have to do a thing. I was not really expecting to get anywhere with this, and it took me straight to the log in page for Hotmail. I looked in his favourites folder but there was nothing saved except for Microsoft's own stuff, and I clicked on the little address bar thing to see where'd he'd been, and it was empty, and I opened his history folder and all it had was Hotmail. So it looked to me like he'd only used it for e-mail. I started to type 'Angelo' in to the username box, and a little drop down menu appeared with 'AngeloInDublin' written in it. I stared. I probably grinned, getting all excited that I'd hacked his e-mail account. So I selected 'AngeloInDublin' and then realised that I would never work out his password. I tried 'Angelo' again, but nothing happened, no menu appeared, no help arrived. I tried to get in with it anyway – just plain 'Angelo'. No joy. And then I tried my own name, which of course didn't work, and then I went through the names of all the people we knew. I tried 'Shelbourne' and 'George' and 'Boilerhouse' and 'password'. I tried random words, my telephone number, then random numbers. Nothing. I looked around the room and tried book titles and album titles. Nothing worked. I gave up. Then I checked what he had set up as a screen saver. I know how to do that. You click on the desktop and choose Properties and Screen Saver, and there's a preview button that turns it on. It was the scrolling marquee, the sentence that travels

244

across the screen from right to left, coming in at different places, again and again. It was a black background. Red lettering.

TIME TO LEAVE ANGELO

What was that? Time for Angelo to leave? Time for someone to leave Angelo? What the hell was that? It really annoys me, that message. It's the only thing in the fucking house that I didn't get. It just makes no sense to me. Who is going to set that up as their screen saver? I stared at it for ages, watching it flicker past me, jerking along, stuttering, stupid, and I just hated it. What the fuck was that about? It was like it was for me. Which I know is daft, but I took it personally. I hate time being called on me, I just hate it. No one does that. I switched the thing off.

I had a final look around his room, wondering whether he would ever forgive me for having been in there, for having seen what he didn't want anybody to see. But again, I found myself wondering what the big deal was. So he kept some porn and wasn't good with dirty dishes. It was hardly shocking.

I went downstairs, and although I had never really expected to find him in the house, I was actually a little relieved that he wasn't dead in the bath, but I was also now lacking any excuse for hanging around. It would have been good if he'd walked in the door then. It would have been nice. We could have written it off against the elbow incident and that would have been that.

I went once more into the big room. There was no curtain on the front window, so I didn't like having the light on. But I wanted to look at the paintings stacked against the wall. I thought about bringing them into the hall, but they were bulky, the pile of them, so I settled instead for crouching on the floor and flicking through them.

There were twelve. They were very different from the

canvas leaning against the other wall. They were smaller for a start, and they were, you know, of things. I mean of people or bits of people, or suggestions of people. So, there was one of two men, I think, two figures anyway; and then a mangy looking dog; and one of a hand with writing on it that I couldn't make out; and a really strange one with a woman in a blue scarf hanging upside down; a washing machine, I think; two naked guys embracing by the sea; a clothed boy under water, bubbles coming from his mouth; a car on a roundabout; a woman in a hospital bed; a man with his face pressed to the ground; and, finally, a pretty shaky one of The Custom House. Actually none of them were much good. I had thought that he would be better as an artist, Angelo. I don't know why. But maybe they weren't even his. I don't know. There was one thing about them though. They were all date-stamped. I mean like photographs – like those photographs you can get if you have a camera that can do that. Little digital orange dates down in the bottom right-hand corner. Not real ones, painted. I can't remember any of the dates though. You wouldn't expect me to.

I left them as I found them and I switched the light off and I wondered whether to go out through the front door. I thought I'd better, given the noise of the garage. I felt weird. Leaving Angelo's house. It was the first time I'd ever done that. Letting myself out. It felt familiar, and maybe it was just that I was glad to have gotten out of there without being arrested, but I felt like I had achieved something. I felt closer. I don't know.

The night was dark, and it was cold, and I walked quickly to the front gate and straight out onto the footpath without stopping, thinking that it would look more natural that way.

I didn't know where to go. I didn't know what to do. Part of me was thinking that I had been stupid, that I had imagined a whole lot of stuff, and invaded a friend's privacy, which is a polite way of saying that I had broken into his house, on the basis that this friend, who had never been particularly consistent anyway, on any level, had stood me up. It was crazy. But part of me felt like I had found something out, though I plainly hadn't, and that I could relax a little now. That I knew more, I knew there was a place, I knew where to come. Or maybe that I knew that there had been a place, that I knew where I might have been, sometimes, maybe.

I walked home. It took hours and I barely noticed.

I haven't seen the woman again. I e-mail Angelo about once a week, but I have never got a reply. I walked to the house a few times, rang the doorbell, waited. I stood outside it once for virtually a whole day. He never showed up. No one ever showed up. Then a 'For Sale' sign appeared in the front garden, and I called the estate agents, and got a viewing, and it had been cleared, emptied entirely, and they could tell me nothing of the previous owner other than that she lived abroad and was doing everything through a solicitor. The opening price was £1.75 million. I passed.

Dolores got engaged to a Dutch guy who thinks I'm hilarious. John Keane is in and out of hospital – at the moment he's in great form, in love, semi-retired, wants me to move into one of his flats. Which I might. The twins are the same, starting an attic conversion or something. Mattie is insufferable, but he comes around sometimes and listens to me.

I think of Angelo all the time. I mean *all* the time. I think sometimes that I made him up. Sometimes I think that it was the other way around. I don't know what that means. I just know that life is a little less without him. It is paler, slower, it has no surprises in it.

Sometimes I think that I will see him again, that I will bump into him somewhere, some night by the river, any river, and that he will scold me for missing him, and that he will tell me stories and let me guess at the truth a bit more. And sometimes I think that I will never see him again, that he has moved on somewhere else entirely, and that if he thinks of me at all it is with some embarrassment, or regret, or some combination of the two – whatever that combination is that doesn't allow you to live in your own life but has you always dreaming up another.

Either way, I'm stuck here, stuck with the memory of him, which is almost entirely unverifiable, which may, for all I know, have come to me mostly in writing it down. If that makes sense. And if it does, does it matter? It comes from somewhere, and wherever it comes from is lost to me now. Gone. Disappeared. And here I am rattling away in the small hours trying to get it back, trying to dig it out of myself as if that's where it might be found. Which is a peculiar occupation. But one that sustains me. I think. For now.

Angelo once told me, I don't know when, that you can only be named when you're dead.

'What?'

'I mean, you know, that it is not complete – that you are only yourself when you're leaving, you understand me?'

'No.'

'Just the same way that you cannot understand what I'm saying until . . .'

I interrupted him.

'Oh right,' I said. 'Until you've finished saying it.'

He just stared at me, and I looked at him, and it wasn't until he laughed that I got my own joke.

'There,' he said. 'You understand me completely.'

That was in summer, when we were mostly together.

That's all. That's all there is. There's no explanation, there's no happy endings, or if there are I'm not in on any of them. They've eluded me. Which is, you know, fair enough. I get the feeling that I wasn't the main player in any of this – that I just caught a glance, and that what I saw was lopsided and blurred and indistinct, and not really intended for me. But I don't know. You know what I know. As much as I know. I've handed it over, all of it. So you tell me.

Tell me.